Wolves of Memory

WOLVES OF MEMORY

Bill James

THE COUNTRYMAN PRESS
Woodstock, Vermont

The Library of Congress has cataloged the hardcover edition as follows:
James, Bill, date
  Wolves of memory / Bill James.—1st American ed.
     p. cm.
ISBN-13: 978-0-393-06188-8
  1. Harpur, Colin (Fictitious character)—Fiction. 2. Iles, Desmond (Fictitious character)—Fiction. 3. Police—Great Britain—Fiction. 4. Informers—Fiction. I. Title.

  PR6070.U23W65 2006
  823'.914--dc22

                                    2006040000

Cover design by Steven Rachwal

Published by The Countryman Press, P.O. Box 748, Woodstock, VT 05091

Distributed by W. W. Norton & Company, Inc., 500 Fifth Avenue, New York, NY 10110

Manufacturing by The Courier Companies, Inc.
Printed in the United States of America

10 9 8 7 6 5 4 3 2 1

Chapter One

'Do you know who I think of myself as occasionally, Col?' the Assistant Chief asked.

'It would be someone very worthwhile, sir,' Harpur replied. 'This opens up a range of possibilities.'

'Frankenstein, Col. I think of myself from time to time as Frankenstein.'

'That right, sir?' Harpur replied.

'You'll ask why, Col.'

'Why, sir?'

'I see myself as concerned with the manufacture of Being.'

'I'd regard that as a true task, a task worthy of you, sir, and you worthy of it.'

'Some ignoramuses speak of Frankenstein as the monster,' the ACC replied.

'That right?'

'I don't say you, necessarily, Harpur.'

'Lately, I haven't thought about him much.'

'Dr Frankenstein was the good, young, idealistic man of science who yearned to produce new life by his own methods.'

'You've always loved a challenge. This is widely acknowledged.'

'I, as Assistant Chief Constable, handling this project, have to make not one but *four* new lives, Col,' Iles replied.

'It's tough but –'

'Shall I read you my instructions? Well, *our* instructions. I don't discount you, Col.'

'Thank you, sir.'

'A memo for the Chief from the Organized and International Crime Directorate in the Home Office, with all the usual secrecy, confidentiality and top-notch security ratings. And they're warranted. Oh, yes, they're warranted. Inevitable.'

'Yes, we've had these before,' Harpur said.

'And then dumped by his Sirship, the Chief, on me. Known as chain of command. Or pass the fucking buck. I'm Assistant Chief (Operations), and this is an operation, so give it to Desmond Iles. That's the gorgeous logic.'

But Harpur saw the ACC did not really resent these orders. He would regard nobody else as big enough to cope. He might be right. The task had to be his. His. 'The Chief has terrific confidence in you already, I expect, although he's so new,' Harpur replied. 'Sir Matthew would probably say to his clerk, "This is one for Dr Frankenstein in person," and the clerk would know at once he wittily meant you.'

'Don't piss me about, Harpur.'

'One quality required in clerks – intuition.'

'Who else could handle this assignment, Col? Who?'

'Some question, sir. What I recall from school used to be termed a *rhetorical* question, I think – meaning it looks for no answer because the answer is built in.'

Iles picked up from his desk a couple of sheets of paper clipped together. He did not pass them to Harpur, as if unsure of his security rating and/or ability to understand without an intermediary. Iles said: 'It's headed "Clandestine resettlement in your area of former Covert Human Intelligence Source."'

'Ah.'

'"Covert Human Intelligence source",' Iles said.

'Meaning an ex-informant.'

'Myself, I don't mind a bit of jargon, Col. It suggests

6

policing is a profession, like chiropodists or window dressers. "Covert Human Intelligence Source" is a more adult, less tabloid, label than supergrass, wouldn't you say?'

'I –'

Iles proceeded: '"Clandestine resettlement in your area of former Covert Human Intelligence Source. The undermentioned and his family/dependants are to be accommodated with all standard facilities of the national Resettlement Scheme:

Ian Maitland Ballion, age 38
Eleanor Carys Veronica Ballion, wife, age 36
Rose Diana Ballion, daughter, age 10
Larry Raymond Ballion, son, age 8

'"The former CHIS and dependants will be housed in a purchased property of the B7 category (detached, four bedrooms, £300,000–£325,000 price.) All costs of this purchase will be met by the Treasury acting through the Home Office. You will provide a short list of six B7 properties from which the CHIS may select the one he and his family find most suitable. The names Ian Maitland Ballion, Eleanor Carys Veronica Ballion, Rose Diana Ballion, Larry Raymond Ballion will cease from the date of this memorandum. These names have become respectively, Robert Maurice Templedon, Jane Iris Templedon, Sian Rebecca Templedon, Harry Charles Templedon. General Register Office and other agencies have been informed. The chosen B7 property and appropriate furnishings will be purchased outright in the joint names of the above Robert Maurice Templedon and Jane Iris Templedon as if through their own funds.

'"You will arrange a conference in a secure site away from police premises [Repeat – away from police premises] at which the family and representatives of all agencies concerned in the CHIS Resettlement Scheme should meet and inter-brief information relevant to the case. These agencies are listed below and have been told that you will notify them of the date, time and place of this conference." I won't read you those, Harpur. It's the usual collection. They are the nuts and bolts of the operation, the artisans, and not to be despised. But it is *I* who has to breathe new breath into this family. It is I who must bring to an end the Ballions' era and out of it form and sustain the Templedon era. This is transformation, Col. This is rebuilding. This is responsibility, Harpur.'

'Always the terrible fear of revenge attacks, on him and/ or his family. But you've succeeded with this kind of concealment and transformation before, sir.'

'True.'

'Beyond genetic engineering, sir.'

'Creation, Col.'

8

Chapter Two

'So, I get used to calling you Robert?' she asked.

She said it big – a lot of breath. It was a kind of accusation. He would put up with this. Weren't there worse accusations around? 'That's right,' he said. 'That's right . . . Jane.'

'And I get used to a new house, a new town in the sticks, new people around?'

They'd discussed this so often, so often. But he stayed reasonable and polite and tried to explain once more. It was a big change for her, he could see that. It was a big change for all of them – her, him, the children. He must go gently. 'I take it as a beginning, a second beginning,' he said. 'We're lucky. Not everybody gets that kind of chance. We can't stay in London. We can't stay anywhere we're known.'

'And the kids?' she replied. 'How do you tell them they've got to become someone else?'

'Yes, dodgy, but it can be done. The police are running this kind of disguise programme all the time. They have experts. Psychologists. This guy masterminding things – Iles – he's got the know-how for these identity capers. He's not a psychologist himself, no, just the police, but he's handled a lot of identity switches. No slip-ups, I'm told. That's why they like using him and his Force.'

'What – there's a whole district of ex-grasses on his ground, is there, like a ghetto?'

'They know how to help people disappear and reinvent

themselves,' he said. 'It's necessary. You can see it's necessary, can't you?'

In a while, she gave a tiny, reluctant nod, but enough for him to see. 'And aren't you sad to find a for-ever stop put on the name Ballion?'

'Yes, I'm sad. Sad some. Only some. I'd rather a for-ever stop is put on the name, not on me.' He knew that once she had accepted the changes she would adapt to them faster and more fully than himself. She liked to go through all the arguments, that's all. She had a university training.

Chapter Three

They assembled as instructed in what had to be called a 'safe house', though Harpur feared the term. It always seemed to him full of vaunting, barmy confidence, or official optimism, a sort of dare to Fate to show it was *not* safe. Harpur thought Fate should be steered clear of. Fate had a lot of form.

They used unmarked cars and parked in other streets, on neutral spots alongside waste ground or garden walls, to avoid resident rage and the attention it brought. No uniforms, of course. Very few of those attending had uniformed jobs, anyway. Most were civilian. Iles had a uniform in soft, superior, light blue cloth, but that came out for ceremonial functions mainly. Tonight did not rate as one of those. Harpur had a uniform, too. He never wore it.

People were individually briefed and given exact, different times for arrival at the house. Most had ordinary, sedate, civilian office jobs and wouldn't be into security. They needed precise instructions. All were told to walk from their vehicles singly, in twos or, at the most, threes, the intervals unequal and spread across a full hour. It was evening and dark, all curtains in the house closed. Over the years a pattern for this type of meeting had been learned, a pattern aiming to hide it *was* a pattern. Iles supervised everything personally and hosted the session. When Iles supervised personally it was very personally.

He and Harpur had visited the place earlier in the day

to make sure things were right. The house was called Meadowland. 'Thoroughness is one of my centralities, you know, Col,' Iles said as they checked. 'I don't mean simple, boring drudgery. Not *plod*, for God's sake. No, a kind of *inspired* thoroughness, becoming in itself a type of . . . well, a type of *creative impulse* . . . yes, in itself. I don't think that's claiming too much, is it? At Staff College I was sometimes known as "Whole-hog Desmond".'

'This is one of your qualities that most would recognize very swiftly, sir. Your Frankenstein aspect isn't so famed, of course, owing to the work's secrecy.'

'My mother used to say, the moment I was committed to some interest or project I would go at it "all out". The very *moment*. This was her phrase, Harpur, "all out".'

'Insights – mothers are famed for them. I certainly don't have anything against mothers.' Harpur knew the ACC also distrusted 'safe houses', but, as the orders said, this kind of conference could not be set up in headquarters. There must be no police connection – no traceable police connection with the Templedons, once Ballions. That requirement Iles would term a 'centrality', meaning that if the Templedons, once Ballions, were traced, Robert, once Ian, would certainly be targeted, and possibly his family.

On their morning call, he and Harpur had found everything ready. Or not quite everything. For the sake of naturalness, the curtains stayed open now, to be pulled over later. They tried to keep clear of the windows. Also, there would be armed support in the garden and on the drive once darkness came and brought concealment. Harpur selected positions for them, pencilled a basic ground plan and marked their spots. 'But one day we'll get a tragedy,' he said.

'Do you know, Col, occasionally, I wonder what they'd call *you* at Staff College, if you were ever going to get there, which you're fucking not,' Iles said, while Harpur finished the sketch. 'These nicknames are almost always good-natured and positive, so wouldn't be to do with your clothes. Tell me the attribute you feel might be highlighted in this fashion, suppose you reached Staff College, as if you ever fucking would.'

'In which direction at Staff College did they think your whole-hoggery revealed itself most strongly, sir?' Harpur replied. 'Though if it's *whole* hoggery I suppose this suggests an all-round quality, or it would be only hoggery.'

'Nicknames – interesting, Col. It's as if people feel short-changed by one's, as it were, *given* identity and wish to impose another selected by them. They insist on defining who, what, one is.'

'Identities. So inconstant, so shifty. Well, our game here, now, isn't it? We're going to transform a family. Try.'

'Tragedy, you say?' Iles replied. 'Oh, yes, possible. Appallingly possible.' Iles's voice turned grave and troubled after the insults, one of those rapid switches of tone and topic he could fall into. They confused many people, and used to confuse Harpur. As to identities, which exactly was the Assistant Chief's? Iles's mother might be able to explain him, or a psychiatrist, given seven or eight years, if the ACC would let one near. 'Schizo' – why hadn't anyone at Staff College given him that as nickname? Not 'amiable' enough? Harpur's method with Iles, worked out over years, was frantic mobility of response – a faltering attempt to match his variations. It could be managed, as long as you never shackled yourself with common sense or politeness. Iles did not prize politeness, neither giving nor receiving. He saw politeness as evasion. He had said on that preparatory, early visit to Meadowland: 'This lad we're hiding, Col – I think of the kids, their safety.'

'Difficult. They're damn vulnerable.'

'We look after them, Col.'

'Certainly, but –'

'We look after them, Harpur. We look after the parents as well, obviously. Wasn't daddy Mr Metropolitan Police Supergrass of 2004, and, as such, the country owes him?'

'As such, as ever. We're good at these makeovers.'

13

'So far.'

'Never lost a former grass or anyone close yet,' Harpur said.

'Have you seen his wife? Dossier pics. Worth a gaze. Eleanor, was. Now, Jane. I don't think I've ever got close to a woman called Eleanor. Definitely not close to a woman called Eleanor who turned into Jane. But in all this, Col, one especially takes care of the children. I mean we, of course. What one is here for. I mean we, of course.'

'Yes.'

'We both have families, you and I, Harpur.'

'Certainly, sir.'

'We know – *know* – the anxieties.'

'Certainly.'

'Know from experience, not from some damn Dr Spock handbook, Col.'

'A very different kettle of fish, sir.'

'What?'

'Experience.'

'Col, don't tell me that a man who's never had children knows – I mean *knows* – actually *knows*, Harpur, knows in his arteries, ligaments, flesh, the concerns about him/her/ them felt by a father.'

'Fatherhood's quite a job. That's been proved over many a century. Think of Saul and Jonathan.' During his career, Harpur had heard Iles do the caring, shepherd-of-my-flock stance more than once. Oh, unquestionably more than once. And it was fairly real. Iles believed in duty. He never skimped on his responsibilities. Resettlement operations would often bring on the ACC's caring aspect. Harpur sometimes wished more people could witness Iles in these roles. At such periods, almost anybody unprejudiced and with normal eyesight could spot true humanity and kindness in him. There had been times, and there were still times, when Harpur felt it a duty to mention this warm side of the ACC to doubters. And doubters did exist. Many

14

decided from their experience of him that he was all brilliant, destructive, selfish savagery.

And, on the whole, people would listen while Harpur tried to convince them. Naturally, they did. They longed for reassurance about Iles. It shook them that he held high police rank. Perhaps they'd even read and learned from that famous thinker somewhere in history who said law and order should be 'in good hands'. Iles himself would often quote this to Harpur – from someone called George Savile? – quote it while showing his own hands symbolically, as if there could not be any better for the task. Well, perhaps.

Now, at their big, evening meeting the ACC gazed around the wide front room where they'd gathered, perhaps thinking this safe house would turn out . . . safe . . . or as safe as any safe house could be. Things might go all right, again. Meadowland had a comfortable *feel* to it, as if it was lived in and enjoyed until the day before yesterday, not simply set up as a venue. Rented? In which case, from whom? Secure?

To Harpur, the pictures around the walls looked reasonable, and originals, not prints. There was a cello propped against the wall in one corner of the room, and full, do-it-yourself bookshelves across an alcove. These held paperbacks as well as proper volumes, suggesting the works might be for reading rather than show. Although Harpur did not read much himself he was not against it, and until his wife's death there'd been a lot of books at home – all sorts, including one called *Edwin Drood*. He got rid of most of them a while ago.

For this evening's meeting, Iles wore one of his great suits, a double-breasted grey, no waistcoat, inevitably custom-made, the trousers cut close to proclaim leg slimness. Iles was fond of his legs. Iles liked most of his physique but not his Adam's apple, which Harpur knew he loathed his father for. That had always seemed unjust to

Harpur, because women didn't have Adam's apples and, obviously, couldn't pass them on.

And then what about those good hands he'd show people as a sign? They were long, slender, well looked after. Yes, you could call them 'good' hands. Just the same, some who came into contact with Iles did not think he possessed the kind of reliability and scrupulousness they hoped for in an Assistant Chief. To them, Iles represented either actual or approaching chaos, and they were terrified. They yearned to believe nobody so roaringly and imaginatively berserk could reach and hold his high post in a British police force, even given the new millennium.

Yes, the unconvinced listened to Harpur's praise for Iles, but then most likely thought back to what they, personally, had noted and quailed from in him. Harpur knew many of them stuck with their own impressions of the Assistant Chief regardless. Such impressions would be deep, difficult to forget.

Chapter Four

Perhaps a reason people married or got long-term shacked-up was to have somebody who *would* ask the important questions, get underneath the show. When she said: 'And aren't you sad to find a for-ever stop put on the name Ballion?' he'd been ready with the true, sharp, unbeatable answer, of course. But, just the same, did that say everything? 'I'd rather a for-ever stop is put on the name, not on me.'

Yes, right, true, sharp, unbeatable. It was why he had a seat alongside her now in this big, crowded room with its cello and chaise longue and books and pictures and cops and quiet men and women from the Ministries. He didn't mind the cello and chaise longue and books and pictures. He was used to middle class culture gear. He'd had the same or similar at home in London, when he was Ballion. His daughter learned the cello and Eleanor – no, no, Jane, now – Jane played the viola. Hadn't he dropped out of college and gone into that rough-house, take-it-and-run career to finance such a fine, nicely equipped life?

They all waited obediently for the fashion-slick performer, Iles, to start his sermon. But Jane's question had troubled Robert Templedon, and still troubled him because it suggested he might be ashamed of Ian Ballion and now wanted to escape at a gallop into someone else, someone with no past and no guilt. That was a brilliant, happy, impossible aim. He had helped put three lads, mates, in jail for terms of between fourteen and ten years. She'd hinted several times that Ian Ballion could not tolerate the thought of this betrayal and so welcomed conversion to Robert Templedon. The charge lingered, half poleaxed him now in this sedate room.

God, oh, God, none of it should have happened – the ambush the arrests, the sentences. He had never meant that. They had promised him, and promised him, and lied. And so, now here he was, sitting mildly among the law and order boys and girls ready for the top law and order boy to preach hope, respectability and eternal craftiness.

Chapter Five

Iles said: 'Welcome, ladies and gentlemen. We are all present, I think, except for the children. They remain at an hotel with a nurse. My view is that they need not be confronted with a battery of police and officials. Intimidating. As resettlement progresses over the next weeks and months, the children will be continuously helped in their adjustment programme by a police colleague, Mr Andrew Rockmain, who specializes in these things, and that should be enough contact with the constabulary for them. I think this wise. They, like their parents, have to learn how to be someone else – a process difficult enough for adults, but very challenging for children, and for Mr Rockmain, as he guides them to their new them.' Iles gave a bit of formal smiling. Harpur regarded this as not too long, in fact too short, but all right. 'I am Assistant Chief Constable Desmond Iles and will be in charge of our project.'

Harpur understood people's uneasiness about the ACC. Iles did have a degree of brilliant, destructive, selfish savagery which went much beyond the standard brilliant, destructive, selfish savagery his rank obviously demanded. And this mode might last for very long spells and come to seem permanent, his essence. All the same, Harpur did now and then try to argue it was *not* the ACC entire. Periods of composure and, yes, tenderness would somehow occasionally take him over and last a surprising while. Schizo. Harpur stuck by the word.

Iles said: 'Happily, I shall have help in organizing things.

It will come from two of my most able officers, Detective Chief Superintendent Colin Harpur, head of CID, standing near the cello, and Detective Chief Inspector Francis Garland, seated on the chaise longue.'

The Assistant Chief nodded at each of them in turn. He seemed to Harpur altogether splendidly dressed – not just the suit, but terrific black lace-ups, probably Charles Laity, and a fashionably wide mauve and silver tie on a radiantly azure shirt. He might have been a private health clinic doctor or TV quizmaster. Iles would regard this conference as important and entitled to recognition in his garb, especially if he wanted to line up one of the women. The ACC said: 'There will be an opportunity to speak with either Mr Harpur or Mr Garland later, or, indeed, both. Don't feel because of their positions near the cello or on the chaise longue that they are impossibly refined. No. Scarcely. They are of our world. Oh, dear, yes!'

Although Iles's clothes sometimes carried a meaning for the day, it would be naive to see in them a prime indicator of his temper. Not long ago, as a kind of self-defence tactic, Harpur started minor research on Iles's garments, attempting to discover whether a particular outfit revealed a state of mind in the Assistant Chief, as, for instance, the lie of a cat's fur might prove *its* state of mind, bristling up when enraged, otherwise smooth. But Harpur soon abandoned this study. He came to recognize that no relationship existed between Iles's clothes and his disposition. He could be deeply manic in one of his large-badged blazers and yet passably civil and rational in the same large-badged blazer only a few days later – the badge signifying some rugby club or Former Pupils posse he belonged to, or claimed to. Harpur didn't know Latin, of course, but he did know *ad hoc*, and *ad hoc* by the mugful he brought to his dealings with Iles. That is, take it as it comes, and give it full whack back to him if rough. Iles expected this. He despised deference as much as politeness.

'Mr Harpur and Mr Garland will handle all day-to-day

problems, should there be any,' Iles said. 'Let's hope the reverse, but they are your contacts, your routes to myself. And if – or *when* – you reach myself what is there to find?' He became intense. 'Above all, you will encounter someone who believes that policing could not function without the use of informants, and that, therefore, such informants, and ex-informants, deserve our total respect. Naturally, they will not get it from criminals. They find only hatred there. And even among non-criminals – even I must admit among some police officers – yes, even there, the informant is regarded as something base and slimy. A tonne of base and slimy names exist to describe him/her – grass, tout, nark, stooly, fink. This is a disgusting and ungrateful error. Police are not the only ones to use secret whispers. Think of all that tragedy-touched wrangling after the Iraq war about who provided key material to BBC reporters on Secret Service doubts about weapons of mass destruction. Such material is never going to come out in formal press conferences. No, there were would-be anonymous, confidential tip-offs, and the public is entitled to such tip-offs or governments could get away with what they liked. Similarly, the public is entitled to the voices who on the quiet help police defeat illegality. Without those whispers, we are nowhere.' His gaze found Templedon. 'Thank you, Robert.' Iles's voice blazed strong and sincere. At times like this, the ACC could be seen as not merely rational but stalwart. Harpur dearly wanted more folk to recognize this. He thought that, if more people did recognize this, the ACC might direct his personality in general a little more towards the sane and affable. Possibly, he would not feel the compulsion then to display the Ilesness of Iles with quite such contempt for the usual way of things.

Of course, some would say the 'usual way of things' could never be the Iles way and that he would be much less if they were. Harpur himself did feel this in part, but only in part. He knew his teenage daughters, Hazel and Jill, would hate it if Iles ever changed. They admired him as he was. This brought tensions, especially to do with the older girl, Hazel, still only fifteen. Harpur wondered if it might be useful to have Iles focused on someone else, even someone as dicey as an ex-Covert Human Intelligence Source's woman.

The ACC continued now to explain to his Meadowland audience the police need for information, and so for informants. Probably not many in the room needed convincing. After all, their reason for being here was to arrange the unbloody future for an informant and his family. The hoped-for unbloody future. No, Iles was speaking mainly to the Templedons/Ballions. The ACC wanted to console and comfort Robert Templedon. Grasses could feel appalling guilt. They knew the terrible scorn directed at them that Iles had referred to. He would try to counter this. It was an instance of his sensitivity and kindness.

This spell of total decency did not last long, though. The ACC smiled again, moving his head slowly from the left this time to take in all the listeners, a kind of 'Guess what's next' teaser. Harpur disliked these preparations. They looked merciless. Iles seemed ready for a change of tone. Schizo rides again. Oh, fuck. The ACC said: 'Now, I have to consider – can't avoid considering – I have to consider that those of you new to the area may soon hear rumours – may already have heard rumours – rumours very familiar to the local people present – rumours involving both Col Harpur and Francis Garland with my wife, Sarah, though not, it goes without saying, at the same time.' His voice approached the screamy. His Adam's apple teetered, like a snooker pink about to drop into the pocket. 'Perhaps you find it unusual that I should wish to speak so openly of this – re my wife, Col and Francis,' he said. 'Yet, it would be foolish, counter-productive, would it not, to pretend such gossip does not exist and to ignore it? No, to mention it is a duty, to you and to myself. It is essential to our cooperation together. What we must ponder, mustn't we, is whether it has any relevance to the delicate and admittedly dangerous scheme for the Templedons we're inaugurating now. What I mean is this – perhaps you will ask – reasonably ask, in view of such reports – perhaps you will ask whether the three of us – myself, Col Harpur, Garland – can work efficiently together in a demanding and potentially hazardous design of this sort, hazardous above all to our principal guest, guests, tonight.'

Now, Iles nodded at the two, waved a hand towards the bit of the city where the children were, and chuckled briefly. It was that ghastly, clanking, death-rattle mirth imitation he could sometimes bring out when aiming to register the very largest disdain, which with Iles could be very, very large. 'Oh, yes, I do understand, I do understand. But let me assure you that currently, when my wife and I discuss such episodes from the past, her principal reaction is amazement that she could ever have regarded either of these persons as suitable . . . well, company. Yes, company, I'd use that term. My wife is a companionable person, no question.' His head drooped for a spell, and he stayed quiet. Harpur could recall the title of a book or film or play or song, *The Company She Keeps*. Did Iles know it? He knew more or less everything. Might he be thinking of it now? People in the room stared at the ACC and were also silent – perhaps transfixed. They sat extremely still. 'Do you know,' Iles said, with a weak shot at a chuckle, 'a tale circulated – a tale you must, must discount, please – a preposterous rumour suggesting I tried to arrange for both Harpur's and Garland's elimination. With detail, including named fees to hitmen. These were, clearly, fatuous slanders. Oh, certainly. Many's the laugh Sarah and I share over the thought of that pair, Harpur and Garland, now. To her – and, even more, to myself – it has become comical to think that either of them might have reached a certain brief . . . well, *familiarity* with Sarah. These laughs enjoyed by Sarah and myself are considerable, extensive laughs. But they are possibly matched by my unexpected shorter laugh or snigger – let's admit it – my *snigger* just now during these few words to you about my agony and consequent supposed plot to have Col and Francis Garland snuffed.'

'I'd put it at more of a chortle or chuckle than a snigger, Mr Iles,' Harpur said.

'Perhaps, perhaps,' Iles replied. 'But the laughter enjoyed jointly by my wife and me over those past relationships is such that we quite noticeably shake, oh, yes, shake I say.'

Rage tears the colour of skimmed milk formed along the ACC's lower eyelids, some spit balls flew, and the way he said the 's' letters in 'is such' and 'shake, oh, yes, shake I say' made them dart across the room like a rodeo whip display, the sounds so nearly tangible Harpur thought they might lash against the cello strings and give them a strum. Sometimes, of course, Harpur felt the ACC's behaviour with Hazel to be a type of retaliation after Sarah, an Iles type retaliation. He said to the room: 'My point in discussing these fairly private matters is to dispel your doubts about the effectiveness of any joint work by myself, Col and Garland. All that past stuff *is* past and has not the least bearing on our present business. We are a combination, and a great one – Col, Francis and myself – and we will look after the lives of the Templedons who were Ballions, guarding them from the many crook avengers who might come into our domain and seek their harm. I could do nothing that would put our scheme, or similar previous resettlement schemes, into jeopardy by having Harpur and/or Garland in any way impaired. This is what I meant when speaking of the foul lunacy of that chatter about hitmen. Full participation of all talents. Oh, certainly.'

Iles glanced fondly, sadly, towards Harpur and then Garland, as a greyhound owner might look at two of his dogs who continually fucked up in races and might be better put down regardless. The ACC said: 'Now, ladies and gentlemen, when I mention these two to Sarah in passing – I mean about matters quite unconnected with

24

when they were helping themselves to her – she will remark reproachfully and yet amusedly to me, "Desmond, love, I –"'

Harpur considered there might have been enough of this and, speaking as loudly as necessary to the large, packed room, said: 'These opening weeks, possibly months, are the most difficult and perilous in any programme for relocating an informant from another part of the country in conditions of secrecy. This is our responsibility in the case of Ian and Eleanor Ballion and family, now Templedon. The secrecy amounts only to a stage, in fact, because our ultimate purpose is to create for the informant a new and full identity – a social identity, neighbourhood identity and work identity, the Templedon identity – which will establish itself and last for the rest of a normal life.'

'And death,' Iles said. 'It will be Templedon on any gravestone. Ballion's already RIP.'

'Once the process is under way, things become increasingly easier,' Harpur said, 'though alertness will always be required and will always be available from our Force.'

Iles's voice grew more or less normal again: 'Mr Harpur and Mr Garland, with the aid of gifted outside advisers, such as Andrew Rockmain, have during several years perfected a remarkably effective system for this kind of work. To Covert Human Intelligence Sources, when they have finished their work, we and police officers and police forces carry an overriding obligation. This is to help them and their dependants disappear into a new life, happy and, as far as possible, in continuing safety. Many admire the skills of Colin Harpur and Francis Garland in bringing about such makeovers. This esteem they have magnificently earned. These are remarkable, devoted men. I am proud to be associated with them.'

'Thank you, sir,' Harpur replied, 'and I know I speak for Francis, also.'

'Proud,' Iles replied.

'This is important to us, sir,' Harpur said.

'And yet,' Iles said, scream-time suddenly on the way back, 'and yet, and yet I admit I'm bound to view them also as –'

'What we have to determine first is where the main dangers to our efforts come from,' Harpur said. 'They are substantial but containable.'

Iles said: 'Friends, I'd certainly categorize myself as of a forgiving nature, and not one to linger over filthy insults offered to one's self via one's wife. My mother would sometimes call me "Turn-the-other-cheek Desmond". However, when I visualize Harpur and/or Garland with my wife, in, say, fleapit hotels, backs of cars, shop doorways –'

'Yes, substantial dangers from many possible directions, but containable,' Harpur said.

'Oh, certainly these dangers are containable,' Iles replied. 'Harpur gets to the centralities instantly. It is a remarkable aptitude for someone at his level.'

'Everyone has been briefed about the need for absolute confidentiality on what happens here tonight, and what follows. I would like to repeat that request,' Harpur said. On the earlier visit this morning he had set up a flip-chart easel near the cello. Now, he drew back the cover to show page one. 'Please make no notes of this material. It is meant only as a general explanation of the possible threats to Robert Templedon and his family, who now will live in our area. If you can memorize salient facts I think that will be enough. For several of you present, the possible hazards in this project are and will remain a very distant, virtually non-existent factor. I refer to the representatives from the Department for Education and Employment, the Department of Health, the Home Office, the Board of Inland Revenue, the Treasury and the General Register Office. Mr Iles always invites members of every organization concerned with the resettlement and disguising of a former CHIS so that you may be conscious of the general circumstances, and may have your undoubted awareness of the need for concealment reinforced through detailed knowledge of the background.'

Iles said: 'Ladies and gentlemen, this resemblance has probably already struck you, but, in case not, may I mention that I think of myself from time to time as Frankenstein, in the sense that –'

'These three names on the chart with head and shoulders pictures are the long-time criminals who were convicted, thanks in part at least to information supplied by Ian Ballion to the police in London, as he then was,' Harpur said. 'They are major law-breaking figures and the sentences in keeping. On subsequent chart pages I will show you the family and syndicate connections of each of the three. It is, of course, from these connections that the main dangers to Templedon and his family arise. There is a kind of underworld "duty" – a perverted duty – to punish, possibly destroy, informants who have been instrumental in sending to jail relatives or associates of villain networks. First, I'll tell you a bit about each of the three.'

'Frankenstein in the sense that it is my consuming wish to bring about new life,' Iles said. 'Some mistakenly speak of Frankenstein –'

'We begin with Lester Basil Melvane,' Harpur said, 'fourteen years for attempted armed robbery and other offences taken into account.'

'New life,' Iles said. 'This is an exciting, positive task – a difficult though achievable task. When I say "I" wish to bring about this new life I mean, of course, "I" with help. Such help will come from many of you in this room and I am grateful. Such help will come from Colin Harpur and Francis Garland. They have a supreme flair, and, odiously disloyal and scheming though they may have been, bringing moral pollution to those whom –'

'Lester Basil Melvane was a member of the so-called powerful "Onset" criminal syndicate headed by his father, Walter George Melvane. This has operated in south-east

27

London from the 1970s. Lester was arrested and convicted with the aid of Ian Ballion, now Robert Templedon,' Harpur said. 'There are known violent offenders among Melvane's relatives, including the father, and, of course, among Lester's associates and friends, who might look for vengeance on an informant responsible for his capture and imprisonment.'

Chapter Six

We'll find you, Templedon – Templedon, once Ballion.
Robert Templedon heard these words, this routine threat, but only in his head. The flip-chart picture of Lester at the safe house session came enlarged from a police dossier, front-on, his features expressionless, just identity, identity. There was, of course, no speech bubble with that vivid promise in it, *We'll find you, Templedon – Templedon, once Ballion.* But Templedon, once Ballion, knew – knew – the Lester lips would have made a grand, cold job of this warning. That was supposing the Templedon name ever leaked and reached the Melvane family and crew. Identity, identity. Oh, God, let's *not* suppose it. Any leak would turn this get-together and its careful arrangements for him, Jane, formerly Eleanor, and the children into farce.

Did it already look like farce? How could anyone explain this snarling, weeping, smiling Assistant Chief Constable otherwise? Back there, far away in London, Metropolitan Police detectives had assured Ballion, now Templedon, that ACC Desmond Iles, down in this suitable, provincial wasteland, was brilliant, reliable, sympathetic. You bet they'd assured him. It suited them. A new existence on Iles's far-from-London, far-from-danger patch for Templedon and family made the heart of the deal Ian Ballion ultimately agreed with them. God, that stinking deal. Had those Met detectives ever actually seen Iles perform? Did they know how he grief-raved about his wife, hate-raved at his two main aides, then went smoochy about them, and then switched back to hate? Schizo? The bugger felt forced to deny he wanted them both dead – an Assistant Chief Constable, for God's sake, an *Assistant Chief Constable* out in Nowheresville decides he must deny ever considering the murder of two colleagues because they'd apparently had his wife, 'though not, it goes without saying, at the same time' – so that was nearly OK, then. Did those Met people know Iles's sick, suffering chuckle? They could *not* know the way he had let his eyes wander around Jane. What kind of police force *was* this?

The sweet, false Met descriptions of Iles reminded him of other cheer-ups and fruity 'Take-our-word-for-it-Ian' pledges he'd been given by the same London detectives. Back before the job, when the job was still only a notion, they promised him there'd be no question of ambush if he grassed the details for them – no arrests, simply prevention through a huge, deterrent show of force at the spot. Just tell them the spot, the time, so this huge, deterrent show of force could be in place and . . . and deter. No encounter, no shooting, no arrests, just deterrence. This would satisfy them, they said – mere prevention. Like that, it would hardly be grassing at all, would it? He'd get no blame from mates or mates' families and pals, no loathing. Police always said what suited – what suited *them*. Naturally. They were police. How had he expected anything else? He'd been a fool? . . .

. . . The jabbering, crazed Iles called it Creation, but really this Meadowland conference aimed at rebuilding. OK, that could be terrific, too. So positive. But you only rebuilt after catastrophe, collapse, devastation, and they – the London Met chums of Iles and Harpur and Garland – had brought plenty of all those . . .

. . . As a matter of fact, Templedon's daughter – Ballion's daughter then, of course – his daughter was cello practising in the sitting room when Lester first called around in Highgate, London, with early, happy ideas for the job – or what he called 'an enterprise'. Lester liked a bit of vocab now and then to decorate his very rickety grammar. Lester brought what looked like sound information, and sound names of those he fancied to make up a stupendous grab-it team. These were Hector Serge Knille and Roy Boon-Mace generally known as Delicate Royston or Royston the Delicate. Yes, great, reliable lads, and reliable all ways – able to do it and not *over*do it. These were people with true CVs, and with something better – the kind of carefulness and clever greed that brought fine luck. Naturally, Lester sounded pleased as he spoke their names. They thrilled Ballion, later Templedon, too.

But then Hector Serge Knille turns out to be unavailable at this particular juncture. It was not on account of jail or pussy quest or wounds, but because his mother now needed twenty four-hour nursing at home, and Hector Serge decided in his big, dutiful way he would be it. Lester said he explained to him that if he came on the 'enterprise', and if it worked, Hect would have cash to buy in any amount of proper, non-stop professional nursing for ma, or to put her in a splendid place with twenty-four-hour attention, clean bed linen daily, smoke alarms, private rooms and all the TV channels. This didn't grab Hector. The second 'if' – the one that said '*if* it worked' – *if* the enterprise turned out good – this uncertainty troubled him right into the core. Anyone could spot that.

Obviously, nobody liked ifs, but they came with the career, and normally Hector would not have minded. Any try-on at taking big funds in transit – and these funds in transit were mighty – any try-on would always have ifs and risks. This could not be like carding a cash machine. Hector recognized that, obviously. However, for him a sick and maybe dying mother was important, and, anyway, he'd seemed to feel he, only he, should attend her, regardless of how rich he got. Hector Serge had always been known as quite fond of his mother, though not gay. You could often run up against quirky emotional things like this when trying to organize a party.

31

And so . . . well, yes . . . and so. And so, Adrian Luke Stanley Foden, picked by Lester as replacement, picked in a great fucking scrabbling rush by Lester, vouched for, apparently. Who by? . . .

. . . Lester had been absolutely cultured about Rose's cello practice. He sat with fine patience listening, no dopey smile of love-it-whatever-it's-fucking-like on view. Instead, his face showed what could easily have seemed lifelong, genuine, wise interest in kids' cello playing, unless you knew what Lester was really like . . .

. . . If you *did* know what Lester was really like, and what some of Lester's relatives and chums of Lester were really like, you'd definitely get big nerves now in Meadowland safe house when the Iles sidekick, Harpur, took them all through his chart details, first on Lester, Royston and Foden, as nabbed at the cash-in-transit disaster, and subsequently jailed for eternity. Then came a run-down of the Melvane family and phalanx. This brought a moment, a long series of moments, when Robert Templedon found himself wanting to howl, 'Yes, yes, I'm Robert Maurice Templedon, not Ian Maitland Ballion, never was Ian Maitland Ballion. The girl on the cello then was my daughter, Sian Rebecca Templedon, not Rose Diana Ballion, and I have a son called Harry Charles Templedon, not Larry Raymond Ballion. My wife is Jane Iris Templedon, pet name Jit, from the initials, as in "every jit and tottle" – joke! – and not, never, Eleanor Carys Veronica Ballion.'

And, confirming to himself and reconfirming, he did definitely notice a flicker of something warm and fleshly for Jane Iris Templedon, or Jit, in that mad dandy, Iles. Were those wounded, wounding eyes on her a bit often and well beyond the call of duty? Hell, this could turn into a situation, couldn't it? Yes, hell. Robert Maurice Templedon's continuing life depended at least partly on that frenzied, immaculate, longing cop. This gave the frenzied, immaculate, longing cop some special strengths in any fight for a woman, didn't it? Pushed to the limit, what if

Robert Maurice Templedon got a bad dose of .45 shells in and around the heart one day or night? The immediate and continuing and reasonable thought would be that the Melvane clan or pals – or Delicate's clan or pals, or even Adrian Foden's clan or pals – had somehow twigged the smelting of Ballion into Templedon and seen off Templedon in the way laid down by powerful tradition within the firms. It went like this – 'Kill grasses, if possible before their grassing works, but, in any case, kill them.' There'd be no need for police to look outside the Melvane or Boon-Mace or Foden families and mates for the executioner.

Iles might be the sort who would note this possibility, this opportunity, and know how to use it. Wasn't there a chilly tale about him?* It said, very unprovably, that he'd personally seen off two villains acquitted of killing an undercover detective – an acquittal Iles didn't care for? Garotting? Jesus. If he wanted Jane, once Eleanor, might Iles do some intelligent leaking in the London direction to get her husband gone? Or might he handle the thing himself, certain it would be blamed on people upset by the jailings? . . .

. . . In those distant, eternally ditched Highgate, London, days, Sian Rebecca Templedon, or Rose Diana Ballion, had finished her cello playing after about fifteen minutes and left him and Lester alone in the room. Once the door closed, Lester started selling the job to Ballion, before he'd even heard what it was. Lester said: 'This would be a girl who deserves the total best, I can see that. Potential? She got it – to be brought out via devotion and money. I'm glad I come, Ian, because it's to talk money – the kind you want. Highgate – a lovely area, and you got to live up to it. Plus, I believe now your talented daughter must have high grade music teaching, plus a tip-top instrument.'

Lester was very creative and positive with loot. He saw it as the route to a more select way of life, or death in the case of Hector's mother. Always he strove for what he

* See *Halo Parade*.

called the 'tip-top'. He had a vision. His robberies were an untiring quest for class, not just for himself but associates. Fourteen years in a max security, when it came, interfered with this mission. Ballion now Templedon would carry the can for that, if his parents and so on could find Ballion now Templedon . . .

. . . 'What we got to ask, Ian, is is the instrument your daughter got tip-top?' Lester had said. 'You need earnings at a glorious level. You're like what used to be called, far back, a patron. In them days, things like Music or Art depended on such patrons – some duke or prince or merchant would see it like a duty to help talent. This now is you, Ian. So you needs such wealth in a great cause.'

He stood and went over to look at the cello. The move reeked of true confidence. You would think he lived cellos. Most probably he had never seen one before, but he knew how to use a chance, whether it was an armoured van with heavy funds inside, or a kid's bit of Schumann. He stroked the wood of the cello lightly, like communing, assessing, getting in touch with the whole history of music, then went slowly back to his chair full of cultured ponder. 'This is something you shouldn't never skimp on, the instrument, Ian. A girl like that, taking her instrument into a college where other kids got tip-top instruments – she's going to feel bad if her instrument is only a so-so instrument because of expense. That makes me sad. It could put her off playing her best, on account of morale. And same with the teacher. You want someone with true tip-top talent, and they cost. Most probably there's plenty around who *think* they got talent and they can give her scales and how to keep her elbow right and, don't get me wrong, her elbow looked great. That elbow looked a natural elbow. For a cello player. But it's the *feeling* they got to get into it all, isn't it? What makes a star. Think of actors. Some of them seem to of got everything – biceps, straight nose, a voice that can be right for whatever – gravelly when it got to be gravelly, smooth for charm. But can they do the feeling? And it's only a *great* teacher who can show them how to jolly this aspect up. Expensive, yes, but what a father would want to give, I'm sure. Well, what I'm bringing now – this is something so you can buy her the tip-top best – an instrument, a teacher. And the best for your boy – whatever he likes. Boys goes more for the guitar. There's high-grade guitars, just like high-grade cellos. Or the greatest soccer boots or training shoes.'

'What's the picture, Lester?'

'I thought of you first, before anyone. I don't mean just because of cellos. Well, I didn't even know there'd *be* a cello, did I? But we worked together already, we know each other.'

'I'll go with that.'

You got judgement. A brain. You was in a college,' Lester said. 'University.'

'A year. I chucked it. Couldn't see the use.'

'All the same. Judgement,' Lester said. 'And nice with a weapon. Didn't you tell me you was in the university gun club?'

'Where I met Eleanor. She stayed on.'

'In the gun club?' Lester said.

'In the gun club and the university. She took her degree.'

'I'm not against that. Women, they got as much right.'

'Sure.'

'And playing something herself,' Lester said.

'Viola.'

'Again, a lovely instrument, as long as you got the best. It's like a handgun, isn't it? There's automatics and then again there's the best automatics. Same with the viola. You got the best for her?'

'Well, I –'

'You first. Then I thought, once you was in, Hector Knille,' Lester said.

'He's a good boy.'

'A true one,' Lester replied.

35

'Right.'

'Personnel – this is my big strength, Ian. Choosing.'

'A skill.'

'I got it. All right, I couldn't do the driving and my gun work is frail, but Personnel – this is a flair.'

'Right.'

'And then, after you two, Delicate Royston – Royston Boon-Mace,' Lester said.

'Delicate's amazing – the way he gets away with things.'

'What we want,' Lester said. 'If you done a what-you-call for Delicate –'

'What?'

'Like for a job.'

'A CV.'

'Right, a CV. If you done a CV for Delicate – I mean, if he was going for a job in a sewage farm or Number 10 Downing Street, that's what you would say – "He gets away with things."'

'I'm trying to work out from these people you've picked what kind of –'

'This is an enterprise,' Lester said.

'In which area?'

'When I tell you, you're going to say, "Lester's coming to pieces. The dim, pathetic sod's talking the so obvious."'

'Sometimes the obvious is –'

'Cash in transit,' Lester replied.

'I did think maybe cash in transit.'

'That's what I mean. Obvious. Obvious to the trained brain, even if you was only at the coll for a year. You'll say, "What else, for fuck's sake? Who does banks in this millennium – cameras, armoured glass?"'

'I was going by the people you've picked. If it's Hector and Royston the Delicate, this is their –'

'And it's yours – yours personally,' Lester replied. 'Your flair – like mine's Personnel. That's what I mean, isn't it?'

'What?'

'*Your* flair is for cash in transit and mine's Personnel. So I pick you because you are the personnel my flair for Personnel tells me I should have because of *your* flair.'

'Subtle. I've done some cash in transit, yes.'

'Some! Some! Enough to get a great house in Highgate and the cars and woman. This is why I said judgement. Special judgement. You had the judgement to get out of that college where they was teaching judgement and use your judgement to pick a trade with real, quick comforting returns. Oh, pardon, that's crude to say "woman" and to put her last like she was just a bought item. But I had in mind you done enough to buy a house and the cars that are up to the mark for a great wife, that's all. Plus a kid with a great cello – I don't say nothing against that cello, regardless of what I mentioned previous. That is a *good* cello – I done a proper scrutiny – and many would consider it as totally all right, which it might be, only I'm saying there could be even better, that's all.'

Lester didn't do alcohol so they were both drinking ginger beer straight from the bottles. He said: 'Hector, Royston, they're –'

'These are controlled people.'

'Right. And me, you, Ian – *we're* controlled people. We don't go blasting off at an incident just for the sake of it, even though you was in a shooting club. Oh, we go armed on this one, of course we go armed. Tell me how to get cash in transit *out* of transit if we don't have a weapon or two to show them. But that's it – to *show* them. You, me, Hector, Delicate Royston - we're not fucking bang-bang loonies, I hope. These guns are to persuade them to pass the contents over peaceful. Remember in the robbing movie with the cop's ear off while that head case is dancing – they're after jewellery and one of them blasts away when it's not needed?'

'*Reservoir Dogs.*'

'And starts all the agony.'

'What cash in transit, Lester?'

'Plentiful.'

'Whose?'

'Ours soon,' Lester said.

'Whose before it's ours?'

'Third World.'

'Third World cash?'

'First World cash now, but *from* the Third World. That's all they can rely on for certain out there – US, Brit, Euro, cash. In the Third World, cheques, bankers' drafts, share certificates – you can't trust they'll ever pay up. That's what Third World signifies.'

'What?'

'Shaky,' Lester said. 'This is well known. Always asking to have their fucking debt written off. Whose mother was it used to tell him, "You're twice the man with a fifty note in your shoe"?'

'Hector's?'

'It could be Hector's. She'd do brilliant in the Third World. That's the kind of thinking. But fifty with a lot of noughts behind, and not in the shoe.'

'I heard she's not too great.'

'Who?'

'Hector's mother. Sick.'

'Hector will be all right,' Lester said. 'That's always going to happen with mothers. Their bodies have took a lot of special stress in life – births and fighting hairdressers so they'll do it the way they want.'

'Which part of the Third World?'

'Africa. One of them countries out there. It's well known.'

'Bit rough some of them, aren't they? The politics.'

'That's what I mean,' Lester replied.

'What?'

'Cash.'

'I don't –'

'Think of someone out there,' Lester said, 'someone

38

nearly tip-top in the line-up but only *nearly* tip-top, so in a dicey position – the head guy scared of him in case he's doing a plot.'

'Like Blair and Brown.'

'There's plots all the time out there, known as coups or putsches. These are words you'll see in the press all the time, meaning, *Me, I want the fucking top job so move over or you're meat.* Someone like that, someone only *nearly* tip-top, he got to be planning all the time how to get up the next step, yes. But also how to get out and fix himself up somewhere else if he got to get out because the top man is so nervous he decides to bring this one just below him to an end before he can try one of them coups or putsches. What's known as pre-emptive.'

Lester had obviously been doing some real background work. When you got down to it, what he was talking about might be only a street hit on cash in transit, but Lester liked to give good, deep explanations of things, on the philosophical side.

'Pre-emptive is a well-known term and I don't want you puzzled by it, Ian,' he said. 'Or perhaps you heard in the college, anyway, even if you was only there a year. History – that's where pre-emptive comes from. A President of the United States called Harry Truman, he was thinking once of getting pre-emptive with Russia, such as nuking them before they could nuke. Or some rugby coach who told his team, "Get your retaliation in first." That's crazy, if you think about it, because retaliation is what you do when it's already been done to you. Yes, it *seems* crazy, but it's clever, too. Diplomats – they all know pre-emptive. Donald Rumsfeld and Iraq – that was pre-emptive. This is, *Hit them NOW in case they hit us, so it gets too late to hit them.* He'd know all about that – the pre-emptive.'

'Who?'

'Our boy,' Lester said. 'Mr Target, who's near the top out there but not the top, yet. He's a diplomat in his country. He's thinking all the time he might get there – Prime

Minister or it could be President. But he knows the nearer he gets makes it more dangerous for him because of the pre-emptive from the one above him who knows our lad is climbing up to be Supremo if he can. So our boy's ready in case he got to exit very fast because the Number One gets so scared of the Number Two getting near that he decides to set his special thugs on him. Meaning – in secret our lad's piling up loot from all the scams they got out there, and maybe needing to move this treasure to another country, say First World, say Britain. He's a diplomat but he got a lot to do with the trade side out there – very dab-in-the-handable in good currencies, not the local dross. They expect that out there, them Third World biggies.'

'He sounds to me as if –'

'Look, things out there are so crooked in one country . . . this is still Africa . . . this country, they got their own oil wells out there . . . I mean, they could be big petrol makers, but things are so crooked they got to buy in their motor fuel from abroad, because the countries selling them the motor fuel give big bribes to officials to get it bought. They don't look after their refineries because if the refineries was working right there would not be no need to buy in and the lovely sweeteners would stop.'

'He can get such big cash loads out – and in, Lester?'

'Our boy brings stuff through Customs unopened being a diplomat. Diplomats got to be trusted. This is a well-known rule for all countries. What's known as "the diplomatic bag". It's more than a bag, really. That's just the name they give it. Anything he brings through – boxes, cases – it's all part of the diplomatic bag.'

'Cash?'

'He's already brought out a couple of million,' Lester replied. 'He's buying property, now London prices and around are not so bad. Investment *and* somewhere to live, if he got to flit. Plus family, wife and women and kids.'

'How do you know, Lester?'

'The money? He's buying with cash. This is bound to be

noticed. Someone comes and puts down £400,000 in notes for a property, no mortgage, no cheque. That got to be unusual. I get word from a girl in an estate agent I used to have something going with and we finished without no bad feeling. She knows she'll get a good gift if we can do something on this enterprise. This is a girl who is sure I act fair with women because when we broke up it was friendly and I put some pounds her way as a true thank-you for all her niceness and so on. They advised him Sevenoaks. He's out in Africa most of the time, so he don't know this scene. She says he asked them to point him to where it's best. This is intelligent. They're buying places for him in Sevenoaks. Ordinary houses in good streets which are not selling too fast there, but it will all pick up. Commuters. And now he's looking for a country place for himself and household, in case. This is up to £3 million. Yes, that's a lot of diplomatic luggage through Customs, but he's got the wind up – he sees signs out there, I expect – and he'll do it. She'll get a date for us.'

'He travels alone? Arrives with his trunks of money for deals alone?'

'No, a minder,' Lester said. 'Also black. Always the same one. His countryman, I suppose, but living here. Perhaps he meets our lad at the airport. The minder might carry weaponry, yes. Our boy can't do that. Even diplomats have to go through screening. But the minder might bring him something. So, once he's here, there could be two weapons, yes. Why we need something to show them. Four of us, two of them. They'll spot the difference. They'll see they could be blasted.'

It had sounded possible, but not very. Would those two, sitting on millions, be ready to cave in gently because the gun balance was against them? It might not be. They could have two each, and rapid fire automatics.

'An ordinary car, Lester? Not armoured?'

'Shogun style four-wheel drive, with the back seats took out to make space for special luggage.'

'So, we'll need the same, or a van, to cart the load away?'

'Delicate's the one for vehicles. You could call vehicles a passion with Royston. He can get just the right vehicle for the occasion, like a genius. Vehicles – Delicate could handle a coronation. He got a sense of style.'

Chapter Seven

'Lester Basil Melvane,' Harpur said. 'Fourteen years for attempted armed robbery and other offences. Officers of the Metropolitan Police, acting on information received, intercepted an armed raid on a vehicle and following an exchange of fire arrested Melvane and two accomplices. These two we shall consider later.'

Harpur, standing by his chart with Melvane's picture up, looked out on the crowded Meadowland safe house room and thought he could see why Templedon's wife – Templedon, Templedon, Templedon – they all had to live with that name now, not Ballion – yes, Harpur could see why Templedon's wife would get noticed by Iles in the Assistant Chief's particular, very positive way of noticing. Mostly, her features showed rich vivacity and poise, and yet also a trace now and then of aching melancholy.

That would be normal enough for the woman of a resettled grass. Harpur had observed such sadness in other women in other previous meetings like this one, in other safe houses. After all, their lives were about to be upended, whether or not they wanted that. The drill here aimed to impose total amnesia on people – the wipe-out of what they were, and substitution of what they must become. Of course, that could not happen. They retained their memories. They did not, in fact, suffer from Alzheimer amnesia. Just the same, the object was to outlaw those memories, discourage them, break people like Jane Templedon from their former selves and selfhood, cancel their pasts. They could have no history, or none they should acknowledge, and certainly not dwell on. They must be persuaded into a kind of suicide – a special version of that phrase, 'process of elimination'. This would always be painful and confusing. On top of that, some of these spouses and partners felt shame at being so clearly linked to an informant. They knew about the hate and contempt brought by grassing. Naturally they did – this meeting and others like it only took place to counter such hate and contempt and what they might result in.

Contrasts in a woman could pull Iles. He would fancy himself skilled not just at spotting this grief beneath the glamour, but probably believed he could bring it to the surface and deal with it – perhaps soothe it away. Iles considered there was quite a therapy side to him. Now and then kindness would unquestionably get into his face and remain a while. He'd told Harpur there were people out there who yearned to yell, 'Oh, comfort me, do, Desmond,' especially women, or possibly only women. He said he certainly did not seek such approaches, but that this urge possessed them whether he was in civilian clothes or uniform at the time.

Someone on the other side of the room said: 'Mr Harpur, since this is a meeting about Mr Robert Templedon, when you mention "acting on information received" do we assume that this information came from –'

'"Acting on information received" is a kind of formula,' Harpur replied.

'Yes, but because we are here on account of Mr Robert Templedon, do we assume –'

'Yes, we assume,' Harpur replied. What use the standard attempt at secrecy? He moved to the next page. It contained seven names:

Vera Melvane, mother.
Walter George Melvane, father.
Donald Lawrence Melvane, brother, known as Solid.
Emily Marie Aspen, sister.

44

Silvester Tom Aspen, brother-in-law.
David Simms Millfloss, associate, known as Optimum.
Justin Oliver Mark Labbert, associate.

Harpur said: 'In your portfolios you'll find enlarged photographs, numbered 1 to 7. These are the family and fellowship connections of Lester Basil Melvane who might be threats to Robert Templedon and his family.' Harpur waited a little while they studied the page. Perhaps Jane Templedon set up memories for Iles. He'd once had a girlfriend called Celia Mars with the same sort of deep contradictions in her beautiful face.* She was dark and slender and to Harpur looked like an Italian princess, if Italy had princesses – but one grieving over lost terrain. She died long ago in a fire, probably before Iles could get full throttle empathy going to treat her downside. Perhaps he continued to search and search for the same mixture of animation and unexplained grief, hoping to match Celia and this time bring help before it was too late. Obviously, a complex, mature personality like Celia's or Mrs Templedon's wasn't what the Assistant Chief sought in Harpur's daughter, Hazel. No fifteen-year-old could provide that mix of qualities.

Harpur exposed the next page of his chart. It contained a small picture of Vera Melvane and a description supplied by the Met. Again, Harpur gave them time to take it in. She wouldn't be a threat herself, but he wanted all present to realize the kind of network Lester Melvane came from. Even desk civil servants involved in this resettlement must be made to realize the importance of total, permanent confidentiality, although their work would never land them in the possible violence.

'This woman, Vera Melvane, is where the main hate will come from, I'm sure,' Iles said. 'What matriarchs are for.'

Harpur always tried not to speculate too much on what Iles *did* look for in Hazel. Possibly because of his own

* See *Halo Parade*.

45

complexity, and his eminence, and his arrant neediness, Iles deserved the love of various women as well as his wife. OK, you smart, insidious lout, but just stay off my daughter.

'In a way, Vera Melvane's hatred is understandable,' Iles said, '– her boy buried in a cell for years on account of that "information received". Oh, one is a police officer and to this extent approves the due exercise of law and order against Lester and the rest, definitely. Yet, one is a parent oneself and can imagine the pain.' He nodded a couple of times and then gave another of those confident, stone-dead chuckles: 'By the way, the child one is parent of is undoubtedly *my* child. The calendar allows no dispute on that. Vasectomies can be reversed. In view of what I spoke of earlier, I must feel sure you're clear on this. Certainly my wife did look for emotional release elsewhere at one stage, even pre-Harpur and Garland. But my child *is* my child, and so I as a parent understand Vera Melvane's feelings and what they might produce. I – we – understand, but we defeat them. We safeguard Robert Templedon and those dear to him. Observing Harpur's unpolished looks, and hearing of his moral looseness with a dear colleague's wife, you possibly wonder whether he has the brain and resolve to repel the kind of people who might come hunting the Templedons. Yes, you possibly wonder, but when it comes to work I have faith in Harpur, regardless.'

'Thank you, sir.' Harpur read the Vera Melvane profile aloud: '"Age 62 years, 5 feet 6 inches, 148 pounds, brunetted grey at most recent sighting, eyes brown, skin fair. No convictions. Dominant figure in the Melvane family and organization with total devotion to husband and sons. Unwavering visitor to any or all of the three now jailed, regardless of distance. Considered unlikely to carry out any attack on R.M. Templedon or family in person if they were traced, but would probably be a powerful motivator

46

and mind in attempting this trace and, if successful, in planning the attack."'

'Exactly,' Iles said.

Harpur went to the next page for Melvane's father. 'This is different. Plainly, Walter George Melvane must represent one of the most likely *actual* dangers to Robert Templedon and family. He will feel an obligation to revenge his son. Such pressures are acute in their culture.'

'*Culture*,' Iles said. 'Doesn't Harpur like a bit of gobbledegook though?'

Harpur said: 'Their culture will require – yes, require – the father and possibly other family males to get after the man they know as Ian Ballion. The Met profile of Walter makes rough reading.' He let them digest it.

Walter George Melvane, age 64, 5 feet 11 inches, 198 pounds, eyes blue-grey, skin fair, hair fair and grey, sparse. Convictions since 1959 for theft, armed robbery, menaces, grievous bodily harm, latest 1992, menaces. Continuing head of London Onset crime syndicate. Onset's activities include, or have included, protection, robbery, drug trafficking, prostitution networks. As father, must avenge for 'face' considerations. Firearms proficient. Lester to have succeeded Walter. Older brother, Donald Lawrence, said to lack drive, creative boldness, organizational skills – nickname, Solid, is meant as dud rating. Removal of Lester threatens future Onset structure and plan for orderly leadership transfer, increasing resentment against informant.

Revenge. It might not be only the Melvanes and their clique who sought that, of course. Harpur came back to a previous troublesome thought – that the ACC's stalk of Hazel could be partly revenge for Harpur and Sarah Iles. The Assistant Chief was handy at revenge.

Harpur said: 'Vera Melvane would probably be one of those urging her husband to action. Please give the photograph and caption of Walter George special study.'

Yes, revenge. Iles sometimes seemed to feel the courts needed special aid. Harpur recalled a case around Celia Mars' time. Two villains and their lawyers managed a Not Guilty on charges of murdering the undercover detective, Raymond Street. Then, soon after celebrating this let-off, the two were grotesquely and mysteriously slaughtered. Or maybe not mysteriously. The acquittals had really enraged Iles. Street's death still gave him appalling pain – pain and shame, for failing to stop it. Emotional surges were part of Iles. Fine, but keep them clear of Hazel.

Harpur thought he spotted a notebook open on a knee over near the curtained bay window 'Please, I say again, nothing written down,' he said.

The woman, from one of the government departments, said: 'This is a lot to absorb. It might help if –'

'Nothing written.'

'But you – you have everything written on the charts.'

'Harpur will eat them as soon as this is over,' Iles said.

Whatever the ACC saw in Hazel, Harpur wished he didn't and still wondered whether Mrs Templedon could shift him away – longed to feel Mrs Templedon could shift him away. All right, this might upset Hazel, but Hazel was a child and the hurt wouldn't last. In any case, the hurt would be stupid, though it might be tough convincing her. Surely, a father bringing up daughters alone had a duty to persuade them that worse things than sessions of brief emotional distress could happen, especially when what could happen was Desmond Iles. Harpur watched Mrs Templedon to see whether she'd picked up any indications of communion from the Assistant Chief, and whether she responded. Some women might sympathetically regard Iles's spells of spit-flying, screaming derangement as signs of an over-sensitive nature pushed off balance for a moment by the world's routine cruelties. Perhaps they'd fail to see that Iles himself was generally one of the world's routine cruelties. Women could be damn tolerant.

Chapter Eight

All right, Robert Maurice Templedon would admit the Meadowland meeting had a plus or two. Of course it had a plus or two, for God's sake. It was meant to keep him alive. For another thing, to be addressed and spoken about as Templedon or Robert so often did help in getting used to this new he, him. People spoke the name as natural. To Templedon, it couldn't be that, not yet, but the repetition did help. When he'd wanted to scream, 'I'm Templedon not Ballion,' it was a bad panic moment, not really a sign that he'd accepted the new identity. The opposite. He'd longed to chuck the Ballion label but found it stuck and stuck. And so, in his head, he'd yelled that desperate denial of what he used to be. Afterwards, he felt ashamed of this spasm. But, hearing people in that room refer to him automatically and easily as Templedon, made the name come across as almost normal. In a few weeks he might be able to regard it as a real part of him. More than a part – as the real total of him, his entity.

'Robert' was OK. It had structure. Not Bob or Bobby. And nobody at Meadowland used either of these. They wanted to give him a real hold on new, respectable realities, and Robert as a name helped. That king – nobody called him Bob the Bruce. It wouldn't be such a strong tale. And nobody called Mugabe Bobby Mugabe, or nobody who stayed alive.

The profiles sent from London had seemed damn thorough – that Melvane dynasty first and, then, as the evening went on, Harpur also showed the family and/or connections of Delicate Royston Boon-Mace and Adrian Luke Stanley Foden. London must be really worried about safety, or why the depth of research? Some on those lists were new to him. He didn't know any of the Foden tribe, and only one or two Boon-Mace people. As soon as they reached home after the Meadowland session he wrote down all names and descriptions he could remember – and to hell with conference rules. He had to keep in mind the full field. People from any part or page of those charts might turn up in the street one day if things went bad, and he had to be able to spot them early.

Near the end of the meeting, the charts had, in fact, been cleared away and there were drinks and general mixing and chat, with constant use of the new names, his own and Jane's. *Get used to them. Get used to them.* This would be a survival condition – for her, him and the kids. Just the same, he could tell that half the people chatting to him felt more interested in what he did before turning Templedon. Robbing had a greater zing to it than this move into lawfulness. Nobody actually talked about that, though. Ballion topics were off limits. Ballion did not exist.

At about 10.15 p.m. they left the safe house and drove home to what Templedon must regard as another safe house, but this one simply 18 Cormorant Avenue, government provided and theirs for ever, or until pinpointed by those on one or more of the charts with a harsh, self-created mission to pinpoint it. Apparently, 18 Cormorant Avenue came from the B7 range of special accommodation for ex-informants. There'd been six in this category for them to choose from. B7 was the highest quality housing offered. Number 18 Cormorant Avenue looked like at least £320,000, even here, out of London. It would still be cheaper and bureaucratically simpler than setting up the family abroad.

Templedon saw he rated as a super-supergrass. What he'd done was an accident and a mistake, but the police still prized him. To get an important Melvane put away for fourteen years and bring the Onset succession deep fuck-up earned major esteem, however the triumphs came about. A crooked hierarchy might be finished because of what Templedon leaked, like wiping out the Romanovs. Plus, Delicate Royston and Foden had been put out of trouble for a fine while, as the Met would see it.

Number 18 was a good, large detached property, two bathrooms and an en suite, in the Dally Grange district, an achievers' area with double garages and wide pavements. Their house had what looked like smart alarms, though probably not smart enough to keep out Walter George Melvane or some of the others if the address grew famous. Barratt, the builders, couldn't do a moat and drawbridge. Plenty of names had been dished out lately and he wondered if the house should have one – not something accurate like Bolthole or Hideaway but a vague, pleasant label, say Repose. New Day?

Templedon thought Walter George Melvane probably ranked as the most dangerous on Harpur's charts. As a matter of fact, Lester had talked a lot about his dad on that first visit – the cello visit – when they discussed 'the enterprise'. Obviously, at this time Walter George Melvane was only a kind of mate and Lester's father, not an obsessed avenger. Ballion days then, not New Day . . .

. . . 'My pa – do you know what he thinks of this job? He thinks fucking great,' Lester had said. 'I always tell him when something's coming up because he got the experience and an eye, he sees the possibles – I mean, not just the *good* possibles, but where the perils could be. He's not scared of perils – he's not scared of nothing – but he thinks perils got to be took care of. What I mean when I say experience. He've seen things go wrong sometimes, or would he of got the form he got? This makes him a bit . . . like, critical. It's good. What he can do is appraisals. What a dad's *for*. He'll really give some big thinking to any enterprise I work on, or Solid, but mostly me because Solid

51

don't come up with ideas, he waits for other people's ideas. He's all right, he's my brother, but I don't want him on this one, and pa also said this is not one for Solid, not his kind of . . . well, skills. He got true skills and he got bottle, you will never hear me say different, but not this sort of skills. Pa thought me, you and two others. When it's cash in transit, he got a big cred in you and respect. Them two – cred, respect – he don't give to many. If you been inside as much as pa you wonder all the time what fucker's going to let you down now. But you – he would never think of you as one who would let him down, Ian.'

And he never would have let them down if things had gone the way they were supposed to go. 'I respect him, likewise, Lester. This is someone who has made his own organization from nothing back in the seventies, and looked after it, made it grow. Positive – always.'

'Positive? He's hot on that. "Things won't come to you, you got to go to them," is what he told me and Solid often. I don't know if you heard the word "proactive". This is getting out there and doing it, not waiting until a chance stands up and calls you. This is my pa, and also yours truly. Well, it been passed down. In the blood. Solid – he got other things. Me – initiative. Pa – initiative. He's *so* keen on that.'

'He's a remarkable –'

'And he got respect for Eleanor, also. The college, and the way she takes care of them kids. He being a family man, he can appreciate a family,' Lester said.

'Eleanor will be glad to hear approval like that from someone of Walter Melvane's standing, believe me.'

'"Standing". That's right. You got the words, Ian. They just comes to you, so easy. That's college.'

'Not much of it.'

'You went that way, I went different, but now, here we are, together. And we'll get a sweet team working. I could tell pa would love to come himself on this enterprise because he always been interested in far continents. This is a thing with him. I don't know how many times he seen that movie, *Out of Africa*, cinema *and* video, so when it's big *funds* out of Africa but in good Western bills this really grabs him. There's something deep in pa that tells him he *ought* to be on such an enterprise because of his flairs. He's sensible, though. He knows he's a bit old these days for a ploy like this, a street ploy. His legs are still great and coolness. He is someone who don't even know how to feel fright. Situations are what pa was born for. Hard situations, I mean. Street situations. But . . . but he's bound to think, and so is my mother, he's bound to think that if it went bad he'll finish life in a max security and this is no comfy thought. Death will turn him wan when it comes, so why get jail-pale earlier? But, look, pa don't think this enterprise *will* go bad – just he's not so strong and quick lately. Well, of course not, sixty-four. Yeah, legs great, but a bit of breathlessness and wheeze – that kind of thing. When you think about it, all sorts in commerce and industry been retired for years when they're sixty-four, getting golf in at the Algarve or Spain, taking it easy because they earned it. All right, I heard Winston Churchill never really got going until he was sixty-six Second World War time, but it's different making them "On the beaches" speeches from doing a street job – tearing into a couple of loaded blacks and humping undoubted big currency wads. If you got breathlessness it could show in a caper like that. Very manual. What I say to him is, he's still the top in Onset, no question, but, like in industry or stockbrokers, he ought to pull back a bit now from the contact stuff. He could become like Chairman – someone who watches everything in the company just like always but not needing to get into the little details, such as waylaying and taking. I don't know if you ever heard the word emeritus, Ian?'

'Well, in –'

'In colleges and so on. You're right. If someone got a job that's emeritus it means they're useful to everything because they're so good at it – which is why in the word

53

emeritus comes "merit", meaning to deserve something –
but some professor who is emeritus he don't have to go in
and write on the blackboard no more or get them reciting
multiplication tables, he thinks bigger, he thinks what is
known as global, meaning policy. Another word you might
of heard of – overview. It could be the same with pa. He
don't need to come and help do a Shogun for its cash load,
he just lets me know how's the best way to do it, and this
would be how an emeritus helps.'

'Strategy, not tactics.'

'Could be that, yes. Pa likes the research I done,' Lester
replied. '"This is a project that been prepared, really prepared" – his own words. What pa would hate for me or
Solid is rush into something, no plans, just hoping for the
best. What he says is, "He hoped for the best" should be on
quite a few gravestones. He said I must really of been
giving it to that girl from the estate agent's the way she
liked if she's coming up with all this grand info even
though it's over. Oh, a nice kid. Young. She and the one
she's with now got a lot of debt on account of being at
university theirselves and they never got over it. Fees. You
was *so* bright to leave.'

'Before the days of fees. I just got so I couldn't see the
point.'

'So there'll be more like you now. Do the government
know what they done for robbery when they said fees? Oh,
we hear about students who got to work nights on directory enquiries or McDonald's, but the cream of students,
such as you, you gets your brain to work in that college
and can see the best way out is get out of that college
soonest and get taking. This girl couldn't see no personal
way of getting into the cash piles like you, Ian, so she
thinks of info to Lester. She can rely on me and a percentage, she knows that. I think she done percentages in
her studies.'

'A driver?'

'What – with them?'

'Yes.'

'No. Didn't I tell you, just the two?' Lester replied.

'Yes, but I thought maybe you meant two plus a driver.'

'If I say two it's two.'

'All right, all right.'

'Oh, look, I don't mind you bringing them questions. This is good. It shows you're thinking, Ian. You're bringing what's known as "input". I don't know if you ever come across that word at all.'

'So, who?'

'What?' Lester replied.

'Drives.'

'Our boy. Main man. The minder's in the passenger. Minding. Hands free. Eyes all round.'

'So who?'

'What?' Lester said.

'Who is he, the minder? What training?'

'Minder training?'

'Right.'

'You mean, what gun training?' Lester said.

'Yes, gun training.'

'Maybe he got gun training. I don't know. If they go for a job as a minder maybe they got to say they had gun training. That's the CV again, isn't it? I expect he's handy, yes. But this won't be no shoot-out. We do it by numbers, four-on-two. They might *think* it could be a shoot-out and we want them to think it. But when they see four-on-two and all of us showing something they'll get the situation.'

'Why I asked about training.'

'What?'

'Troops – SAS, that kind, they're taught how to handle things even if there's more of the others. That's what a minder always has to be ready for.'

'Well, my tipster girl – she got no way to know that, have she, the SAS?' Lester replied. 'This is a girl in a Bromley estate agent's. She can't say to some black she only met once or twice in deals, "Was you by any chance

SAS? Do you know how to blast the enemy even if there's more?" How could she bring that into the conversation? I know the SAS do have blacks. This is not racist. But this girl would not even think of asking along them lines. She wouldn't say, "Can I see your weapon," would she?'

'We operate from one car?'

'Get ahead, cut in and stop him. Then we're out at them before he can reverse,' Lester said. 'Traditional. Pa said, just because something's the old way of doing something it don't mean it's not the best way. He said think of childbirth. They got all kinds of ways of getting there these days, such as donors and IVF, but the old method still got a lot to be said for it. Delicate will get perfect vehicles for this, I know. What Delicate can do is visualize. He can see a scene, a future scene. All the details. At the end we're all with the funds into the blocking car, and then another big one not too far away for a switch. This is going to be bulk, the cash – why Delicate will get big vehicles.'

'Hit them where? What traffic?'

'They'll be on their way to the estate agent, Bromley way, which sells Sevenoaks way stuff. Not too much traffic. Not exactly country, but not too much traffic. Now, I know, you think, "Oh, we stop him, and then some noble fucking public-duty folk on the road box *us* in with *their* vehicles." But we'll be too quick. It got to be less than three minutes. Pa said, "Less than three minutes, and two if you can do it. Abort if it gets to four." I say, "I got a fucking stopwatch in this enterprise?" He said, "Abort at four. You'll feel it when it's four." Meaning, *he* would be able to tell four, because he had a lovely feeling for clocks, small and big hands, he could always sense just where they'd be. It's like a gift, the way some are with the sax or juggling. Anyway, it's going to be less than three. I got a spot on the map. I can show you the spot on the map. I showed this spot on the map to pa and he thought about right. He said, "Geography, crucial." I suppose I knew that already for a street hit, but I give him a kindly nod, like "Thanks for this

56

revelation, pa." He's great, but sometimes he can be obvious. They gets like that – the ageing. We got no date yet. This is weeks ahead, maybe even more. Our lad – the diplomat with the exit funds, it's a tricky thing for him at the other end getting it all together and ready to pack. What you said – Africa, it can be rough out there – thin buggers in combat gear, strutting and sniffing, cocking weapons. The officers been to our army college, Sandhurst, half of them. A lot of smiling, with them bright, hard teeth they been chewing bark with, but, yes, rough.'

'Daylight?'

'It got to be daylight. It got to be office hours for the estate agent, most likely early afternoon. That's how it been previous. But, of course, we'll be masked up. The thing about Hector – he loves a mask and he's great with unexpecteds. He got the sort of face that's best with a mask. Hector's one who don't flap. Something slip up with the plan and he can deal with it. What's known as adaptable. It's a great plan. I think great, my pa thinks great, but a plan is *only* a plan and there can be little matters not in it – things nobody could think might happen.'

They'd been sitting opposite each other in armchairs with their soft drink bottles. Now, Lester stood and walked over to the cello again, carrying his bottle. He had a bit too much weight but the walk was nimble enough. He'd be all right in the street. He put a hand on the cello as before. 'You think how it would be, Ian, if your little girl, Rose, gets to be really great as a player, so one day she's up there on the platform doing a solo in, say, the Albert Hall, and she's rehearsed it and rehearsed, such as Sir Edward Elgar, and all at once what happens, a string snaps? Now, she have done all that rehearsing, got all the tricky bits all right, but that was with the full lot of strings. Now she got to be able to keep going, use just the strings she got left, known as improvise. This is what I mean about Hector – he don't just break in pieces because it's not in the plan, he'll think up straight away how things got to be changed.'

Lester returned to his chair. He had a small smile on. He looked pleased to have found this lesson in the cello string crisis. He said: 'Someone like Solid, he could be grand and solid if the plan is going how he been told it will go, but if there's some little matter not in it, he got no imagination to do something not in the plan. He's my brother and I love him, but I got to say that. I already said it to him, so this is not behind his back. He knows it's right. Imagination? He never fucking heard of it.'

'What sort of little matter you scared of, Lester?'

'Someone like Hector – this is a thing he's born with, imagination, like pa with clocks and time and initiative. All right, Hector's close to his mother, and this could be a gift that come to him through her, like initiative come to me through pa, and he takes care of her now from gratitude. When he's looking at her in the bed and maybe hearing her cough or groaning, he says, "This is the lady who give me imagination. I owe to her." People can get all sorts through a womb, which is why the old way of getting them pregnant could be best.'

'We should think of a stand-by in case Hector can't come because his mother's sick.'

'Oh, she might be sick, like you say, Ian, but Hector will understand. He'll see his mother could have all the best there is – treatment and looking after – the best, if he gets into this Africa money with us. You heard of BUPA at all? This is in case you're bad and can pay for hospital. Pa and ma are in BUPA, of course. He wouldn't let her go into an ordinary NHS hospital, on a trolley in the corridor.'

'Just a *possible* substitute for Hector. In mind in case.'

'Solid's never going to be right for this,' Lester replied.

'Maybe, but someone else as a reserve?'

Lester leaned forward in his chair, like a rush of aggression. 'You think I'm scared of Solid?'

'Scared? How do you mean?'

'You think if I let him in on this hit I'm scared he'll do so fucking good with snatching the Africa money he could

be the one to get boss spot when pa goes, the . . . like, heir,'
Lester said. 'He's older, yes.'

'Not at all. I –'

'Solid's my brother and he's all right, but he –'

'It doesn't have to be Solid. There are other people.
Think of someone good you could bring in if Hector won't
do it.'

'I got this persuasive side to me,' Lester replied. 'Many
have noted this. This is one of the things for leadership.
You got to be able to what's called "bring the work force
along". This means talk to them nice so they'll do what
you want. Solid – I don't think he could do that.'

'Well, yes, I know, you're good with chat, but –'

'I can talk to Hector and he'll soon see this is an enterprise spot-on for his ma. Could not possibly be more spot-
on. If there's one thing I truly believe in it's helping the
sick and old and this road tickle is so right for that. Look,
good funds in untraceable notes and funds nobody except
him and his minder care about keeping account of too
much because them funds been piled up from scams in a
country where it's *all* scams and heavy stuff. Maybe them
funds should not even of been brought into GB. Like they
don't exist, not officially. The beautiful side of this enterprise is, we're taking stuff that's not really here. This is
dirty money but some of it can be turned good by spending on real medical brains and all the care for Hector's
mother. When I think what we can do for her in this
operation it really excites me. Operation! That other kind.
Yes, if she needs an operation there'll be money to put her
right up the front of the queue, no fucking Health Service
four-year wait. That's how it fucking is now, isn't it –
you'd-be-lucky hospitals and people who done college but
on the bones of their arse for years from fee loans? Did you
vote for them?'

Chapter Nine

'Here's a lady who hasn't even been living in this area for long and yet she's come to visit you, dad. She was a bit worried about whether it was all right, I think – sort of *nervy* – yes, nervy is what I'd regard it as – but we said, Of course all right, because quite a few come here asking for you, and our address is in the phone book for anyone who needs you – as a police officer, I mean.'

'Certainly all right, Jill,' Harpur replied.

'We said this was one of your kinks even though senior, to be in the phone book because you like to be at the nitty-gritty. When she heard you were not here she wanted to go but I thought things definitely seemed urgent, or most probably, owing to coming in a taxi – so we said come in and wait, you might soon be back, depending. And she didn't want us to call you on the mobile in case you were in the middle of something, so we said come in and wait.'

'Fine,' Harpur said. 'Thanks, Jill. Mrs Templedon and I have already met.'

'Yes, she said she knew you,' Hazel replied.

'Not just Mrs Templedon but her husband as well, obviously, has come to live here,' Jill said.

'Yes, I believe so,' Harpur replied.

'And their children, obviously,' Jill said.

'Yes, I've heard about the children,' Harpur said.

'Heard how, dad?' Hazel asked. 'From Mrs Templedon herself? You've been in contact?'

'Generally,' Harpur said.

'What's that mean?' Hazel said.

'Yes, generally,' Harpur replied.

'What's it *mean*?' Hazel said. 'I don't understand how you know Mrs Templedon if she's only just come to live here.' Harpur's daughters could be vigilant.

'Mentioned,' he replied. 'I've heard it mentioned. About the children.'

'But where?' Hazel asked.

'They're all getting used to being in a different city, which is strange for them, obviously,' Jill said.

'Good,' Harpur replied.

'Does everything have to be "obvious"?' Hazel said.

'If it's obvious,' Jill replied.

'So why say it if it's obvious?' Hazel asked.

'All people say obvious things,' Jill replied. 'If people stopped saying what was obvious nobody would talk at all, except teachers.'

'It's bound to be an upheaval for the family,' Hazel said.

'I expect so,' Harpur replied.

'I believe they were in London before, so they'll notice a big change,' Hazel said.

'Such as the children having to start a new school,' Jill said.

'Yes,' Harpur replied.

'But not here. They'll go to boarding school, although the boy is only eight,' Hazel said.

'Some boarding schools will take children very young,' Jill said, 'for parents who might be living abroad, say ambassadors or tax dodgers in the Cayman Isles.'

'Yes,' Harpur said.

'Mrs Templedon is sure they'll settle down in boarding school very well,' Hazel said. 'We had quite a talk with her about this while waiting for you, dad.'

'Yes,' Harpur replied.

'I don't think I'd really like to go to boarding school, although I'm thirteen,' Jill said. 'Matron. Prep. But I'm sure

Mrs Templedon's children will *really* like it. I don't know their names. I did ask, but –'

'Most children soon settle down in boarding school,' Harpur replied.

'How do you know?' Jill said. She poured Harpur some tea and buttered a bun for him. They were in the big sitting room. 'Haze and I told Mrs Templedon you might be out looking at the scene of a crime, because you liked to be at the nitty-gritty, even though senior, like I already said.'

'As,' Harpur replied.

'As what?' Jill said.

'As I already said,' Harpur said.

'Dad likes to be at the nitty-gritty, even though senior, *as, as, as*, I already said. Often he's on about "as" and "like". You'd think he was educated.'

'Often it's necessary,' Harpur replied.

'What?' Jill said.

'The nitty-gritty,' Harpur said.

'He also does surveillance,' Jill said.

'Yes.' Or no. He'd been occupied with Iles for the last hour and a half. During a crime data conference, the ACC went into another rage fit about Sarah and Harpur and Francis Garland, and Harpur quietened him down by a lot of intelligent praise for his slip-on black shoes and Windsor knot tie, then took the Assistant Chief for a drive and some air along Valencia Esplanade, towards what had once been the docks. Harpur knew this trip would buck Iles up. He loved the Esplanade, loved the richness of the name and its suggestion of busy, steamship sea trade in the city's past. The Esplanade took him into history – but history before the Sarah and Harpur matter or the Sarah and Garland matter. The Esplanade also had more recent pleasant elements for Iles. He was fond of a bright, ethnic tart who worked this district, though Harpur didn't recall seeing her about lately. Perhaps she had given up the game or moved to Shepherd Market in London where the money was grander, grander even than the ACC's. As they returned in Harpur's car, Iles had said: 'Did you get good glimpses of that Mrs Templedon in the safe house, Col – the line of her shoulders, the very perceptible lips?'

'We'll look after her, sir.'

'Well, yes.'

Now, in his sitting room, with Mrs Templedon occupying an armchair opposite and holding a beaker of tea in her hand, Harpur could examine her shoulders and lips. He didn't go all that much on shoulders, but could see that these shoulders certainly had a line. But then, he thought most people's shoulders probably did or the body would look ramshackle. Perhaps for some hallucinating moments Iles really believed he had created the Templedon family in his Frankenstein role and would therefore look very hard at things like Mrs Templedon's shoulders, checking he'd done a decent job. Her lips seemed certainly perceptible or very perceptible. How many people's lips were not, though? Harpur felt perceptibility might be built into lips because of where they came, smack in the front of a face. Jill said: 'All right, the children are going away to boarding school but they will come home at holiday times to a little-known place which they'll have to get used to, obviously.'

'And I'm sure they will,' Harpur replied. 'Mr and Mrs Templedon can help them with that, because they'll have grown more used to the new address.'

'Oh, we're *really* talking the obvious, are we?' Hazel said.

'Well, I hope they can help them,' Jill said.

'When Jill says Mrs Templedon was nervy – I wouldn't say *nervy*,' Hazel said, 'I'd say tense.'

'Tense *and* nervy,' Jill replied. 'Or perhaps they're the same. If somebody is tense, that could *make* them nervy.'

'Nervy seems to mean out of control,' Hazel said. 'I don't think it's something that should be spoken in front of a person – that they were *nervy*. It's like telling someone they have a twitch.'

63

'Our mother was murdered as part of a case, you know,* Mrs Templedon,' Jill said.

'What's that got to do with now?' Hazel asked. 'What's it got to do with Mrs Templedon coming here?'

'So we know about nervy and tense, Mrs Templedon,' Jill replied. 'That made us all nervy and tense.'

'Always she has to drag this in,' Hazel said.

'But dad's found a great girlfriend for himself, called Denise who's a student in the university here although from Stafford,' Jill said. 'Perhaps he'd found her while mum was still alive, but they were both a bit like that owing to being born in the sixties. Literature, French, lacrosse, everything – that's Denise. She knows a poem about the death of a wolf through defending her cubs from hunting dogs, but the mother wolf never complains, she just gets on with it. She's much younger – that's Denise, I mean – younger than dad, well, obviously, but she doesn't seem to mind. She's not here now, owing to revision she has to do in her university room for exams. Many other poems, besides the wolf. But often she is here to make great breakfasts.'

'I think Mrs Templedon might want to speak to me privately,' Harpur said.

'Well, I expect so, 'Jill replied. 'She wouldn't come in a taxi if it wasn't something private and important. Anyone could tell that. What Hazel would call the obvious obvious. This must be something really urgent.' She filled everybody's cup from the teapot and then settled again in a chair, sitting on her folded legs.

Occasionally, people would turn up unscheduled like this looking for Harpur at his house, 126 Arthur Street. And, if he was out, his daughters generally took care of the visitor with chat, tea, and a cake or biscuits until Harpur returned. Both girls liked conversation and tried to get callers to open up through genuinely interested questions. It could be a fucking pain. Harpur wished they'd be less

* See *Roses, Roses*.

social, more like kids – shy, for instance, or indifferent. But he did not want to load rules on them. That would be poor fatherhood, and they had only one parent now. Although this meant big responsibilities, he felt he shouldn't browbeat or restrict them on that account. They must develop their natural styles, no matter how damn pushy and endlessly intrusive.

Of course, when young or youngish attractive women like Mrs Templedon called, his daughters always grew especially edgy and would try to find out whether the stranger had nothing to do with police work at all, but might be a girlfriend, possibly here to nail Harpur about something intimate and worrying. Several aspects of his life Hazel and Jill hated. Harpur recognized it. They were very fond of Denise, and felt he should look after this relationship and value such luck, given his age, fashion sense and job. They would nose away non-stop. Harpur knew how to block interrogation, but they would still nose away, especially Hazel. Harpur saw she considered it a duty to protect him and keep tabs on his outside activities. He was only in his late thirties, after all.

'Luckily, the boarding school takes girls and boys, so they'll be together,' Jill said.

'Oh, yes, that should be a help,' Harpur replied.

The Home Office would meet school fees. Routine. Ex-Covert Human Intelligence Sources with children always had the option of school boarding for them – not Eton or Roedean, but somewhere reasonably all right. The private school system would probably collapse if it lost all ex-informants' children. The thinking was that to separate youngsters from the parents for a good chunk of the year might be marginally more secure. Harpur wondered. Schools could be traced. Schools didn't usually have defences. In any case, as Jill said, pupils came home in the vacations.

'It's on account of his work that Mr Templedon and family have moved here,' Jill said.

'Yes, I expect so,' Harpur said.

'I don't know what his work is,' Jill said.

'Ah,' Harpur replied.

'I don't understand how you met Mrs Templedon,' Hazel said. 'Have you been in contact?'

'These days, few can count on staying in the same job and in the same locality for a complete working life,' Harpur said.

'You,' Jill said.

'Not if I go higher.'

'But will you?' Jill asked. 'Des Iles says you won't.'

'That's just him being playful,' Harpur said.

'Do you know Mr Iles as well as dad, Mrs Templedon?' Jill asked. 'Mr Iles is an Assistant Chief. Some say he's mad, others just glossy. Hazel thinks –'

'Quiet, slug queen,' Hazel said.

'Des Iles runs most things, so I wondered if you knew him as well as dad,' Jill said. 'Often he'll call here, as a matter of fact – supposed to be police stuff, but it's only if he thinks Hazel is home. Although he's married he still likes coming here. That's the way with some people, isn't it?'

'Which?' Mrs Templedon said.

'He wears a leather bomber jacket. He's got a crimson scarf worn like casual,' Jill replied.

'Worn casually,' Harpur said.

'So, what's the matter with "like"?' Jill asked.

'Nothing, except how you use it,' Hazel said.

'Dad could never have a crimson scarf worn casually,' Jill replied. 'He'd look like a toilet door with a tassel on it. Is that "like" all right, like? Mrs Templedon said her husband's work was business. That's why they had to move – because of business. But this is a word that covers a lot, such as bulk lipsticks for many shops, or wheat from the prairies.'

'People in business have to be very ready to up sticks and go somewhere more favourable,' Harpur said.

'But we don't know what *kind* of business,' Hazel said.

'"Business" does cover a lot,' Harpur replied.

'Such as catering or hi-tech?' Hazel said.

'Those could be business, yes,' Harpur said.

'Is it through business you met Mrs Templedon?' Hazel said.

'Many's the way people come across each other,' Harpur said.

'People in business use a lot of taxis,' Jill said. 'They can get them on expenses.

'It would be an idea now if you two girls went into the other room and Mrs Templedon and I can have a talk,' Harpur replied.

'Are you all right with that, Mrs Templedon?' Hazel asked.

Harpur crossed to the sitting-room door and opened it for the two girls to leave. Jill said: 'When you've had your talk with dad, maybe we can all come together again and discuss the various matters.'

'Out, please,' Harpur said.

'If Denise comes we'll try and keep her with us,' Jill said. 'She gets like unhappy if she sees dad with another woman in private, Mrs Templedon, even if the woman is married. French books she studies are full of things about what's referred to as "liaisons" in private spots. It's not all poems. There's one quite well-known book she told us about, called *Madame Bovary*, where the married lady is in a coach with another man and they just keep driving and driving around getting very close to each other not just because of the way the coach was bumping them about. Probably the coachman couldn't see them. It's not like being in the back of a car when the driver might watch what was going on through his mirror. That's one advantage of the old days. But the drawback would be no pill.'

'Although dad looks rough he can be quite understanding,' Hazel said. 'Many are surprised at this.'

After they'd gone, Mrs Templedon said: 'For this conversation I'm going to call him Ian.'

Harpur said: 'Well, we'd hoped you –'

'What I'm going to be talking about – why I'm here – what I'm talking about is Ian as Ian.'

Harpur said: 'All the same, it would be best if –'

'Yes, Ian. As a matter of fact, I usually manage the rechristened state better than he can, but not today – not when I'm talking about . . . not when I'm talking about what I want to talk about with you. This sudden trouble with names – it seems part of a pattern. I found I couldn't speak the children's names to your daughter when she asked. Obviously, I wouldn't give her their true names. But something stopped me speaking their new ones. I didn't want to lie to her. So, I stayed quiet. She'll think I'm damn rude.'

'The name changes are only a device. They don't actually alter anything about Robert, or about any of you, do they?'

'I think they do. Robert Maurice Templedon is a grass, a retired grass. Ian Maitland Ballion was not a grass, or not until –' She left this, couldn't complete it.

'A safety measure, that's all. Like a suit of armour – the knight inside is still the same man,' Harpur said.

'He doesn't feel like a knight. I know he doesn't. I know what he feels like. He feels like a grass. A grass put out to grass.'

'For now, perhaps. It won't last. It will become easier for him. You must get into the new identities. And we'd prefer not to use the term "grass", anyway.'

'Oh, Covert Human . . . whatever.'

'Covert Human Intelligence Source,' Harpur replied.

'Another name change.'

'It's a good description, accurate.'

'And non-abusive,' she said.

'Yes, non-abusive.'

'Soft soap. Politeness. Evasion.'

68

'Why should grass or snout or nark or fink or snitch be better?'

'They're shorter. A lot of words bring a lot of cloud, a lot of disguise.'

'I don't believe it's –'

She said: 'Look, why I came – oh, I know I shouldn't come at all, really.'

'It's best that contacts with the police are very few and carefully done. We've worked out a procedure during other resettlements. It's wisest to stick with that.'

'The taxi was a mistake?'

'Well –'

'Taxi drivers talk, I suppose,' she said. 'But if I'd brought the car I'd have had to explain to Ian where I was going. I didn't want that. He'd have stopped me, most probably. I'm supposed to be out for a little stroll, that's all.'

'I'll take you back and drop you off not far from the house.'

She sat gazing at him. He had the idea her perceptible lips were going to speak something alarming. 'I think he plans to go and see Lester Melvane's father,' she replied.

'See Walter Melvane?'

'Right.'

'He can't.' Harpur felt bewildered, appalled.

'Why?'

'He can't,' Harpur said.

'I watch him, listen to him, listen to what he leaves out as well as what he says, and that's how it looks. He wants to explain. He wants to make us all safe and say sorry to the Melvane lot, clear himself, as much as possible. This is a loyalty thing, and all kinds of other things.'

'He can't.' Harpur's brain had stalled, wouldn't let him move on.

'Can't what?'

'Can't clear himself with them. Can't undo things,' Harpur replied.

'Perhaps not,' she said. 'It's done. Lester's down for fourteen. And the rest for nearly as much.'

'What makes you think he'll try it? What *exactly*?'

'There's no exactly.'

'But why?'

'I told you – I watch, listen.'

'What has he said?' Harpur asked.

'Oh, he doesn't announce over breakfast that he thinks he'll pop up and have a word with Walter George Melvane and his tribe.'

'No. What, then?'

'I know what he thinks – thought – about grasses. It's standard, isn't it? Contempt. Endless contempt.'

'Thought? The past? It's the past that troubles you?'

'Even the police who use them feel this contempt, show their contempt sometimes. It's why they've dreamed up the jargon name for them – Covert Human . . . and so on. It's to conceal the disgust.'

'You heard Mr Iles condemn that kind of harsh, stupid thinking.'

'Of course he did. It's his job.'

'He believes it. I believe it.'

'You wouldn't convince Walt Melvane, or his wife, or Lester's brother. You wouldn't convince Ian, either. That's why I said I'd call him that. What he used to be. And if he goes to see Walter George Melvane and can put everything right he'll be Ian again for keeps, won't he – all this mad Templedon fiction gets flattened by a Skud?'

Harpur heard the front door open. It would be Denise. She had a key. 'The people he helped put away deserved to be put away,' he said. 'They brought guns on to streets and put passers-by at hazard, as well as their victims.'

'Possibly. That's not what it's about, is it?'

'What *is* it about?' he said.

'Grassing.'

'Yes, sometimes people do feel bad about it afterwards.'

'Ian feels bad about it.'

70

'People get over this, just as they grow used to the name change. It doesn't happen at once. But it does happen. Always it happens. I'd ask you to try and convince him it happens. You don't want him to go to Walter Melvane, do you? That's suicide. The whole resettlement structure destroyed.' Yes, like blown all ways by a Skud.

'He's not interested in the resettlement structure, is he? I'm not sure I am, either.'

'It brings you out of a crooked life,' Harpur said.

'*Our* life.'

'A crooked life. And very dangerous now.'

She frowned and stayed quiet for twenty seconds. 'Well, yes, I know.'

'If he goes to see Walter Melvane he –'

'No, he really believes he can explain,' she replied.

'How explain? Lester's in jail.'

'Explain it wasn't meant to happen.'

'What wasn't?'

'The raid on the Shogun.'

'This was a four-man, heavily researched, organized job. It came unstuck, but it had been planned. Yes, it was meant to happen.'

'The planning had been more or less ruined because that psycho gunster Foden was brought in as replacement for . . . well, I don't say who for. Would anyone *plan* to work with Foden?'

'Oh, a personnel switch, that's all. The plan stayed as before.'

'The plan didn't involve even the possibility of shooting.'

'They all carried guns,' Harpur said. 'If people go armed they're thinking gunfire. That, plus their records, meant big sentences.'

'They carried to scare. All right, from the start Ian was doubtful it would work like that. He thought the whole ploy very risky, but feasible. And then when Foden joined and Ian heard him talk, the more he knew there could be bullets and a disaster, which almost happened. So he –'

The sitting-room door opened and Jill came in: 'As a matter of fact, Denise did arrive,' she said.

'Yes,' Harpur replied.

'You knew?'

'I heard her.'

'I thought perhaps you hadn't heard her,' Jill said.

'Yes, I had.'

'She didn't send me to interrupt. She didn't want it.'

'Right,' Harpur replied.

'But I thought if she came in and talked to Mrs Templedon everything would be all right.'

'Everything *is* all right,' Harpur said.

'If she could see it was just definitely work, not –'

'Yes, work,' Harpur replied.

'But if she could *see*.'

'How could she see?'

'What?'

'It's work,' Harpur said.

'Like the atmosphere. Sorry, not "like". The atmosphere.'

'What atmosphere?'

'I said Mrs Templedon came by taxi. So it had to be urgent. Meaning it must be work, only work.'

'Naturally,' Harpur replied.

'But cool – Denise could see the atmosphere is cool. Not emotions. Not Mrs Templedon crying because of some letdown in a personal matter.'

'Denise will understand, if you tell her it's work.'

'What *kind* of work?'

'Police work.'

'Yes, but what *kind* of police work? That's what Denise will ask.'

'Confidential.'

'Ah,' Jill said.

'Confidential police work.'

'But you won't say what?'

'Because it's confidential. I can't.'

'Denise will ask and ask me.'

72

'No, she won't. She knows some work has to be secret.'

'I'll say confidential, but with a cool atmosphere.'

'Businesslike,' Harpur replied.

'Sometimes Denise is quite all right about things like this.'

'Mostly,' Harpur said.

'She behaves like that mother wolf in the French poem – putting up with rotten things, making the best of things, "in the path of life which Fate has set you on".'

'Denise won't want to be compared to a she wolf,' Harpur said. 'And there aren't any rotten things. Will you go now, please, Jill.'

'Yes.' She went out and closed the door.

'Look, they had a good, controlled team together,' Mrs Templedon said.

'He talked to you about jobs?'

'You're asking, was I a moll?' she said. 'No, he didn't. But he's talked since, because he's ashamed. He doesn't want me to think of him as a fink.'

'He did a service and –'

'A good, controlled team,' she said. 'He knew there'd be risk – this was a hit – and, yes, they took guns – but Ian thought it might just about work the way it was supposed to work – not a hit at all, really – an interception, with a lot of big shouting and pistol waving. He stacked all the factors against one another – the dangers and possible gains – and decided the thing came out positive. Close, but positive. He'd do it.'

'I see,' Harpur replied. 'And then Foden?'

'And then Foden. A good, sensible lad pulls out – domestic reasons. In comes Foden. Do you know about him?'

'I do now.'

'Ian knew *then*. Suddenly, the odds are different. The balance has shifted. The dangers become huge and stupid

73

because Foden in a raid with a gun . . . is Foden in a raid with a gun. Wild.'

'So why didn't Ian – Robert – pull out?' Harpur replied.

'Yes, why? Scared of looking yellow? A breach of loyalty to Lester? These would be big considerations for Ian.'

'Perhaps.'

'So Ian gives a whisper to some Met detective,' Mrs Templedon said. 'He describes what's planned and where and tells them to do a big, showy job of stopping the cash car just before the spot Lester has picked for their hit. Just before. You understand? This makes the raid impossible because the area's full of cops. But, in Ian's scheme, they would be there, not because they'd been tipped off about the raid, but because they'd heard the cash load might be tainted somehow. End of project – the Lester project. It can't happen. That's how Ian saw things. The detective would get glory because the money in the car might not be legal money. To Lester the police swoop should look like bad luck, nothing else. He and the other three would abandon the attack, and be in no danger of arrest or gunfire. Great. Ian told me he was *so* pleased with the scenario.'

'But that's not how it went,' Harpur said.

'Our Met friends decided they could get the cash car *and* the Lester crew. They stayed hidden until the attempt started and then swamped the scene and took in Lester, Delicate and Foden. Ian they let get clear – so he could become Robert Maurice Templedon. You people look after your helpers, don't you?'

'And he's going to tell Walter George Melvane all this, for God's sake?' Harpur said.

'It's not just because Ian wants to get the old man to call off the vengeance party. Ian's desolated. Humiliated. A face thing. It kills him to know old mates think he's a grass.'

'No, that doesn't kill him. Talking to Walter George Melvane will,' Harpur said. 'Walter George Melvane

74

thinks – knows – Ian Maitland Ballion is the man who put his son away. He won't make pretty distinctions. He probably wouldn't believe the tale at all. To Walter Melvane, all that matters is Ian Maitland Ballion talked to the police, and as a result Lester's inside. This is why Ian Maitland Ballion has to stay permanently and untraceably disappeared. You and I, Mrs Jane Iris Templedon, should both talk to Robert Maurice Templedon and stop any relapse.'

'I don't want him to know I've spoken to you.'

'Grassing about grassing? We have to look after him, Mrs Templedon.'

She went into one of those pauses again. Another big topic on the way? 'Listen, Mr Harpur, this is not vanity, but I see Iles gawping at me.'

'Oh?'

'I wonder whether he'd mind if Ian was taken out of the scene.'

'We've got to get back to calling him Robert, Mrs Templedon,' Harpur replied.

'You don't answer.'

'Did you ask something?' Harpur replied.

'Are the things they say about him right?'

'Who?'

'Iles.'

'Which things?'

'You know. The things they say about him.'

'Which things?'

'Men he thought killed an undercover cop but got off in court. He dealt with them?'

'People who *did* kill an undercover cop.'

'How can you be sure – if the court said, "No."'

'The rumours about Mr Iles are . . . rumours. Outrageous rumours.' Harpur felt he'd better say something like that.

'Yes?'

'Mr Iles is concerned about you – concerned about all your family. That's why he might appear to "gawp", as you call it.'

75

'Yes?'

'When might he go?'

'Ian?'

'To see Melvane.'

'Do you really understand the loathing he feels for him-self?' she said.

'You don't know when?'

'I'm guessing, aren't I? I'm guessing that he means to go there at all. It's all guessing.'

'Yes, it's guess,' Harpur said. 'All guessing. Probably your imagination. That's natural enough, given the stress.'

He thought he must show politeness and called the girls and Denise in before Mrs Templedon left. Jill introduced Denise to her. In this kind of formal, hostess role, Jill was good. 'The thing about a chief superintendent is he's never really off duty owing to one situation after another,' she explained, 'so a work meeting can happen at any time or in any place, not just the nick. I certainly believe this.'

'Oh, great. We're impressed,' Hazel said.

'Many a note might have been made at this meeting but owing to being in confidence such notes would not be available for us to see now,' Jill said. 'A meeting like this could be about almost any topic.'

'Certainly,' Harpur replied.

'And the thing about work is, dad doesn't *have* to tell us the topic covered in the meeting, and sometimes it would be really wrong to tell us, on account of being confidential,' Jill said.

'Right,' Harpur said.

'This is not unusual,' Jill said.

'Hardly,' Harpur replied.

'I know Denise understands,' Jill said.

'Certainly,' Harpur said.

'Perhaps to do with Mrs Templedon's children,' Hazel said.

'What?' Harpur said.

'The meeting,' Hazel said. 'It must be serious. I mean, needing someone of your rank, dad.'

'This meeting covered several points,' Harpur said.

'If it's urgent. Children *can* get into situations where things are urgent,' Hazel said.

'We're not the sort to listen against a door to hear what's going on, Mrs Templedon,' Jill said. 'That's Hazel and me, I mean, because of being a police family and being used to it when people come for private matters. And Denise wouldn't listen against a door, either, because we all felt sure it was definitely work in there, not some carry-on, so it would be sneaky and wrong to listen.'

'This is true,' Harpur replied.

'What *kind* of points covered, dad?' Hazel asked.

'Mrs Templedon had some genuine problems,' Harpur said.

'Yes, I expect so,' Hazel said. 'This would be why she came here.'

'Exactly,' Harpur replied.

'But what *kind* of problems?' Hazel said.

'You said, *had* some genuine problems,' Jill said. 'Does that mean they're gone now because you could deal with them, dad? Or maybe Mrs Templedon could tell us herself.'

'Mrs Templedon had some problems which I didn't know about previously but now I do so I'll be able to look at them,' Harpur replied.

'It wouldn't be Ilesy getting after her the way he does, or anything like that, would it,' Jill asked, 'in view of Mrs Templedon's undoubted beauty and that sort of thing? Does she know Iles? He likes many types.'

'Slander sow,' Hazel said.

In bed Denise said: 'Colin, what I noticed was sometimes when you or the girls called her Mrs Templedon she didn't seem to respond. I thought she glanced around as if expecting to see someone else of that name.'

'I wish Jill knew the difference between "as if" and

"like",' Harpur replied, if that was a reply. 'What's the grammatical rule?'

'And then she'd make an effort and get herself into focus again and become absolutely Mrs Templedon, like an actor at rehearsal going in and out of character.'

'Oh, I didn't spot all that,' Harpur said.

'This was a woman with real stress.'

'Jill said "nervy".'

'I saw it here, I saw it in the car when we took her back.'

Of course, it had been Hazel's idea that Denise should make the trip with Harpur and Mrs Templedon. 'I was glad you came,' he said. 'Some woman-to-woman chat. It soothed her.'

'Why did we put her down where we did – not her house?'

'That's part of it,' Harpur said.

'What?'

'The situation.'

'How?'

'Yes, part of the situation,' Harpur replied.

'She mustn't be seen in contact with you – with police generally? Why not? But she came to your house. Hazel told me it was by taxi. Did Mrs Templedon make a mistake turning up like that?'

'She didn't have to walk far from where we dropped her,' Harpur replied.

'Where does she live?'

'It's a reasonable area, low on the mugging chart. High-powered Neighbourhood Watch.'

'The girls are so funny, aren't they, Col? Funny but nice.'

'How?'

'Thinking I'd go possessive and evil because you're talking privately to a woman.'

'Yes.'

'She's very beautiful,' Denise said.

'In some ways, I suppose so.'

'Which ways?'

'I occasionally got that impression.'

'Very striking mouth and lips,' Denise said.

'Ah. I didn't spot those, but, now you say, yes, I think you're right. Perceptible lips.'

'Well, it's in the nature of lips to be perceptible, surely,' Denise replied.

'True.'

'So, what did you mean?'

'Yes, of course, lips are bound to be perceptible or the area below the nose would look blank.'

'And the way she carries herself. It's a strange thing to say, but wonderful shoulders – narrow and with a lovely line.'

'Yes, perhaps shoulders *are* important. Yours, for instance. The slope is so refined.' He sat up in the bed to look down on her alongside him and stroked her right shoulder.

'But I honestly never thought she was other than work,' Denise said.

'Your shoulders are great as shoulders but also great because what's all around – your face above, obviously, and then all the rest of it. These are shoulders with what you'd call in your academic game a "context", I should think.'

'Actually, I don't get much kick from shoulders – having my shoulders touched, even by you,' she said.

'Who else touches them?'

'But I can see the point of shoulders, for holding T-shirts up or pushing doors open.'

'The Venus de Milo. Terrific shoulders.'

'Most people go on about her arse,' Denise said.

'I've never noticed that. I don't touch *only* your shoulders.'

'No, you don't, do you? No, you don't, do you?'

Chapter Ten

'Walt, I want you to believe – please believe – it was never meant to happen like that. All right, you'll say, "Fuck meant, who cares about meant? Lester's inside for ever. His mother's down for ever. The future of Onset, fucked up for ever, maybe." I know. I know. But ask yourself, Walt – please ask yourself – would I come here, to London, your ground – the risk – would I come if that's how it was meant to go at the Shogun? I'm talking to you now like this, but who could be sure I'd have the chance to say one word if I stuck my head inside your door? And it's not just the risk, is it? It would be like crowing if I came here free and nicely accommodated – a detached property, lawns front and rear back there – and sporting Laity slip-ons and gold leaf cuff links when Lester's inside. Like mockery. Would I do that? Am I the sort who'd do that? I mean, Walt – my pedigree.

'All right, you'll say, "Fuck pedigree. I don't know what fucking sort you are now. I didn't think you were the grassing sort, did I?" But this grassing – all right, it *looked* like grassing – a *sort* of grassing – but it was never supposed to be, I swear. They've given me a new name, a grass's name, ex-grass's – Robert Maurice Templedon. Two first names, Walt, to make it thorough, the same as my own or yours. Coming here like this, I'm blowing it all away. I'm telling them to stuff it, aren't I? This is me, Ian, junking all the secrecy, all the disguise, all the expense, the smart house, all the cop care. I read in a *Sunday Telegraph* report complaints from a one-time supergrass in Northern Ireland because he says the police haven't looked after him right. They hid him away, yes, but what he calls "in poverty" – a council house. Me nothing like that. I've been given luxury, Walt. But do I want it? What I want is for old friends to feel all right about me. Forgive me. Forgive me for a terrible, mad mistake. Not anything deliberate. Forgive me for trusting a cop. Friends like you, Walt. This is me – me, Ian – not Robert Maurice Templedon, here to tell you how it really was and maybe – maybe – comfort you and Vera a fraction, and clear myself, oh, yes, clear myself. All right, you'll ask, "How can we be comforted when Lester's still doing big time?" and you'll say, "Fuck clearing yourself, we can't help on that. How could you ever clear yourself?" And I can understand this attitude, believe me, Walt, but I still had to come. Doesn't this signify?'

He rehearsed this slab of tortured plea mentally most days at home, pacing the new Templedon Cormorant nest in case he ever did get so sickened by shame he actually made the trip to London to see Walter George Melvane. He'd thought of it, even hinted at it, but could he do it? Impossible? Perhaps. In any case was the speech too long? Would he get the chance to talk so much, if at all? He had other versions of the statement. One of them left out the bit about comforting Walt and Vera, because it was so obviously mad and might make Melvane mad, or madder. Lately, Templedon read another newspaper report. This one told of a grass, possible grass, forced to drink petrol then set alight.

Templedon's alternative version also dropped the 'I swear' and 'believe me' because they sounded like someone who knew he looked a frightened, crawling liar. It seemed only right in an imagined get-together like that to give Walt some words, too, so when he did these runthroughs Templedon acted out the arguments with himself – well, not acted *out*, acted *in* – in his mind.

And then Templedon had a third prepared spiel which,

in fact, came out much longer – came out longer, happy, triumphant. This one assumed Walt was gloriously won over by the opening words in one form or the other and instead of throttling or torching him asked for a proper, all stages account of what happened on the day and leading to the day, a 'Talk us through it, Ian, would you, please?' The trial had brought out parts, of course. But in these make-believe scenarios that Templedon concocted for himself, Walt wanted more, and wanted it without all the angling and twisting and doctoring of a courtroom.

Easy to give. Robert Templedon's memories of the whole course of things had been brushed up and sharpened by that flip-chart in Meadowland a few weeks ago, and commentary by the scruffy, thug detective, Harpur. Someone there whispered Harpur was a fair-haired image of Rocky Marciano, heavyweight boxing world champion of the 1950s. Templedon remembered photographs of Marciano in the ring hammering Joe Louis and thought Marciano looked more sensitive than Harpur. Every time Harpur brought up a main name on his chart, Templedon had reglimpsed in memory catastrophic moments from the cash raid. That raid should have been beautifully, intelligently impossible.

His bargain with the police said they must move in on the money car before any attack by Lester's team could reach it. The police would have good pretexts. The cash might be dubious. And there'd be two men illegally packing guns. But, of course, the loaded Shogun arrived on Colex roundabout at just the time Lester's tipster promised. And the roundabout or twenty metres after it was where Lester intended the hit, a spot approved by Walter. In the Rover's front passenger seat that day Lester gave a little gasp, as though amazed by his brilliance and the rightness of his information. 'Nice, Lest,' Foden said. This was precision. This was fucking disaster. Yes, nice, Lest. This was real fine-tuned planning. This was jail.

The big Shogun appeared entirely as Lester's girl source

had told him – what must be the diplomatic maestro driving, bodyguard alongside, and no other interested-looking vehicles ahead or behind stuffed with cop posses in baseball caps, about to make a pounce. So, where the fuck were they? Ballion, suddenly well on his way then to turning Templedon, saw betrayal, saw a ploy, saw a police operation built on a police operation.

As scheduled, Delicate Royston moved the Rover out for the interception in Ensign Road. They all had pistols ready, Lester's, Foden's and Ballion's in their hands, Delicate's holstered for the moment so he could drive. They went fast around the Shogun and blocked it just as schemed, beauti-fully, really Delicate and delicate, and then Foden yelled like a frenzy, 'They'll shoot. The fuckers will shoot,' raised his Browning and would have fired himself at the Shogun, but Lester skewed around in the front seat and knocked the gun to the floor. It was as if Lester knew Foden might go off like that and was ready for him. Why did he let him into the job then . . .?

. . . And so, suppose Templedon *did* ever go to see Walter Melvane, he would say, if he had the chance to say much, or anything, 'It all started to deadfall, Walt, when Hector Serge Knille sent his apologies and we had to take Foden . . .'

. . . Naturally, there had been a Harpur chart page for him at the safe house: ADRIAN LUKE STANLEY FODEN, AGE 36.

Yes, some had *three* first names, but they didn't do much for Foden. The chart concentrated less on Foden himself than on his relations and friends, of course – as possible threats to Templedon and family. They came listed under-neath Foden, those Harpur rated as most dangerous in red capitals. How did this backwater cop know who were most dangerous anyway? The Met had briefed him? If Templedon visited Walter Melvane it would be to show him how dear Adrian Luke Stanley, brought in like that, had raised the risk too far – beyond sanity. Risk and cash-

83

in-transit jobs couldn't be separated, but the risk had to be sensible . . .

. . . Templedon might say: 'You know Adrian Foden, Walt – knew *of* him before all this. Normally, we wouldn't let the bugger anywhere near. Wild. Very suddenly, though, and unexpected Lester gets the cash car's time-table from his estate agent contact, and at about the same moment he hears Hector's final no to a share in the job. Confusion. I don't say panic, but confusion, bad hurry. We're looking for someone who's done transit work, some-one not locked up or under the eye on bail, and someone needy enough to get brave. Foden. Foden? Dodgy. *So* dodgy. But available.' If he was offering this to Walt, he would not say Foden had been Lester's idea, or that Lester had been so bloody sure he could talk Hector around that when he found he couldn't his brain crashed, went zombie and picked the first replacement in sight. Best not kick Lester in front of Walt. Lester had taken enough kicking . . .

. . . Lester had brought the final news of Hector's refusal on another visit to the Ballion Highgate house – but this time Lester came jam-packed with fury and hate. 'That fucking Hector – he won't. Tell me, you ever heard of a lad who'd miss a ducky enterprise like this on account of his admittedly personal mother?'

'Hector's always been –'

'Mothers – they got a place in things. I respect quite a few of them, don't get me wrong. Of course I do. Umbil-ical.' Lester was plump in the face and body, large-headed, his hair spike-cut and mousy. Fatness made some people look evil, some childlike and jolly. Lester, the second. It could be a help if he needed to fool people and seem harmless. When a lad with all that depth to his cheeks pretended to be interested in the cello, many could have believed it. Music or a pork butcher's shop would seem his kind of career. It did happen fairly often that he needed to fool people and seem harmless. 'There's many a mother

84

who deserves quite good care,' Lester had said. 'My own mother – plus others, no question. Yours, for sure, also. Mothers got an undoubted call on us. But Hector – all my most considerate conversation and he still won't come in. This is conversation with a theme and true detail.'

'Hector – pretty well indispensable to the job, isn't he, Lest? Maybe we should –'

'Out of my share – I said *out of my individual share* I'd pay for nursing and all bedside treats during the enterprise, plus for the full day and night after so we could party the way people got to party after an enterprise like that – real pricey, spruce girls and Krug – and he done a lot of wholehearted-gratitude-for-the-offer-believe-me-Lester rigma, but he still says he got this duty, the cunt, this sickroom duty, feeding fucking consommé and mopping the brow in a sonnish manner, believing no one else could.'

'Hector and his mother have –'

'I don't know. Is he asking for a princier share on account he's so great at transit jobs? All right, I'd never deny it. He's sure he's the fucking star and wants top loot? How? Myself, as I said, he could chop nursing fees and the cost of damson jelly off of mine, but can I promise him more than you or Delicate Royston? Can I? This is a four-way split. We're equal. Think of Royston, for instance. He's from a family – them Boon-Maces – who been brought up to get their due in a deal. This is a "that's-mine-if-you-don't-mind" lot.'

'Hector was important. He can deal with unexpectedness.'

'Hector *was* important.'

'Maybe vital? Look, Lester, should we –'

'Hector was important but he's not the be-all.'

'Readjusting so near the date –'

'I'm not thinking of Solid,' Lester replied. 'Solid's fine for many enterprises but I don't see him OK for this.'

'No, right.'

'You thinking something when you say "No, right"?' Lester sounded a bit poisonous.

'Thinking something?'

'Look, like I said previous, don't fucking tell me I'm scared he'd do so great with the Shogun he'd look like the succession to my pa at Onset, being older.'

'No, of course not, Lester, I –'

'I been in touch. It's lucky I know the scene. Personnel. Luckily I always got a list of likelies in my head for any kind of enterprise. That's just basic leadership.'

'Not Solid? So –'

'Adrian.'

'Adrian? Adrian Foden? You mean Adrian Foden?'

'I had a really good and helpful conversation with Adrian,' Lester said. 'I didn't mention Hector dropped out mother-struck. Obviously. Adrian don't need to see he's only fill-in on account of Hector and his fucking ma. You got to consider morale and respect. That's another management ploy. Would I say to him, "Oh, Adrian, care to make up our quartet on account of Hector Serge Knille not being around at the last moment through Florence Nightingaling?"'

'Foden – he's –'

'He's hungry. He got nothing troublesome attached – no tag, or awaiting trial, or reporting in, or regular woman to start shouting about pros and cons and unpicking his backbone. I done a proper all-round check. I'm not going to believe him, am I, on something like that?'

Appalled, scared, Ballion had said: 'What we wanted in this operation, Lester, was a controlled episode. That's the essence. The thing about Foden is –'

'I explained all that. Well, naturally. I gave him some real conversation on that exact topic. The control topic. It was the very word I used with him, "controlled", and he understood it. I could definitely see he understood it for this task, regardless of how he used to be.'

'Foden, in a set-to, when the other side is black and carrying weaponry – Lester, this is a –'

'I told him, "No Rorke's Fucking Drift." He've never actually killed, you know, Ian – white, black or Asian. Something else I done a personal check on. In fact I don't think he even ever had a hit,' Lester replied. 'He might blast off, but he never had a hit. It always been only like, show. He'll be all right . . .'

. . . Templedon would give all this to Walter Melvane, if the meeting ever did happen. It would be worded – shaped – so as definitely to offer no suggestion Lester messed up when he asked Foden, although, of course, he did mess up and big when he asked Foden. This had really shocked Delicate as well. Delicate was a worrier, anyway, but bringing Foden in *really* worried him. Although Delicate had a snob side through the Boon-Mace lineage, he objected to Foden for a few other reasons, too, especially the up-down-down-up state of his mind, what Delicate called 'labile'. A Boon or a Mace was something very distinguished in animal feed during the sixties, and the hyphen must show this family thought themselves on the climb, at least until Royston's off-centre career started to get known. His nickname had come because he went to a manicurist every fortnight. Many women envied his cuticles. Delicate did not look aristocratic exactly but definitely not Devil's Island, either . . .

. . . Soon after Foden joined, Lester had brought Delicate and him to Ballion's house for a policy meeting. It was then Ballion started to feel *really* troubled. All right, before *any* cash-in-transit operation he would feel troubled. Now, though, anxiety nearly flattened him. Once again, Rose was practising the cello when these three arrived, and although Lester and Delicate listened with good attention until she finished, anyone could see Foden thought the wait an arse pain. Ego. *He* wanted the forefronting, not Rose. You could *feel* the ignorance. If he heard the word Schumann he'd think a cobbler. He was half bald in that tufty, ragged sort of way many are, like bogland symbols on a map, but he still thought all spotlights loved him. Obviously, you could not judge how someone would do a cash-in-transit job from what he thought of the cello, but it showed he was all self and didn't understand consideration for mates and a mate's daughter. This was the thing, wasn't it? He could only think of himself.

When Rose left and they began to talk about the job, Foden was into it right away, gabbing more than anyone, although he'd only just had the invite. He chortled about how easy it would be, because all it fucking was, he said, was lifting money from 'slob nation material' – how he regarded the Shogun pair. If they even thought once of resistance they wouldn't have time to think again on account of his 9 mm shells ripping their chests apart. But hadn't Lester said he talked to him about control? Did the fucker Foden hear any of it? Lester said Foden understood, but Lester thought he could talk anyone into anything, including Hector. Yes, wild had to be the word for Foden, or apprentice maniac. Probably he would *like* to be called wild, thinking it meant animal power . . .

. . . 'Look, Walt,' Templedon would say, *might* one day say, 'Foden was problematical. Anyone could see it, even then. He wanted a gun battle, longed for it. He should have joined the paras. You could tell the money wouldn't feel so sweet to him without shooting. For satisfaction, he's got to conquer it – like Hitler with France. That's his nature. I wouldn't say a psvchopath, but frothy, extreme. As if he was on some sort of upper all the time. He *needed* violence. There are people like that. All right, so you'll ask two things, Walt. You'll ask, Didn't Lester spot all this in Foden? And you'll ask, Why didn't I stop Lester going on with it or try to stop him? Fair questions. I'll answer straight. First I think Lester had all sorts of thoughts, a mix. This was *his* operation and he'd planned and polished it. He'd hate to give it up on account of someone's mother however much he respected mothers as a group, and especially his own, obviously, Walt. Lester would have thought himself weak and poor on leadership if he'd folded. This job was to show that if the Onset shahdom came to him he'd be fine with it.

'And me? Why didn't I persuade him against? Well, I did try, but not head-on, I admit. I wouldn't have liked him to regard me as yellow, feeble. I gave him a hint now and then that we should quit because of Hector. But, no, you're right, I didn't really try to stop him, and I would never pull out. Delicate the same. I could see he felt like me about Foden, but Delicate also felt like me about Lester. It was a kind of loyalty, a kind of respect. Built in, isn't it, Walt? So, my answer was, I'd tell the police – tell that Detective Constable Callic, who's always sniffing around – tell the police there'd be a car full of maybe funny money plus two naughty loaded pistols and they could do a big ambush before we were due to hit, meaning we'd have to be spectators only and safe. OK, so no loot, but no jail and no bullets our way. No chance for Foden to start his barrage. We'd watch, then drive home. A disappointment, yes. Never mind, though. There'd be other heaps of cash in transit to take, and perhaps when Hector's mother had died or done a recovery, he could come in and make things satisfactory.

'But, of course, Walt, the police wanted more than the money wagon. They wanted Lester and Delicate and Foden as well. Smart, smart. They stayed hidden, so bloody brilliantly hidden, until we did the Ensign Road stop on the Shogun, and then they were everywhere, fucking everywhere, Walt, six-to-one against us, nearly all weaponed, girls included. This was never the deal. Nowhere near it. This was two-timing. Do you see what I'm getting at when I say it was a special kind of grassing – if it really was grassing at all, Walt? Call it a "Save Lester" grassing. It should have kept him free and at the same time left his valuable and wholesome pride in himself undamaged, a famed pride built over years through you and your undefeated family. You see, Walt, he wouldn't have chickened out of a hit – couldn't blame himself for a failure. The hit would have become a no-no, That's all.'

And Walter would give it all his thinking, all his years of knowledge and rough cleverness and then reply, wouldn't he: 'I'm content you come, Ian. I'm not going to call you Robert because what you just said was what the Ian I knew and know would say. You been misunderstood, Ian, I can see that now. Thank God you had the bravery to come and explain. What we asked – what we was bound to ask, wasn't we? – what we asked was, how did you get out of it, the raid, when three was taken? Skill? Luck? Magic? Fix? And no charges after, though we knew you was there because we'd heard the team from Lester. He checked it over with me, didn't he, start to finish and the crew? So, what it looked like – what it looked like when you was not took was police gave you a path out, and then arranged to forget you was a part of it and could be done like the other three. Your reward. They'd settle for them three, but one could go. You. This was the deal.'

'Yes, in a way, but, Walt –'

'And that's what it still looks like, but the difference is, now I can see it right. *You* didn't plan it, *they* did. You never thought this ambush would happen because your raid would never even start. So, *their* plan was collar three and make sure you got out and was not identified. They fucked you up and fucked up Lester and Royston and Foden, but they did look after you after. This they'll do sometimes. They're police but they'll still stick to a deal, or one part of a deal, anyway.'

'Right, right, Walt, *so* right,' Templedon would reply . . .

. . . And right it was. Because of Foden and his 9 mm they'd been maybe half a minute late out of the Rover. The gun lay on the floor at Templedon's – Ballion's – feet and he bent to pick it up, not to return it, of course, but to make sure the shoot-on-sight sod didn't rescue it himself. When

Templedon stepped out of the car he had two guns, like a Wild West film, but automatics, not revolvers. At least, fire power from the pair would be the same as if Foden still had the Browning. Probably Lester jumped out first, running around the front of the Rover to get at the driver's door of the Shogun, wagging his own Browning and yelling "It's a robbery!" in case they hadn't twigged. Templedon was slowed a bit more by having to open the door while both hands held a gun. But he made it to alongside Lester and screamed the same sort of message – couldn't recall the words now. The plan was still the same plan, regardless of Foden – do it all by noise, show, threats.

Perhaps Foden had it right, though, and the two in the Shogun really would have started the gunplay. If you'd piled up millions for yourself in a hard African country, then managed to get the millions out and into Britain, you were not going to let them go because a few lads shouted at you. When Templedon came up from recovering the Browning, he could see through the Rover window and Shogun windscreen the minder start to pull something big from a shoulder holster. 'Hit the fuckers,' Foden yelled and grabbed for the gun in Templedon's left hand, his Beretta. But Templedon shoved him off, got the door open and made for Lester at the cash car.

That feel of the road under his shoes, like *through* his shoes, all the gravel bits and small slope, he could still get it now in recall. The first people on the moon – they would probably feel the first step through *their* soles for ever. Like that. Moments that made a life. Perhaps it would all work even *with* Foden. Then, above their own shouting, he heard the boom of a loud-hailer, 'Armed police. Drop your weapons. Drop your weapons now.' Of course, by then Templedon had been more or less ready for this. If the Shogun wasn't stopped by the law earlier it was because . . . because it would be used as bait now. The simplest logic told him that. Why hadn't it told him before he made the deal, though? He looked away from the Shogun

91

and saw them all over, black flak jackets, black baseball caps with POLICE in white letters – spelling things out for the dull and confused, like Lester's 'It's a robbery!' No time for doubts. The minder did not fire. Maybe the double shock was too much for him – first the Rover and Lester, then the swarm of baying officers with their dull-shine weaponry.

'God, we're done,' Foden sobbed. They took him first. Had they heard he adored the smell of cordite and might get hasty? They clobbered him to the floor. He was unarmed, but they would not know that. Still no shots. That didn't make the sentences any lighter for Lester and the other two, though, because of their previous. Having the guns with them was nearly as bad as firing.

'Get along, lad,' one of the baseball caps muttered to Templedon. 'Left into Highton Street and keep running. You'll be met. Nobody will follow. Ditch the armament soonest.' And Templedon ran . . .

. . . Now, he longed to think that after this battle report Walt would cry out: 'You wanted to take care of our Lester, it's obvious, not get him sent away, and you done it the only way you could find. Bravo! Bravo, Ian! What I want to say at this juncture is "Welcome back from being that Robert Whatyoucall. You're Ian Ballion again and Eleanor is Eleanor and the kids just as always. Identity? It's what we're born with. There can't be no altering, not ever. Monkeying with names? It don't signify. How could it? There's no need no longer for you to be Robert Whatyou-call. No need to go police-side and skulk and hide like a rat in a drain. Oh, yes, I'll explain it all to Delicate's lot and even Foden's. They'll understand, no question."'

Then, Walt would call out to his wife, Vera, and give her this true picture, run over all the detail in loving detail. She'd step across the room and embrace Templedon, pat-ting his back with real affection. Speaking into his ear, she'd say: 'I know – I always knew – how it looked must be wrong. You'd never want to hurt Lester, or even Delicate and Foden. You'd never cuddle up to cops. That's not Ian Ballion. Next time it's a visit we want you to come with us, don't we, Walter? Max of three – they'll allow that. This will signify to Lest that we know – *know* – you're all right. He don't need to organize something fierce for you and yours from inside, which was a possible, as things stood till now. Knowing you're all right – really *knowing* – will solace him through the years he'll still be in there. He'll turn milder, easier, and maybe get his parole earlier. Thanks, Ian.'

Yes. YES, YES! This is how his peace visit would turn out, wouldn't it?

Of course it fucking wouldn't. They'd have him killed. *Have* him killed? Walt might want to do it himself. Or Vera. What else were parents for?

He ought to concentrate on being Templedon and safe, and ditch the sloppy fantasizing and fiasco memories. Learn this, Templedon who was Ballion – when you ran up Highton Street after the ambush you were running into an eternally changed and disinfected existence, and you'd better understand that, stick with that, even if you do slide back into Ballion reminiscence now and then, and the Ballion moniker now and then . . .

. . . Actually, he did not have to run very far on raid day. A big, black, unmarked Vauxhall waited at the first junction, engine running, a woman in plain clothes at the wheel. One rear door was open and that smarmy, nosy, maybe-one-day-soon-high-fly detective, Piers Callic, stood near and called his name, 'Ian, Ian. Here.' Ballion went to the car and climbed into the back. Callic slammed its door and took the front passenger seat. The Vauxhall moved off at once.

'What the fuck?' Ballion said.

'I know, I know,' Callic said, 'some little amendments to the script.'

'Different from fucking promised.'

'We got you out, didn't we? You'll be fine.'

'But you –'

'Out of my hands, Ian. I don't get to run jobs where a couple of million's involved.'

'A couple of million and three people.'

'Well, six, including you and the two with the booty,' Callic said.

'I mean the three I put on a plate.'

'Three we've been after for a real while,' the driver said.

'They'll give you a lovely future, Ian, all of you – the family,' Callic said. 'Think of it as a beginning.'

The Vauxhall took him to a safe house, the first of the safe houses he'd be seeing from now on – a Hackney safe house, and then, after a couple of hours, they drove him to a taxi rank and told him to go home and get everyone ready for immediate relocation to an address outside London that Callic gave him verbally and told him to memorize, immediate meaning the same day. They'd be issued with their new names by local police as soon as they arrived. A sub-department made them up and really tried for suitability.

And his new name was Templedon. Had it become stupid now to fight that? Should he give up on the dream scripts starring him and Walt, with Vera as a walk-on? Weren't those playlets pathetic? He would never commit the new idiocy of a journey to see Walt, would he – Walt and Vera? Settle to it here, Templedon who was Ballion. Settle to this decent house in this decent street – or not a street, Cormorant *Avenue* – in this decent district.

OK, then, today he would take all his family out to the local castle. He wanted to get a through-and-through feel of their adopted city, the way he got the feel of the special tarmac under his soles on a raid. The castle was a big feature. People went on about it, said you *must* see the castle, it amounted to an *experience*. They made it sound like some sort of initiation. But, all right – good for him, good for Jane, good for the children. In the months since

Ensign Road and Highton Street the family had moved around from secret refuge to secret refuge until now they were installed, permanent. In a couple of weeks, the kids would go to their school. Before this, he'd like them to build a little background in their home city, take on stability, solidity. A genuine castle with a motte and bailey ought to give them that, surely.

Then this evening, after the castle, he and Jane would sit in on the last but one 'readjustment session' which the cop named Andrew Rockmain had been doing with the children. Apparently, although this Rockmain held big police rank – Commander – he was also a top-flight psychologist who specialized in the problems of former grasses' offspring suddenly required to change their identities. He brought off a big success with a family resettled in Cardiff or somewhere like not long ago, Templedon heard.*

As they toured the castle he found himself now and then placing a hand on the thick stone walls. They had probably done some good defending in their time. The idea heartened him, though he couldn't have said why. Walt Melvane wouldn't be coming after him with a longbow. Yes, stability, endurance – he needed these as much as the children did, and when he passed a palm along the lumpy stonework he could almost persuade himself he took some of its strength through the contact. This castle, this city, were what counted now for all of them, not imagined, listen-to-me-do, love-me-do apology trips to Walt Melvane, nor eternal re-creations of that police-schemed shambles around the cash car.

When this afternoon on their outing Templedon explained what he could to the children about the castle, he made sure he frequently used their new names. These were parts of the same process of adaptation. They had begun to accept the changes now. Rockmain helped with that. At first, they'd been difficult about the switch – sullen and resentful, not able to understand why it was happen-

* See *Forget It*.

ing, not *willing* to understand why it was happening. Rockmain had said: 'Typical' and stayed unfazed. By the time they went to the new school they must be ready to respond instinctively to the new names, must be on their way to forgetting they had ever been called Rose and Larry. Rockmain specialized in making kids forget, the way other police specialized in Traffic.

Tricky. Now and then, Templedon could himself slip into calling them by their previous names. Today he took care. Jane seemed better at it. She never reverted. Did she see the hazards more clearly? Was her mind free from the kind of daft clouding that came to him when he pretended he could make it sweet with Walt, sweet *again* with Walt, and with Delicate's and Foden's sweet relations and/or sweet buddies? So hopeful, so mad. Sometimes he thought he must have caught from Lester that naive belief in his own talk powers. Look where it got *him*.

After the evening meeting with the children, Rockmain said, his voice clangy with optimism – he was hot on optimism: 'I'm pleased. My view is that the children have almost completed their journey to Templedonness and will be content to abide there and competent to abide there.' The session had been in an hotel suite and a nurse took the children home to Cormorant Avenue afterwards.

The two police, Iles and Harpur, joined the meeting now. Always they avoided contact with the kids for fear of worrying them with more police faces. The police faces worried Templedon himself, though. 'Yes, it's the cockroach experiment, you know,' Rockmain said. 'This may sound unpleasant and demeaning, but it *is* important. From these lowly insects we have learned the memory can only take so much. If you push a lot of fresh data in, previous items will be shoved out from the other end to make space. This is what has been accomplished with Sian and Harry and will continue. It's rather like a computer memory. The capacity is measurable and limited. Maybe we should be grateful. I'm happy to tell you that Robert and Jane instinctively realized what I try to do and have been able to complement my own work with the children. For instance, I hear that this afternoon, Robert, you took them to a castle and chatted about some of its features and history, no doubt calling Sian and Harry by their new names. This kind of exercise is brilliant. Their minds will seek to contain such information – such very regional-specific information – and in doing so will progressively lose recollections from their previous environment. And this new, pressing information will be associated with themselves, in their new persons that is, as Sian and Harry. The information itself will be vivid and will bring vividness also to their new names. Psychologists refer to this as "conjoint place syndrome". I've written on it, but absolutely no need for you to buy that book.'

'Also called brainwashing, yes?' Jane Templedon said. 'Or is that too simple and dated? Sluice away one personality, fit another. All right, so I've let this happen to the children. No option. Don't worry. I see it, accept it. I won't backtrack. But I don't like it. And it's no treat to hear you learned what to do to them from dirty bloody insects.'

Rockmain spoke considerately, softly: 'No, not at all like brainwashing, Jane. And "the dirty bloody insects" do give us a real pointer. Cockroaches, yes, I'm afraid so. A gang of them were put in a cage where half the floor had been electrified and gave them a bad shock. They learned to keep away from there. Then all are removed. Some get placed in hibernation. The others carry on normal cockroach life. After a while, all are put back into the original cage. Only the ones who hibernated remember to steer clear of the electrified area – because they've had no new experiences to crowd out recollections of the pain.'

'The Cockroach Kids,' Jane replied.

Templedon wanted to shut her up and wanted to sympathize with her. How things were these days. He put an arm around her shoulders: 'Look, Jane –'

'I'll wear that, too,' she said. 'Jane.'

'Look – yes, he's working on their brains et cetera, and their memory, but they're still our kids,' Templedon said. 'Nothing changes this. Some memories – they can be ditched, no damage. Memories of little things – they're just . . . well, little, not important. It's the now we've got to think about. The four of us, we share the now, a new now. All right, it's made up for us, it's made up for us by people like Iles, but it's ours. We take it over, put our mark on it. This is a family with the love and strength for that. And they're still our kids and we do what we can to make them safe – and keep ourselves safe.'

'I've said I can let it happen,' she said. 'I *have* let it happen.' She released herself from his arm. That hurt him – these cops watching, Iles watching. You never knew where you were with her, whatever name she used. She thought she had a right to views and she'd spout them. She wanted a part in things. People like Jane would never realize they were carried by a big earner and ought to be grateful and keep quiet sometimes. Templedon blamed her parents. They'd both netted good, high-level civil servant incomes and pensions, and so their daughter thought money came by itself if you had a bit of ability, like natural. She didn't see it had to be ripped away from others. She didn't know much about competition.

Or she hadn't seemed to see or know when they first met at that university gun club. She'd easily outperformed him there, because *daddy* brought her up to shoot, in a range and on the moors. But she didn't crow or appear to make any big effort, just took it for granted she'd be better than anyone else. She'd adjusted her views about money now, obviously. That started once she realized the kind of game he went in for after goodbyeing his college degree. If someone like Lester called at the Highgate house to talk business, anyone would wonder what kind of business someone like Lester talked. In any case, Templedon tried not to have too many secrets from her. On the whole he believed marriages should be like that. But she still kept some ways of regarding things from those earlier times. *Life's lovely and easy, just enjoy it.* This could enrage him. She'd never really cottoned to the presiding, inescapable gospel of take.

'I don't want to mess up anything,' she said. 'Just having a useless moan. Brainwashing – it seemed a fair, familiar term for it, that's all.'

But it had never been her way to do useless moans. Templedon wondered if he was putting her through too much too fast – wondered whether he was putting himself through too much. Lately, in the papers he read about abandonment of a case against Flying Squad detectives accused of corruption because a police grass became sick from stress and couldn't give evidence. Templedon understood. And the pull to get back to what he was previously, and what they, the family, were previously, returned – the pull to grow glib and more or less truthful face-to-face with Walter Melvane and put things right.

'No, really, I do find the term "brainwashing" definitely won't do, as a matter of fact,' Rockmain replied, giving his hair a slow palm smooth to signal anger. 'This is not *The Manchurian Candidate*, Jane – the wish to take over others' minds and direct them into some evil, unnatural purpose, as happened in that film. What I do is help people – mainly children, but also adults – help people move out from one crumbling framework to their lives and set themselves up happily in another.'

Iles said: 'Myself, I'd like to get rid of certain clinging memories, Andy. In some ways they're comic, admittedly. My wife, Sarah, and I chuckle at them jointly now. The retrospect. But they also . . . Could you help me with that? I'm thinking of the memory when I first discovered about Harpur and –'

'You'll hear people actually say they're seeking a "framework" for their lives,' Rockmain replied. '*My* objective is to show how to break through one such framework, destroy it, smash it asunder because that has suddenly become necessary, vital, and find something different, more suitable, safer. I'm proud of this work. I might have been a university psychology don, you know. Too far removed from things, I decided. What I'm doing contributes more to the collective good.'

'Some would argue that a vile, recurrent recollection like mine of Harpur or Garland and my wife could shove even the most balanced, temperate mind – and plenty of these exist, I understand – shove even the most balanced, temperate mind towards disorder,' Iles said. 'I know there are folk who, observing me, when I am suffering one of my agonizing interludes, fear I have –'

'In the matter of eliminating the past and its awkward, binding influences,' Harpur said, 'I understand some experts favour the Saul of Tarsus approach rather than cockroaches.'

'This must be quite a toss-up,' Iles said.

'I don't dispute Harpur's point,' Rockmain replied.

'Saul of Tarsus?' Iles said. 'Harpur's good on both the Bible Testaments – that kind of thing. His parents sent him to Sunday School as a child, though classes didn't seem to reach the bit in Hosea, is it, Col, about controlling the dick at noonday and, yea, also when the sun hath sunk and shadows fill the land? Old Hose could be strict.'

'Now, since it's been mentioned, you'll probably all want to know what we mean by the Saul method as against cockroaches,' Rockmain replied. 'I'll explain.'

'Oh, God,' Iles said.

Rockmain said: 'It refers to the instant, now-you-see-me-now-you-don't, total conversion of someone from one identity to another. So, Saul is struck down on the road to Damascus and immediately becomes St Paul. As Harpur suggests, it's true there is a view that this is the best, briskest, all-out way to accomplish the kind of switch required in resettling informants and their families. Just one, uncompromising blast of information – like: "OK, you were so and so and your life was such and such. Now you are someone different, and these are the details of your new circumstances and life so take them aboard at once and get used to them." Fine, fine, possibly for adults, who instantly and vividly see the perils in their old name and being, and therefore the immediate need for a total switch. Aliases dished out like the dole or a new suit of clothes. But can children grasp this? Can they abruptly decide to be someone else? I don't believe so. Gradualism. Essential. Thus, the roach syndrome. At the new school, when they get there, more and more fresh, formative experiences will come upon the children and always, of course, in the names of Sian and Harry Templedon, since the school knows them only as such, and must, of course, know them only as such. It will be as if they have no past. *Tabulae rasae*, as my old friend, Johnny Locke, the philosopher, has it, meaning blank pages, waiting to be written upon.'

'I hope that's true,' Templedon said.

'Obviously, obviously,' Rockmain replied. 'This is a crucial element in the transformation.' His voice fell a degree. He grew less bouncy. Something had happened inside. Templedon felt baffled – always felt baffled by Rockmain's personality. Did anyone know him properly? Templedon thought Rockmain might be perve in some way, but probably not with children. He would have slipped up by now, surely, when so much of his work involved kids. Thin, shortish, he looked almost frail, his neck wispy. He wore expensive denim and very narrow-fit black shoes. Too much lip wetting. He was smooth-faced and kept his fair hair long. From time to time, he arched his back, like modesty, and gave a crawly little smile that aimed to win you over. He did this as Templedon watched, then said: 'May I add, though, Robert, it is not the children I worry about now.'

Templedon stayed silent. He thought he could sense what Rockmain meant. It alarmed him.

'I worry about *you*, Robert. Yourself. Oh, pardon me,' Rockmain said. 'I don't mean this to sound uniquely applicable to yourself. All ex-informants who have helped put mates away show one, common massive characteristic – shame-stroke-guilt, the wish to rectify things with the family and pals of those jailed.'

Templedon realized suddenly that he'd better amend at least part of his estimate of Rockmain. Templedon had thought of him as a smartarse, capering fool, probably with a big degree from one of the big, smartarse universities. Well, yes, he remained smartarse and he capered, but not a smartarse fool – just a very sharp-eyed smartarse smartarse. He'd seen others in Templedon's state, and could at once spot the symptoms now. In a way, that comforted Templedon. Was all the dream stuff with Walt Melvane only typical of a retired supergrass, then, not special to him, not ludicrously unique?

Rockmain said: 'There's a French phrase, *nostalgie de la boue*. Oh please, now *please*, don't be afraid of a foreign language, I beg. Literally, a longing to get back to the slime – a suppressed urge in sophisticated societies to return to primitive times. But it could refer also to the crook turned lawman who longs to resume his old comradeships and values – uselessly, dementedly wishes to undo the cataclysm for chums that he – as a grass – helped bring about. One observes this in you.'

Iles said: 'I can understand such a feeling – the yearning for one's community and its approval. At Staff College I was known as "Desmond the –"'

'But now there's a *new* community for Templedon,' Harpur said. 'It provides our local castle, as well as a detached house. This community frees him from the rotten power of villain ex-mates.'

'Obviously, everyone remembers that poem by de la Mare,' Rockmain replied.

'Ah, another Walter,' Iles said.

'It's called "Jim Jay",' Rockmain said.

'Harpur won't have heard of it,' Iles said. 'He's from

what's known as "the university of life". Poetry was not on the syllabus.'

Rockmain recited: "'Do diddle de do, Poor Jim Jay –'"

"'Got stuck fast in Yesterday,'" Iles said.

'My job – to get people *un*stuck, liberated from Yesterday,' Rockmain said, 'because Yesterday is degeneracy and peril.'

Jane Templedon said: 'Please tell us some more about this nostalgia, Mr Rockmain, the terrible impulse to revert, despite degeneracy and peril.'

'A community has its own effective bonding elements,' Iles replied. 'These are what *make* it a community. For instance, it can be the continuous, loot-driven fucking criminality previously practised by Ballion alias Templedon around London highways and further with his associates. Crooked teams demand perfect loyalty. Or, in the more normal community, inhabited by most of us, one of these bonding elements might be – and an *admirable* bonding element in this case – one of these bonding elements holding things together might be the continuing prevalence of marriage, despite some slackening. Oh, yes, marriage. But then along comes someone like Harpur, spots a marriage where he fancies the wife and –'

'Yes, tell us more about this dangerous nostalgia for the mud days, would you, Mr Rockmain?' Harpur said.

'Ah, have you also detected it in Robert?' Rockmain replied. 'The absurd wish to reject everything that's been done for him and the family and return.'

Templedon tried to keep some hold on the chatter. People cut across, stuck to their own obsessions, ignored one another, as in most talk, but here he felt a unique kind of special chaos. Always this seemed to turn up when Iles turned up. There was the vital matter of Templedon's own and his family's safety, but also other half barmy strands, mainly from Iles, of course, that seemed almost to throttle everything else. Templedon found it frightening to hear himself spoken about as though not present, as

103

though some dodgy item to be dealt with in the best way possible.

'Yes, tell us more about this hazardous nostalgia, would you, Mr Rockmain?' Harpur said.

'Let me come at it in roundabout fashion, would you? You see, along with worries about Robert, one of my prime problems here is Mr Iles,' Rockmain said.

'Andrew has such lovely bluntness,' Iles replied with a great, friendly grin, mail order direct from hell, Templedon thought.

Rockmain laughed a small amount to counter this grin. 'I've been told my frankness, bluntness if you like, will kill me one day,' he said.

'Oh, dear,' Iles said.

'Yes, kill me,' Rockmain replied.

Iles said: 'You'll have the consolation, Andrew, of knowing that the minister summing you up for a pitifully sparse yet gloating congregation at the funeral would certainly refer to your lovely bluntness. I can see your casket – small, though above child-size.'

Rockmain said: 'I don't in any way question Mr Iles's devotion to his wife and his continuing rage with Harpur over the affair, the betrayal, but Mr Iles himself looks about for extra woman-flesh, girl-flesh, and this is relevant, crucial, to our present problems. In my view.'

'I don't actually see any problems,' Iles replied. 'We have a normal resettlement programme on the go.'

Templedon wondered if he was watching some sort of internal police battle. He *knew* he was watching some sort of internal police battle, but how big? Did these two, Iles and Rockmain, detest each other? Well, of course they detested each other. But would it go to such a point that Templedon's security and his family's security were forgotten?

Rockmain said: 'I know from previous encounters that Mr Iles adores logic. Here's some for you, Desmond, then.

If you're buzzing around Mrs Templedon, which I, of course, observe you are – no great psychological insights required to determine that – if you're buzzing around Jane Templedon, it follows that for Robert to invite the awful, appalling hazard of talking to Walt Melvane or Delicate Royston's people or Foden's, would obviously suit you brilliantly. Robert Templedon might get himself slaughtered and removed, leaving a clear run to Jane. Perhaps you would place no obstructions in Robert's trip to annihilation, Desmond.'

'Yes, I've thought of that, naturally,' Templedon answered.

Harpur said: 'This is foolish. I believe – a guess, but a reasonable one – I believe Mr Iles thinks of himself as like Frankenstein. That's not the monster, as some folk imagine, but the experimenting genius.' Harpur always disliked hearing Iles attacked, especially when the attack seemed based on truth. The Assistant Chief was needed – uncrushed, vehement, wily. Things would start breaking up if Iles got destroyed, or even part destroyed. 'The ACC is greatly proud of what he justly refers to as his creations, such as Robert Templedon out of Ballion, and, in fact, would almost certainly not favour his destruction, either brought about personally or by some other method. Regardless.'

'Thank you, Colin,' Iles said. 'You bring empathy, as well as observation.'

'You say "regardless", Harpur. Regardless of what?' Rockmain asked.

'Jane Templedon,' Harpur said.

'I've noted in the past that the warm whiff of woman gets to Mr Iles in a rather . . . well . . . a rather disturbing manner,' Rockmain said.

'What the fuck does that mean?' Jane Templedon asked.

'The Bathsheba syndrome,' Rockmain said.

105

'Biblical again, for God's sake?' Iles asked.

'Second Book of Samuel,' Rockmain replied.

'Harpur will know it,' Iles said. 'I told you, either Testament. He's a damn concordance.'

'King David sees Bathsheba, a married lady, having a wash . . . items exposed . . . that kind of thing . . . and David fancies her, has her, gets her up the spout,' Rockmain said. 'Then he puts her hubby, Uriah, in a battlefield hot-spot so he's killed and can't be a nuisance any longer. See any comparisons? I think so.'

'Harpur will definitely know this bit if it's to do with galloping sex,' Iles said.

'I see Mr Iles as not so much like Dr Frankenstein as King David,' Rockmain replied. 'In the Bathsheba context. Similar appetite, similar ruthlessness.'

'David wrote the Psalms, didn't he?' Iles asked. 'Many of those I wouldn't have minded writing, as a matter of fact. Consider number 13. Up my street. "How long wilt thou forget me, O Lord?" Often I feel like crying out movingly in those terms. I weep. It's not good to be forgotten to the degree I'm forgotten. Unjust.' Templedon wondered if Iles would weep now. He paused, obviously terribly sad about his state. In a while, though, he resumed. '"How long shall mine enemy be exalted over me?" Exactly. Exactly. "Lighten mine eyes lest I sleep the sleep of death; lest mine enemy say, I have prevailed against him; and those that trouble me rejoice." I expect you'd be surprised to hear I have enemies who'd rejoice if things went hellish for me, Mrs Templedon.'

Rockmain said: 'So you see, Robert, for you to cave in to sentiment – to what I've perhaps pretentiously labelled that *nostalgie de la boue* – if you cave in and visit Walt Melvane it would really delight Mr Iles. I don't imagine you'd want to hand him this sort of triumph, would you?'

'Oh, yes, I've many an enemy, difficult as it is for people

106

to believe,' Iles replied. 'It comes with the job, of course, but there's extra, too, wouldn't you say, Col? Harpur's one of the people I wholly trust, except, of course, when it comes to –'

'Thank you, sir,' Harpur said.

Chapter Eleven

Jill said: 'Here's Sian Rebecca, dad. She's ten but nearly eleven and she lives just over there – not in this avenue but her back garden is just behind *this* back garden, over that fence. But they don't call it "back garden" in this sort of avenue, they call it their "gardens". Although it looks like only one garden they say "the gardens". This is how Coral knows her, from being in her tree house trying to bop magpies with a catapult and looking down into Sian Rebecca's gardens and talking to her over the fence. And then inviting her to the party although younger. I think that was kind because Sian Rebecca is new.'

'Yes,' Harpur said.

Coral Ann, the hostess child, took Sian Rebecca by the arm and drew her away to see a litter of kittens in the garage. 'And you come, Jill,' Coral said.

'In a minute,' Jill replied. 'And this is the funny thing, dad – you might know it already – Sian Rebecca's other name is Templedon and I think her mum might be that same lady who came to our house the other day, if you remember, called Mrs Templedon – Templedon not being a very *usual* name. I don't think Mrs Templedon ever told us the names of her children, did she, although I did ask? Sian has a brother whose name is Harry Charles and he's eight. Do you know if Mrs Templedon who called at our house to see you had children with these names?'

'Mrs Templedon?' Harpur said. 'Oh, yes, she came to the house, didn't she?'

'Is it dodgy?' Jill replied. 'Is it police stuff and really dodgy?'

'What?' Harpur said.

'Mrs Templedon. The one who came to the house.'

'Dodgy?'

'Well, you say what's so obvious "Oh, yes, she came to the house, didn't she?" *I* just told *you* that. This is how you answer when you don't want to answer – just by repeating what's just been said and giving a dopey smile, all sweet but a brick wall.'

'That right?' Harpur said.

'What?' Jill asked.

'Me – answering by not answering and giving a dopey smile which is a sweet brick wall.'

'So, *is* it dodgy?'

'It would be better if you didn't say to Sian Rebecca that her mother came to our house,' Harpur replied.

'Why?'

'It would be better,' Harpur said.

'Her mother *is* that Mrs Templedon then, is she?'

'I expect so,' Harpur said.

'You know, do you?' Jill asked.

'It would be better if you didn't say she came to our house,' Harpur replied.

Sian Rebecca joined them again. 'Is *your* dad like this, Sian Rebecca?' Jill said. 'Like difficult?'

'*My* dad's called Robert Maurice Templedon,' Sian Rebecca said. 'Many know this. They say "Robert" when they talk to him. And mum. She says "Robert". I say "dad", like always. But mum says "Robert".'

'Well, yes,' Jill said. 'Her brother is called Harry Charles, which are both royal names, you see, dad, but not Sian Rebecca.'

'That's a fact,' Harpur said. He'd come to take Jill home from Coral Ann's party, his half of a ferrying duty.

Sian Rebecca said: 'My name is Sian Rebecca Templedon.' She sounded dogged and aggressive, as if expecting someone to disagree.

'Yes,' Harpur replied. He had seen pictures of the two Templedon children, but only fairly basic dossier shots. Now, he could look properly at Sian Rebecca, once Rose Diana. She was fair, like her mother, tall and a bit bony, blue eyes large and uncertain, her thin body tense, as if scared a rough-house might start. They were in the garden or gardens. It was still warm, but beginning to get dark.

'I don't mind if people call me just Sian or Sian Rebecca,' Sian Rebecca said.

'Same with Coral, whose party this is, dad,' Jill said. 'Is a house as big as this and with gardens known as "a property"? Coral had a pony as her present from her mum and dad. Some call her just Coral and others call her Coral Ann, which is also right.'

Harpur didn't know Coral, or Coral Ann. She was a new friend of Jill's from the martial arts club, thirteen today, and celebrating with a houseful. A big houseful. Yes, a property – Chessington Avenue, which, as Jill said, backed on to the gardens of Cormorant Avenue and the Templedons' house.

'I can easily remember my name,' Sian Rebecca said, 'even if none of it is royal.'

'I expect so,' Harpur said.

'Well, most people can remember their own names I should think,' Jill said. 'Except when they have that disease – you know, dad. Waking up in hospital and no idea and no papers or anything to show who she is.'

'Amnesia.'

'Because, obviously, people have grown up with their name – and the mother and father calling out that name from when the person was just a baby,' Jill said. 'At first when they called out that name a baby would not understand what it meant, obviously. A baby would not know this was *her* name, because she wouldn't even know what names were at that time. In the hospital they put a label on the baby's wrist with its name on so it won't get mixed up with other babies all looking the same, like wrinkled and pink, but obviously the baby would not even know what a label was and definitely would not know what a name was. They just scream and sleep – they don't realize they've got a name. But then when her mother and father keep on calling her Sian Rebecca as she's growing up it would go right into her head so that when they called it she could tell it was to do with her. Like a cat or a dog. If you keep on calling a cat or a dog Delphine or Rex the cat or the dog will get to know it is being spoken to and will come purring or wag its tail. It would be only for certain sorts of animals – animals with a brain a bit like ours. It would be no use calling a wasp by a name or a goldfish most probably, even many times. But us and some animals – this is how names work, isn't it? Those kittens with Coral – they wouldn't know their names yet. I mean, if they've got names at all. It's too soon. But later. So when I was just tiny, dad and my mother would call me Jill all the time and I would be able to tell after a while that Jill was me. My mother's dead now, Sian Rebecca, but I'm sure she and dad used to call me Jill when I was small, and this sound of the letters J. I. L. L. would soon get to seem me to me. I couldn't spell it then, obviously, or write it down, but after, say, months or a year I knew it was me. This is called identity or ID.'

'I can spell Sian Rebecca Templedon and write it down,' Sian Rebecca said. 'Sian is Welsh, and sometimes it has a little squiggly thing on top of the letter i but I don't have to do that, and Rebecca is from the Bible, right at very near the beginning, so it's important, but *my* Rebecca is spelled R.E.B.E.C.C.A., but the one in the Bible is Rebekah, R.E.B.E.K.A.H., but this doesn't matter. The one to remember is R.E.B.E.C.C.A. At first I used to think two Bs and only one C. But that is not right.'

'It's a lovely name,' Harpur said. 'The wife of Isaac.'

'Dad knows the Bible,' Jill said.

'That's the *other* one, the one that's R.E.B.E.K.A.H.,' Sian Rebecca replied.

'Most probably this would be the Hebrew way of spelling it if it's at the beginning of the Bible, because they all spoke Hebrew then, didn't they, dad?' Jill said.

'Oh, yes,' Harpur replied, 'although it was after Babel – when all the other languages got going.'

'I told you he knows the Bible, Sian Rebecca.'

'I don't have to remember how to spell it in that old way,' Sian Rebecca said. 'Some names are much easier to spell than Rebecca.'

'Jill,' Jill said.

'A name like Rose is easier to spell,' Sian Rebecca said. 'But that's not my name. No.'

'No, indeed,' Harpur replied. He thought he could hear Rockmain's instructions and guidance in this child's struggling efforts to get accustomed to the new self.

'Well, yes, I like the name Rose. I don't like all names from flowers, but I like Rose,' Jill said. 'I don't like Violet or Lily.'

'Sian Rebecca is easy if you're just careful,' Sian Rebecca said.

'Who told you about that old way to spell it?' Jill asked. 'Your mum and dad?'

'I think it was just so I'd know Rebecca was a *really* old name and important, so I'd always remember it, but not the way they used to spell it in Hebrew,' Sian Rebecca said.

'You won't forget it,' Jill said. 'I mean, everyone calling you it since you were a toddler – your mum and dad and your brother and all the friends here and teachers at school. Did someone tell you about the first Rebecca in the Bible, but spelled a different way?' Jill asked.

'Genesis,' Harpur said. 'Most people know about her.'

'Famed,' Sian Rebecca said.

'Are you Welsh, then – I mean, the name Sian?' Jill asked.

112

'We live just over the fence at the back of Coral's gardens,' Sian Rebecca replied.

'Yes, but before,' Jill said. 'Coral said you haven't been there very long – she knows because she had another friend in that house – what's *your* house now – and she used to help her do magpies, but they moved.'

'Cormorant Avenue, number 18,' Sian Rebecca said. 'This is my address.'

'Yes, but before that where did you live?' Jill asked.

'We lived elsewhere then,' Sian Rebecca replied.

If anyone asks where you lived before, just answer 'Elsewhere.' That would be Rockmain's wisdom, along with the memory aids to her new names.

'You lived in some other city?' Jill said.

'Yes, elsewhere,' Sian Rebecca said. 'Cormorant is a bird which is a great fishing bird. It sits on, say, a wave and then suddenly goes under if it sees a fish and swallows it. It is a famous bird with a tuft on its head. In China they tie a cord around its neck so it can't swallow the fish it catches and people can get the fish back to eat for themselves.'

'Who taught you all this about birds?' Jill asked.

'I would never forget Cormorant Avenue if I know about tying the cord around in China,' Sian Rebecca said.

'That's clever,' Harpur replied.

'Is that why someone told you about the cormorant, so you'll remember your address?' Jill said. 'Who told you? Your mum and dad?'

'Number 18 I can easily remember,' Sian Rebecca said. 'My brother is eight, so just put a one in front of it.'

'Yes, easy,' Harpur said.

'But later he'll be nine,' Jill said.

'It won't matter then,' Sian Rebecca said.

'Why?' Jill asked.

'I will have it in my head then, *really* remembered,' Sian Rebecca said. 'So, I won't think our house must be number 19 because he is nine. Eighteen will be in my head, like my names, Sian Rebecca Templedon. That's exactly who I am now. And Templedon is easy – like temple, like a kind of church, you know, and don, which could be short for Donald, like Donald Duck. If you bring them together, you see, you have Templedon.'

'Donald Duck after church,' Jill said. 'Who told you to remember your name like that?'

'It's useful,' Harpur replied. When he set out to collect Jill, the nearness of the two addresses – the party address, the Templedon address – hadn't struck him. Different avenue names. Jill had been picked up and driven here by the mother of another friend, and Harpur was to take them back. Hearing about the Templedons now, he would have liked to get clear before one or both of Sian Rebecca's parents arrived for her. This kind of unforeseen social connection was not good. Too close, too many ends. But perhaps Sian Rebecca could do the walk back around to the parallel avenue alone. Or she might climb the back fence. He thought probably not. It was almost dark. The girl couldn't know this area yet, and he had the idea that her mother and father would not want her unaccompanied. The fence might be tough in a party dress.

'Many names are like this – Temple and don, two pieces, even more,' Jill said. 'Think of the star, Justin Timberlake, which, when you think about it, is two words put together for his second name.'

'Castles I know about, as well as birds,' Sian Rebecca said.

'Which castle?' Jill said. 'Do you mean *our* castle?'

'A keep,' Sian Rebecca replied. 'Nearly all castles have a keep. This is where they would all get to if it was attacked because the keep had the strongest walls. Also in castles, towers, a bailey, a moat. Also a portcullis. I've been learning a lot of new words and remembering.'

And would they do their job and push out some of her previous memories, as Rockmain had said?

'Did you have a castle where you used to live before?'
Jill asked.

'Elsewhere,' Sian Rebecca said. 'I lived elsewhere.'

'Did you have any portcullises there?' Jill said.

'Elsewhere,' Sian Rebecca said. 'But now I live in 18
Cormorant Avenue. Also, the cormorant spreads its wings
out in the sun when it wants to get them dry after all the
diving. This makes it very easy to remember. I can think of
it in my head. It's black and very, very still, with its wings
spread out, and when I think of that I think, This is a
cormorant and so I live in 18 Cormorant Avenue.'

'Our street is Arthur Street,' Jill replied. 'I could think of
King Arthur and his Round Table if I forgot where I lived.
He wouldn't want to live in Arthur Street, though. He
liked it down Avalon way.'

'Here's my mum, come to get me,' Sian Rebecca said.

'Ah,' Harpur replied. 'I'm Colin Harpur.' He put out his
hand and Jane Templedon responded and briefly shook it
almost as if they were strangers. He wanted that impression. As few people as possible should know of her links
with the police. Gossip could leak, even from a harmless
gathering like this birthday party. Other parents had
arrived to pick up children and there were Coral Ann's
mother and father. Jill knew Harpur and Mrs Templedon
had met, but he'd asked her to keep quiet. And at resettlement meetings the Templedon children were always gone
by the time Harpur and Iles appeared. 'My daughter and
yours have become friends, I gather, Mrs Templedon,'
Harpur said.

'Oh, good,' Mrs Templedon said.

'Sian Rebecca told me you live on the other side of the
fence, Mrs Templedon,' Jill said.

'Yes,' Mrs Templedon replied.

'We live quite a long way off,' Jill said.

'Oh,' Mrs Templedon said.

'Called Arthur Street. The houses are not so big, or the
gardens,' Jill said.

'I'm sure it's very nice,' Mrs Templedon said.

'It's all right,' Jill replied.

'My mother is Mrs Jane Iris Templedon,' Sian Rebecca said. 'Many know this.'

Jane Templedon was in an ankle-length, Laura Ashley style floral skirt and off-white blouse. You could see how the child's thin body would develop into this kind of elegant long figure, leaving behind the boniness. Jane had the same sort of wide blue eyes but more confident, no uncertainties. As the party ended, thanks and goodbyes were big in the garden or gardens. Jill and Sian Rebecca went over for a last look at the kittens. Mrs Templedon stood close: 'Can we meet, Harpur? Not your house. And not mine, naturally.'

'I don't know if that's –'

'Your daughter was very good – the conversation – as if we'd never met.'

'Sometimes she'll do as she's asked.'

'He'll go, you know. He's getting worse.'

'Robert?'

'Getting worse – the regrets, the stupid shame. What did Rockmain call it – "nostalgia for the slime"?'

'He'll go to Melvane?' Harpur asked.

'He would. So I've decided.'

'Yes?'

'Yes. I want to go myself – get there first.'

'To Melvane? That's –'

'Come with me,' she said. 'Please. I know it's at variance with the whole –'

'It's unthinkable.'

'He'd believe you if you told him Ian's – Robert's – tale.'

'I don't know his tale.'

'Of course you know his tale. The grassing that wasn't supposed to be. Anyway, I'll remind you. Where can we meet?'

'There's a World War Two concrete defence pill box on the foreshore at the end of Valencia Esplanade.'

'When?'

'When suits?'

'Eight tomorrow evening,' she said.

Jill returned, ready to leave. She had found Isabel, the friend she came with, and they joined Harpur and Jane Templedon near the rockery.

'Nice to meet you, Mr Harpur, Jill,' Mrs Templedon said.

'We're going home to 18 Cormorant Avenue now,' Sian Rebecca said. 'It's easy to remember because –'

Jill said: 'One day perhaps you and Sian Rebecca can visit us in Arthur Street, Mrs Templedon. It's simple to find.'

'A nice idea,' Mrs Templedon replied.

In the car, after they had dropped Isabel off, Jill said: 'What's it all about then, dad?'

'You were grand,' he replied. 'As if talking to someone just met. And you hadn't asked Sian Rebecca if her mother, Mrs Templedon, called on us?'

'I thought it was a bit dodgy when Mrs Templedon came,' Jill said.

'Yes, I remember.'

'So I didn't mention it.'

'Good.'

'What's it about, dad?'

'Confidential.'

'Police confidential, or just you and Mrs Templedon confidential?'

'Police confidential, of course.'

'Honestly?' she said.

'Of course.'

'That quick talk at the end of the party – police confidential?'

'Of course.'

'All right. If you say.'

'Thanks, Jill.'

'And Denise believed it was a police matter when Mrs

117

Templedon came to the house, didn't she, and no crabby jealousy like Denise is sometimes?'

'None at all.'

'But, look, dad – like Sian Rebecca has been taught to remember her own name and keep saying it.'

'As if.'

'As if she was scared she'd forget her own name and address. I mean, dad, she's ten, nearly eleven. All right – a new address, but her name's not new, is it? And the address, anyway. So hard? If she wants to remember where she lives she's got to think of a bird drying its feathers and then her brother's age and stick a one in front. Someone been telling her these tricks? Has she got something wrong with her? I like Sian Rebecca, but weird. When she said "Rose" it was like that was really what she wanted to be called.'

'As if.'

'And "elsewhere" all the time like . . . as if . . . she didn't know where she had been. Or as if she didn't want to say. Yes, what I thought is she gets lessons about how to have secrets. Who does it? You? Des Iles? Why?'

'"Elsewhere" would be absolutely accurate,' Harpur replied.

'Well, yes, of course it's *got* to be accurate, hasn't it, if she's only just come to that house, because before that she must have been elsewhere. Obviously. But . . . well, "elsewhere" could be anywhere in the world.'

'Right.'

'It's stupid. I mean, she's not telling us anything – the way *you* do your brick wall. And the way Mrs Templedon didn't answer when I asked the names of her children in our house. Clouds and big gaps everywhere. It's like weird. It's weird.'

'There are people like that.'

'Is "like" all right like that, then?'

'Of course.'

'Like what?' Jill replied.

118

'They keep some things to themselves. It's habit. Nothing for you to get bothered about.'

'I'm not bothered.'

'I thought you were bothered,' Harpur said.

'But something weird about names. The way she kept on.'

'She's new. Perhaps she feels she has to tell people who she is,' Harpur replied.

'And tell them, and tell them?'

'I should think she'll stop that soon.' Harpur was not keen on lying to his daughters, but what else when you had someone as nosy and bright and persistent as Jill, plus a duty to keep the Ballion family secret and secure?

'I don't know many children who go to boarding school,' she said.

'No.'

'And her brother.'

'Some people believe in that,' Harpur said. 'It's normal for them.'

'What?'

'Sending the children to boarding school.'

'It costs, doesn't it? I mean, real fees, with extras for music and archery. Are Mrs Templedon and her husband rich?'

'People make the sacrifice.'

'It *was* a business matter, wasn't it?'

'What?'

'Talking with Mrs Templedon again just now. Does she say "Elsewhere" if you ask where she was living before Cormorant?'

'I don't ask.'

'Why?'

'It doesn't matter where she was before,' Harpur said.

'Don't you need her history . . . like her *background* – if it's a business matter? A police matter. I thought police were all about dossiers and records.'

'No need for "like".'

'Don't you need her history – if it's a police matter?'

'No, it's to do with now,' Harpur replied.

'What is?'

'The business matter. The confidential business matter – police matter. To do with the present and the future, especially the future, not what's gone.'

'Why? Is what's gone bad?'

'What's gone is gone.' God, he hoped so.

'And her husband,' Jill said.

'What?'

'Where is he?'

'Number 18 Cormorant Avenue, I expect.'

'Do you know him, too?'

'He wasn't with her when she came to the house,' Harpur replied.

'No, I know he wasn't. There you go again with the brick wall.'

'It was kind of Coral to invite a younger girl to the party. She's a stranger to this area and this will help her get to know other children.'

'I thought we were talking about Sian Rebecca's father.'

'He wasn't with Mrs Templedon this evening or when she called at our house, if you remember,' Harpur replied.

'Yes I remember. What's all this about, dad?'

'What?'

'You – not answering.'

'I expect on other occasions Mr Templedon *will* be with her,' Harpur replied.

'And then she says – that's Sian Rebecca says – she says, "I say 'dad' like always."'

'Should be "as always",' Harpur replied.

'"I say 'dad' as always. But mum says 'Robert'." Well, of course she calls him Robert, if that's his name. She's explaining stuff that obvious because it *isn't* obvious to her. You would think her father's name had only become

Robert lately and now she has to tell people about it and when she does that she's reminding herself about it as well. Do you see what I mean, dad?'

'What?'

'Weird.'

Chapter Twelve

Robert Maurice Templedon and his son Harry Charles walked down the garden of 18 Cormorant Avenue to the fence. It was too high for Templedon to see over, just what you'd expect in this kind of B7 neighbourhood, to use a term from the relocation papers. B7 meant top-grade suburbia, official reward for a former top-grade informant. As Jane said, the lawns were obviously supergrass grass. Standing near the fence, Templedon could make out the sounds of a kids' party coming to its end as evening moved towards night. Jane would be there now. She had gone around to Chessington Avenue to collect Sian Rebecca and walk back with her. Harry was too young to be invited and Templedon had taken him out in the late afternoon for a burger and Pepsi as compensation. Since they all became Templedons, Robert Maurice saw a lot more of his children. The family cowered together. When he and Harry returned, Jane had been just leaving to fetch Sian.

Now, Harry heard the laughs and shouts and grew curious. At the fence, Templedon put the boy on his shoulders so he could perhaps spot Sian. But daylight had almost gone and there were low-branch willows and beech at the bottom of the Chessington Avenue garden, one beech with a solid-looking tree house in it. Harry wouldn't be able to make out much. 'Call her name,' Templedon said. He liked having the lad on his shoulders. It made him feel fatherly, ready to put the child's wishes first. He had to speak upwards to him. Templedon knew he was not always so selfless, so sweetly parental. That pressure rested on him now though – to be parental, more parental. At a time of bewildering and perhaps cruel change for them, the children needed this. And possibly Robert Templedon needed it himself. He felt reduced, diminished, since he ceased to be Ian Ballion. His new Templedon character had to be built up and plumped out. One whole area of the Ballion side of him must be cut away – the lawless side. Whatever he replaced it with should be, above all, legal. Doing more in the dad line suited and might help – might help him put aside for good that urge to visit Walt and all it meant. 'Yes, call her name, Harry,' he said.

'Her name is Sian Rebecca Templedon, isn't it?' the boy replied.

'That's it.'

'Shall I call that?'

'Why not?'

He shifted about on Templedon's shoulders, wanting to be lifted down. 'No, I won't call her.'

Templedon set him on the grass. 'You could have told her it's time to come home,' Templedon said.

'I know the address.'

'Of course you do.'

'It's 18 Cormorant Avenue.'

'Right.'

'A cormorant is a bird and it's easy to remember because in one country they tie a cord around its neck to stop it swallowing the fish. Also, it spreads its wings very wide sometimes in the sun to get them dry. I know it's number 18, because I'm eight and put a 1 in front.'

Oh, God, oh, God. 'Great, Harry,' Templedon replied.

From where he stood near Templedon, the boy yelled towards the fence, 'Sian Rebecca,' once and not at full power. Templedon saw Harry wanted to show he could do it – remember the names perfectly – and wanted to please his father. The yell was a token, more or less private between them. To shout her name with a chance of getting it heard and answered would have chilled the boy because of its newness and strangeness, and he couldn't. Templedon detested what had happened to the kids through Rockmain, the fashioning of their minds, refashioning.

Hell, couldn't they get back to where and who they'd been, all of them? A crazy, mixed-up thought – a pile of mixed-up thoughts? Yes, he saw that. It went like this, didn't it? Because he'd become Templedon he'd also become more fatherly. And because he'd become more fatherly he saw and hated what Rockmain had done, was still doing, to the children. Therefore, despite all his resolves he wanted at times to junk the Templedon state and resume as Ballions – which would probably mean he became less fatherly!

As a matter of fact, he had a new, better speech ready for the maybe London trip. Was it eternally only maybe, and never to take place? Maybe. He'd come to realize that Walt Melvane would never swallow all that other stuff he'd prepared and rehearsed and rehearsed to himself about the cock-up at the hit. This was only wordage, spin. He knew now it had been stupid even to think of it. Thank God that's all he did do, think of it. Rubbish. But he'd worked out a terrific, different approach.

A death. This death would really say a lot to Walter Melvane and his wife, Vera. It would say a lot, but not just a lot, it would say absolutely what was needed.

Once this death had been done, he'd be able to murmur in a conversational way, no theatricals, to Melvane: 'Walter, I suppose news has reached you and Vera about DC Piers Callic, the Metropolitan Police officer. Probably it's not necessary for me to tell you, Walt, who killed him and why. I'm confident you'll see the message.'

Yes, he meant to speak it exactly like that – a certain vagueness and formality, so Melvane would realize this was not just purple mouth burble but a true statement, founded on a definite act, the completely necessary wipe-out of Callic. Vera must be mentioned repeatedly as well as Walt. This showed that, by deleting Callic, Templedon intended a message to the whole Melvane family, and it was a message of true regard and wholehearted friendliness, even love. By killing Callic, Templedon felt he would take over all their revenge duties, and at the same time make revenge by them against himself no longer right.

Harry went ahead of him at a trot, past the goldfish pool and gazebo, to the house. 'Careful now, Harry,' he called. 'It's nearly dark.'

The boy waited for Templedon to catch up and then took his father's hand. 'My names are easy to remember because of Prince Harry and Prince Charles,' he said 'who are well known because of royalty.'

'That's it.'

'And Templedon is like a temple, which is a kind of church, and then don which could be short for Donald like Donald Duck in old films on TV.'

Oh, God, oh, God. 'You've got it,' Templedon said. The boy's hand in his did give comfort. The trust made Templedon want to live up to it. He felt vitalized. This was a kid looking for something that stayed the same among all the changes and, for the moment, anyway, Templedon's hand would do. What he'd told Jane still stood – the children would always be theirs, regardless of surface changes. Well, of course. Did it need saying? But maybe now even the most basic and obvious things needed to be said between her and him, made clear, because their lives had lost almost all the usual certainties. Templedon wanted those certainties back. This meant he wanted Ian Ballion back, even if Ian Ballion did not often go in for holding his son's hand. It hurt him to realize he, Robert Maurice Templedon, had been devised by that rambling, mad fucker, Iles. Like cloned. Templedon had reversed things again. He longed now for the old solidity of Melvane and his grab-all flair. When he reached Walt, and he was sure to, wasn't he, wasn't he? – when he reached Walt, and had given those few introductory remarks on the due slaughter of Callic, Templedon would go on . . .

. . . 'I expect you'll remember Detective Constable Callic, Walt, but in case not here's his details. They're important. I *know* you'll see they're important.'

And most probably Walter Melvane would reply that everybody knew Callic. 'He was the one who sniffed and snooped around like an everlasting mission, wasn't he? Looks like he sniffed a bit too much in the wrong place at last.'

'Not exactly sniffing too much, Walt,' Templedon would reply.

'What then?'

'Betrayal.' Templedon liked the way some words seemed to signal what they meant, so, probably, even if you were foreign and didn't know the language you'd understand. 'Betrayal' was a word like that. He'd string it out when he said it – b-e-t-r-a-y-a-l. Darkness and two-timing seemed built in. Of course, Melvane would be thinking at first that Templedon himself had carried out all the b-e-t-r-a-y-a-l that interested *him*. But Templedon wanted the elimination of Callic to end this sick notion. There was a revenge side, yes, but Templedon also wanted the killing to tell Walt of reconciliation, of restored comradeship, of respect towards a true, fine dynasty, the Melvanes. He thought words beginning with 're' often had a good, warm feel to them – others would be renewal, reconstructions, repairs. And all these came from someone called Ian Maitland Ballion, not Robert Maurice Templedon . . .

. . . It was dark but still warm in the garden and Harry and Templedon stood outside near the open french windows. Not much noise on the other side of the fence now. Harry continued to hold Templedon's hand. Templedon did not mind this too much. 'Dad, Mr Rockmain said if I ever think I am Larry Raymond Ballion, this is wrong.' It was almost a question.

'Well, yes, it is. For now.' For now. Of course, Templedon recognized that his Callic plan and a happy return to the respect and friendship of Walt might never get going. More fantasy – like his earlier ideas for the trip? So, he must keep thinking Templedon, and keep Harry thinking Templedon, not Larry Ballion. *For now. For now?*

'He said I shouldn't even remember those names and I must always try not to, but I said I couldn't help it, I didn't know how to stop remembering them because . . . well, because they used to be me, didn't they?' The boy sounded ratty and sad, as though fed up with trying the impossible.

'Yes, they used to be you.'

'He said that my name, Harry, was like the other name, Larry, so it would be easy to remember, but the first letter is different, being an H not an L.'

'Yes,' Templedon said. 'I can see that.'

'Mr Rockmain said the best thing is, if I think sometimes by mistake I am Larry Raymond Ballion, I must make myself forget it. Keep on telling myself H not L.'

'That's the way,' Templedon replied. 'Mr Rockmain really knows about these things. He looks strange but he does know about these things and he's quite clever. He's all right with you, is he?'

'I don't know what you mean.'

'Just talks to you? Nothing else? Either of you? He doesn't get too close – anything like that?'

'He talks – about names and things like that. But sometimes I forget to forget the names from before.'

'If every time you forget to forget it you say to yourself, "I musn't forget to forget about Larry Raymond Ballion and I must remember I am Harry Charles Templedon," then, one day, the names Harry Charles Templedon will push the other names right out of your head – that's out of your memory – for ever.'

'I know. Mr Rockmain said that.'

'It's true. They proved it with some insects.'

'Sometimes Sian Rebecca forgets to forget the names Rose Diana Ballion. She told me. The name Rose is not like the name Sian so it might be harder for her to remember her new name,' Harry said.

'Did Sian tell you she forgets to forget?'

'Only sometimes she forgets to forget.'

'You can help each other,' Templedon said.

'How, dad?'

'Keep calling her Sian Rebecca. Call her this a lot. And she must call you Harry Charles a lot.'

'Mr Rockmain said that.'

'It's right.'

'He says Sian Rebecca or Harry Charles a lot. He never forgets to forget we were the other names. He knows we were those other names, I think, but he can forget them.'

'He wants to help you. When it's breakfast, for instance, say, "Good morning, Sian Rebecca." This will be a clever way to start the day and helpful – it will help you *and* Sian Rebecca.'

They heard Jane and Sian come in at the front door. Harry freed his hand and went through the french windows to see them and ask about the party. Templedon stayed outside alone. He felt split. He would go worthily through that Rockmain stuff with Harry, while half his mind schemed how to leave it all for ever behind.

It would be a tricky one knowing whether to carry something when he went to see Melvane after doing Callic. This was not because a gun holstered under his jacket or in his belt or pocket would be spotted and might make Walt even jumpier and rougher. If you were careful with an automatic it needn't show an outline – not like some big revolver. He had wiped over and chucked Foden's 9 mm Browning soon after the raid and kept the Beretta. This could nestle into the body reasonably all right, although nine inches long. But if you had something like that aboard it could somehow change the tone of a meeting – the *feel* of it, its mode. A gun meant you had decided even before the first words that Melvane could be peril. Wrong atmosphere for a helpful discussion. You would be wondering all the time if he was going to pull and if he did whether you could be quicker, like some ancient, corny Western movie on TV. 'Draw!' All that shit.

This meeting planned by Templedon would not involve confrontation and competition. A peace meeting. Otherwise, there would be no reason to slaughter Callic, except for revenge, and revenge as *only* revenge was barmy and infantile. He recalled another movie that came up on TV, a Woody Allen tale, where a crazy Italian character won't stop screaming, 'Vendetta, vendetta, vendetta' because he's been upset by someone. Comical. Pathetic. Unpositive. If you killed anybody you wanted a step forward from it, not just a chortle . . .

. . . 'Callic's the lad I gave a pre-whisper to about the raid, Walt,' he'd explain. Obviously, this was sure to be a danger moment – the admission, because that's what it amounted to. It would be before Walt heard the reasons for that pre-whisper. And if Templedon had a pistol on him his hand might more or less instinctively sneak towards it at that moment, only through thinking of possible rapid defence, not starting anything, but the move could happen. Melvane, noticing, of course, might go for his own gun then. He'd have one on him, even at home. Or some of his people would possibly be around, either in the room with them, or ready, and they could start blasting. Pre-emptive, as Lester called it. The disaster route.

Templedon decided, more or less definitely, that he would carry no weapon for the coming call on Walt. He wanted to walk into the Melvane place like what he was, a true admirer and colleague, someone whose first class attitude to the Melvanes could never be stifled by turning Templedon. Of course, he would have to take a gun to London with him to deal with Callic. Occasionally, he regretted getting rid of Foden's Browning, well buried in one of those early, safe house gardens, because that calibre gun was a real stopper. But he had wanted to retain nothing of Foden's and especially not a gun. It might have a history. The Beretta would do now, and afterwards he must get rid of that, too. The Thames could be a beautifully useful river, so big and grubby and unsearchable. His daughter had learned part of a poem when they were in London and would recite it. A line went, 'Sweet Thames, run softly, till I end my song.' The Thames might have been different then – sweeter, and all right for poetry. But it was still all right for other things.

He would tell Melvane. 'When I say I "gave a pre-whisper about the raid", Walt, what I mean is I gave a whisper ON CONDITION. That's the nub, isn't it, Walt – ON CONDITION? It was on condition he got his boys and girls to hit first, so *our* hit could never happen. He says he's only a DC and can't control things once he's told his chiefs. I'd like to have heard *how* he told them. Did he even mention the pre-whisper was ON CONDITION? Or did he just say, "One of my tipsters tells me we can get Lester Melvane, Delicate Royston and A.L.S. Foden in one swoop." He wanted the glory, didn't he? This was Callic looking for a big future. But, all right, let's suppose he *did* do it the way he agreed with me, and say his bosses reply, "Forget about bargains, Piers. We don't do bargains. You're not entitled to offer deals. You're a DC. We bag the buggers. We've been trying to long enough, haven't we? It's too long since they were inside." I admit, it's possible the big brass did take over. We're talking about millions and an international angle. But what I ask then is, Why didn't Callic return the whisper and tell me what his chiefs had in mind? I would have said "Thank you very much, Piers," and let Lester know the police plans. Result? Abandon the raid. Yes, a let-down, but we're all safe and we wait for something fat and easier when Hector might be available again if his mother had passed on, or managed a remission, and there would be no spot for that wrecker, Foden. But this is not their thinking, is it? Piers Callic and his chiefs consider everything will be fair and decent if they take Lester, Delicate and Foden and make a nice exit path for me to get out on, a running path at first, and then a path to the hideaway and new names.

'Well, Piers Callic knows now that Ian Maitland Ballion does *not* believe this was a fair and decent answer, Walt. Or, to be accurate, Piers Callic doesn't know anything now, but he did know for a second or half a second before he got the bullets in his skull. I didn't need to explain. I didn't hang about. But he would understand. And, Walt, I'm certain you understand, too, now, and I'm sure Vera will understand when she hears about Callic. This death is a symbol, Walt. This death is me speaking personally, loyally, honourably to you, Walt – to you and Vera and to Lester himself.'

And, in this scene, as Templedon saw it, Walt would come forward and embrace him. This was another reason for not carrying a pistol, because even though it might be properly hidden under suiting, when Walt held him in his arms like that he would feel any gun shape, even a small one. He might not be actually doing the embrace just to check on armament – not frisking and disguising it as affection. It could be a genuine, emotional move by Walt. People like Walt did have emotions, no question, and not just the emotion hatred. But if he accidentally rubbed against the outline of a piece, it would tarnish this happy, noble session based on Callic's good extinction.

After the embrace, Walt would probably go to the door, open it and call: 'What do you think, Vera? Who do you think done that Callic in the press?'

'Callic?'

'That law boy with the brainbox holes.'

'Oh, *Callic*. You said because he nosed too much, Walt.'

'I didn't get the full picture.'

Vera might come forward and see who was with Walt in the room. 'Not Ian?' she would cry out, joyfully.

'Ian,' Walt would reply. 'And do you know why?'

'Why?'

And when Walt had explained, she, also, would embrace Ballion. Definitely, he could not risk taking a gun there. It would be even more gross to press the lump of loaded metal unavoidably against this old lady's body than against Walt's, although through clothing layers. She was a mother, and with absolutely no charges ever, everyone said. 'Ian, this is such a fine, telling gesture,' she would murmur into his ear, while still holding him with grand fondness. She might turn to Melvane and say: 'We must send flowers, with a Deepest Sympathy card, Walter – really get a stab into Callic's family.'

But perhaps Walt would reply: 'No, V. Callic was a person, not just a detective. His family are people. He's dead. That's enough. We don't abuse the body.'

Or, in an alternative to this scene, it could be Walt who said send the flowers and giggle card and Vera who objected. On the whole, Templedon preferred his first version with Vera's malice and Walt's humaneness. Templedon wanted to believe Walt had a humane streak, because Walt was top of the firm and a dangerous one who had to be convinced . . .

. . . Templedon went into the house and closed the french windows behind him. 'Sian Rebecca enjoyed herself, didn't you, Sian Rebecca?' Jane said.

'It was nice,' she replied.

'Great,' Templedon said. 'Harry tried to look, didn't you, Harry? I lifted him up.'

'Yes, but it was getting dark,' the boy said. 'And trees in the way, and like a wooden thing.'

'A tree house,' Templedon said.

'So, you couldn't see anything, Harry?' Jane asked.

'No, I couldn't see Sian Rebecca,' he replied. 'I shouted for her. I shouted her right name, Sian Rebecca, didn't I, dad?'

'Oh, yes, excellent.'

'How about me?' Jane asked.

'You are Mrs Jane Iris Templedon,' Harry said.

'Yes. Could you see me?' she said.

'No, nor you,' Harry replied.

'Time for Harry to get ready for bed now,' Jane said. 'And Sian, best change from the party dress.' When the children had gone upstairs she said: 'Sian's got a new friend. You'll never guess.'

'Who?'

'A child called Jill Harpur, daughter of that big cop – you know, the mangled-looking one. Mr Flip-chart.'

'How do you know she's his daughter?'

'He came to pick her up.'

'They won't like that – a social meeting,' Templedon said. 'Too many possible complications.'

'Just polite chat, like strangers.'

'They still won't like it.'

'Tough. We didn't choose our neighbours. The child hostess meets Jill Harpur at a martial arts club.'

Sian Rebecca came back down in T-shirt and jeans. Templedon said: 'Mum says you met a new pal called Jill.'

'She's nice but she asks a lot of questions,' Sian Rebecca said.

'What questions?' Templedon said.

'A lot of questions – like where before this house in Cormorant Avenue, and about castles and if I'm Welsh, because my name's Sian now, not Rose.'

'She's interested, because you're new, that's all, love,' Jane Templedon said.

'Mr Rockmain has shown you how to answer the questions, hasn't he, Sian Rebecca?' Templedon said.

'I said "Elsewhere", dad.'

'That's a good answer,' Templedon said. It was always important to have replies ready in case the sharp questions began . . .

. . . If Walt Melvane came back at him with a lot of queries, even after hearing who did Piers Callic in affectionate, heartfelt tribute, Templedon would have perfect

133

answers in stock. He had prepared a barrelful to dispose of whatever Walt or Vera asked. He could anticipate. Templedon believed he understood their psychology. He believed he understood the psychologies of many, like Foden's as gun crazy. It was an instinct in him. All right, all right, Rockmain was the pro, the psychology expert, but Templedon trusted his own insights and made his preparations from them. With the grassing, for instance, there had been the insight first, about Foden, and then the preparation – lining up fucking Callic to mercy-kill the raid. The preparation went wrong, yes, but due to a double-cross. But maybe he should have applied some psychology to Callic and spotted he would jiggle the deal.

Walt might ask – and this would be the really basic one, the tough one, the one you could definitely expect from someone like Walt, even if he did have several decent strands – he might ask, 'Nice job on Callic, Ian, but what good to do him, except it makes one less of them – it don't get Lester out, and you put him in there?'

'Callic put him in there, Walt.'

'Don't see it.'

'Callic – he two-timed.'

'Callic was police.'

'Sure but –'

'Callic was police. That's all they know.'

'What is, Walt?' Templedon would stay patient, go along nicely with Melvane.

'Two-timing.'

'A bargain with police – it *is* possible, Walt.'

'They think we're shit. They don't bargain with shit.' Yes, That was the message from the raid. Templedon saw it. And Walt would say it, most probably, and then a bit more: 'They'll listen and talk, especially listen. They'll promise. Of course they will. But they don't think any of it counts because *we* don't count. None of it counts except the bits they want to count, such as the promise to get you out of it when Lester, Royston and the other was took.

134

That's one part of the bargain they said all right to. They got a phrase for it. Latin, or something like that.'

'Quid pro quo.'

'Now and then they'll do something like that.'

'It wasn't in the bargain, Walt.'

'It was in *their* bargain. *Get dear, fucking Ballion away, because he's our fucking man and we might need him somewhere else one day.*'

'What I mean about doing Callic. It's to show I was never their man, Walt. It's to show I was conned.'

'They was police. That's what police do. Con.'

Templedon would get true sorrow and shame into his voice at this spot: 'I know it now, Walt. I wish I could have talked to you, for guidance – your experience.'

And Walt would answer something like: 'Well, you could of talked to me, couldn't you? You *should* of talked to me. This was about my boy, Lester. So, you should of talked to me.'

'Time – a rush, Walt.'

'You saying my boy went at it too fast, no tactics, no sense?'

'Never, Walt. But things came at him, at us, in a gallop. This was Hector and his fucking fading mother, and then the urgency from Lester's contact – exactly when, exactly where. I had to be quick – no time for discussion.'

'Lester – he got a lot of time. Fourteen years.'

'I've come unarmed, Walt.'

'I can see that, or something tiny.' But Walt might go on: 'Do you know how that looks to me, coming here clean? That looks to me like a fucking insult. That looks to me like you thought you would get away with it. I'm some sort of push-over?'

'Never, Walt, never. This was on account of respect and friendship.'

And then Templedon could imagine Walt would at last give a little nod and a little smile to signal that, all right, despite the harshness act, he did believe the tale and did

135

appreciate the fine fragrance and rare timeliness of Callic's head blown open. Walt might do the embrace as this stage, as in Templedon's other scenario, and might call out to Vera, also as in that other vision, praising Templedon, endorsing him amply, welcoming him back as Ballion.

Rerun. Templedon really liked the sequence that came next, so he'd enjoy it again, word for word. If you had a good fantasy, make it work, and work. 'What do you think, Vera? Who do you think done that Callic in the press?'

'Callic?'

'That law boy with the brainbox holes.'

'Oh, *Callic*. You said because he nosed too much, Walt.'

'I didn't get the full picture.'

Vera might come forward and see who was with Walt in the room. 'Not Ian?' she would cry out, joyfully.

'Ian,' Walt would reply. 'And do you know why?'

'Why?'

And when Walt had explained, she would do *her* embrace. Then she might say about sending the flowers to Callic's funeral so as to rub it in with the family, and Walt would protest because he had some kindness in him somewhere. Or the other way about. Templedon still wanted Walt to be the tender one . . .

. . . 'Did Jill Harpur's father ask *you* where we used to live before 18 Cormorant Avenue, mum?' Sian Rebecca asked.

'No, just ordinary chat about the party,' she said.

'If he did ask you, would you just say, "Elsewhere"?' Sian Rebecca said.

'That's the best,' she replied.

'But would grown-ups think that was all right, just to say "Elsewhere"?' Sian Rebecca said. 'Is it silly? Would a grown-up say, "Yes, I expect it was elsewhere – like sarcastic – but where?"'

'It would be crazy in a party if you said "Elsewhere", Sian Rebecca, and then mum came along and said something else, wouldn't it?' Templedon replied. 'We're a family. We all have to say the same. That's what families do. Didn't Mr Rockmain tell you that?'

'Well, yes,' Sian Rebecca said, 'but –'

'"Elsewhere" is definitely the best,' Templedon replied.

Chapter Thirteen

Walter Melvane said: 'Well, this trip you made been a real
kindly move by you in a personal gesture, Eleanor, and
you also, sir.'

'Thank, you, Walt,' Eleanor said.

'Yes, thank you, Mr Melvane,' Harpur said.

'I know Vera thinks the same, don't you, V? And so
would Solid, I'm sure, if he was here.' They were in the
Melvanes' big, tidy sitting room.

'Oh, yes,' Vera said.

'I call you Eleanor because that's the name I knew for
you from way back with Ian. Eleanor Ballion.'

'Of course,' she replied.

'I know you got another name now which got to be
eternally confidential,' Melvane said. 'Well, that's obvious.
And Ian – same for him. I would never ask what them
names are because they are what's called in the police way
"cover". Yes, cover. The police are always *so* grateful to
their finks – and why not, because these finks sell their
friends to them? – so they always gives them good cover
afterwards.'

Harpur thought, thank God Walt Melvane *did* call her
Eleanor not Jane, and Ballion, not Templedon. It showed
the resettlement was working. It showed the cover
covered.

'The new names – they're something we've been landed
with, Walt,' Eleanor said. 'Sort of government issue, like an
identity card in some countries. We might not want it but

it's . . . it's something we've been landed with – as part of the new scene. It's important – and *not* important.' She was here to win him over and secure the safety, if she could, of Robert who'd been Ian. Her voice crawled and wheedled. But OK. That was the game. She had to do an acting job – give Walt all the sweetness and respect she could concoct. Harpur considered she seemed to handle it all right so far. They'd been here a while. She'd already explained to Walt and Vera how the cash-in-transit tip-off had gone so wrong.

'We understand that – how you been took over – don't we, V?' Melvane said.

'Oh, yes,' Vera replied.

'And I expect one of the ones who gave you them new names and also gave you the . . . what did you call it? . . . the "new scene" . . . I expect this officer with you now gave you them new names and the new scene. And he comes to make sure you don't use them new names here, because it would spoil the fine, tuck-you-away-somewhere scheme they got and spoil that new scene you mentioned. You got to be secret people now, haven't you? And not only now – for ever. There's people around who remember and remember, and they don't forgive.'

'I wanted someone with me, Walt, that's all,' Eleanor said.

'Someone who's not Ian,' Vera said.

'At this juncture,' Eleanor said.

'I should think you're acting *for* Ian, dear,' Vera said. 'On his behalf, yes?'

'He doesn't know I'm here. I don't want him ever to know,' Eleanor replied.

'He's a lucky boy – having someone to . . . well, someone to do all this travel for him,' Vera said.

'I thought it might help,' Eleanor said.

'And it's clever,' Vera replied.

'Clever?'

139

'Well, he might of come himself, if you didn't do it first,' Vera said, 'and then . . . well . . . it's different when it's you.'

'I knew you and Walt could be . . . I knew you could be reasonable,' Eleanor said.

'Some have remarked on this about Walt – that he can be reasonable,' Vera said. 'Often he gets a kick from that, the dear. This surprises some people.'

'And this officer, he haven't got no name at all, not while you're here with us, I mean,' Melvane said. 'He got to be known as just "the officer". This also being what's called "cover".'

'We thought it would be better like that, Mr Melvane,' Harpur said.

'I expect you did,' Melvane replied.

'I'm not important – just back-up,' Harpur said. 'I could be any officer.'

'You're not though, are you?' Melvane replied.

'I regard it as noble to come with her into our home like this,' Vera said. 'This is kindly, as well as police craftiness. Yes, kind. I don't smell no sex between you, but, of course, you're clever folk.'

Melvane said: 'When you was planning this kindly little trip I expect you said to each other that if Walt gets to know the officer's name he could do some tracing. All right, it's a different police outfit, not the Met, but if this officer is some important officer, even from another Force out in the shrublands, if this officer is important, and if I do some phoning or e-mailing and describe him, that face and his clothes, maybe I could find his Force. And if I found his Force I would also find the place where Ian and Eleanor are, and the two children, Rose Diana, aged ten, and Larry Raymond, eight, though these having different names now, but their ages unaltered, obviously. This was how you would think when you decided to do this visit together.'

'Don't be offended by that, Walt,' Eleanor said. 'They're

precautions, yes, clearly. Basic precautions, given the set-up we're in. Look, I –'

'And when I say most probably an *important* officer, that got to be so, haven't it, if he's the one who helps with your new names and the new scene in some secret spot? You wouldn't put some DC on a job like that. This is too big. This is like bringing out a new car model. This is to give the world a new family in a new scene, like born again. If they're thinking about a new shape Mercedes S-type they don't ask the puncture lad in the garage to sketch something out for them, do they?'

Melvane had a merry period of laughter over this, blue-grey eyes lively. Vera joined him. Harpur didn't mind the merriment. It was better than rage and gun-slinging. Did Walt write gags for Bob Hope before turning to robbery and so on? All the same Harpur found the tone of things eerie – the chattiness, the politeness, the creaking humour. Did Melvane want to lull them? To him they might seem a brilliantly promising way to locate the lad he knew as Ian Ballion, the lad who'd grassed his son.

Once, early on in the meeting, Walt had left the room, apparently to ask a staff girl to bring in drinks. Soon afterwards a tray appeared. But Harpur wondered if Walt had really left to order someone to tail Harpur's car when he and Jane Templedon, née Eleanor, departed after their work of intercession. From what he remembered of the dossier, tailing was the kind of artisan job Solid might be good at. Now and then, Harpur thought it had been a farcical error to come here. Oh, more than now and then. He'd tried to say so in that defence post meeting with Jane when they discussed this trip. He *had* said so, but she wouldn't hear. And he'd capitulated. If not, he knew she would risk it alone. The car was from the police pool, an old Escort, and Harpur had fixed false plates. Walt might know someone who could get a glimpse of registration records on the Department of Transport computer.

'That's why I believe this officer is probably an important officer in his own patch, and he would think, "I could be findable, so it got to be a matter of 'just call me officer',"' Melvane said. His voice was mild, maybe part of that lulling ploy. He had a squarish, big-chinned face, heavy lips, thin, unfriendly eyebrows, but not necessarily a face you would associate right away with menaces or a daddy's obsession with revenge.

'We thought it would be an insult to you, Mr Melvane, for me to take some false name, which would have been so easy,' Harpur said. 'We knew you'd see the realities – the absolute requirement for cover – and we decided to recognize this and not play about with a piffling alias.'

'Eleanor's got a piffling alias, hasn't she?' Vera said.

'That's what I mean,' Harpur said.

'What?' Vera replied.

'You see the realities. It would be absurd to try to fool you,' Harpur said.

'But for Eleanor to call herself Eleanor Ballion here, now, is a way of trying to fool us,' Vera said. 'It hides the name she and the family live under today in that new scene.'

'That's what I mean,' Harpur said.

'What?' Vera replied.

'You see the realities. It would be absurd to try to fool you by calling myself Detective Sergeant E.G. O'Trip,' Harpur said.

'Oh, I get it! Humour I love,' Melvane said.

'I felt that about you from the start,' Harpur said.

'Humour I love, regardless,' Melvane said.

Vera said: 'He do. How often Walter have remarked to me that humour always got a place, regardless?' She had a long, perky, well-balanced face, but frowned now, pushing everything up towards her hairline, while she tried to work out how often Walter had remarked to her that, regardless, humour always had a place. This might involve going back years.

'When I say "regardless", re humour,' Walter Melvane replied, 'what "regardless" signifies is, it don't matter

142

what's being talked about, such as Lester doing fourteen fucking years.' The mildness cracked for a second, then resumed. 'But would Lester see the joke? I think it's reasonable to ask that. Yes, reasonable.'

'We notice on visits to him that Lest is not into jokes so much as he used to be,' Vera said.

'I been in worse slammers,' Melvane said.

Eleanor said: 'I didn't come here to joke, believe me, nor the officer. We came to make sure you understand – really understand – why it's not right to think of Ian as a grass. Not *reasonable*. Not reasonable at all. I've told you he foresaw things might go haywire because of that idiot, Foden, and what he wanted to do was stop it, for the good of everyone. I'd like to know – long, long to know – whether you accept that.' Her voice sank towards whisper as she badgered them. 'Do accept it, I plead with you. *I've* told you, and the officer confirms. Walt, Vera, please say you believe what we've put to you.'

'Of course, what you're telling us is what in a court situation would be referred to as "hearsay",' Melvane replied. He gave the word plenty of weight. 'The judges and such don't go much on hearsay. Not at all. The officer must know that. You, Eleanor, pass on what Ian told you about the grassing and the officer passes on what you told him about Ian and the grassing. This officer didn't have nothing to do with the raid and the trial. Well, obviously he didn't. They wouldn't ask him to look after a grass, would they, if he been one of the ones who did Lester? This officer got to be someone far off and no connection. So, how could he know if it's true, what you said Ian was thinking of when he finked the raid?'

Melvane had it right, of course. More and more this mission looked to Harpur like the botch he'd dreaded. But, at the foreshore blockhouse back home, when he struggled to talk her out of the idea, she stayed immovable. Yes, she said she'd go whether Harpur came or not. She would prefer he did, but he was not crucial. He couldn't stop her, of course. She could go where she wished. 'There's a huge risk Melvane could trace you, and if he traces you he's traced Ian and the children,' Harpur had said. 'All he needs to discover is the area, the town. After that, narrowing things down to where you live wouldn't take him and his long. The resettlement scheme falls.'

'I suppose you want it to continue so Iles stays stuck on me and leaves your daughter alone, Harpur,' she'd replied.

'*Is* he stuck on you?'

She became embarrassed then and went to stare at out at the sea through one of the blockhouse gun slits. 'All right, I know it still sounds arrogant. I mentioned it earlier, didn't I? But yes, I think so.'

Harpur wondered if she read his motives right. 'I want it to continue because it means you and Robert and the children are hidden and safe,' he said.

'If he goes to Melvane himself the resettlement scheme's finished, anyway, isn't it? He will be offering himself. He'll be telling Walter Melvane, "Here I am and I am what I was."'

'He might still offer himself, even if you got to Melvane first,' Harpur replied.

'Perhaps. But we'll have prepared his way. Perhaps we can soften Walter Melvane. We'll convince him that Robert hoped to do something good . . . something . . . well, yes, positive, constructive.' She turned away from the gun slit and faced him in the blockhouse shadows. 'You'll say, "What if we *don't* convince him?" We will. Even if not, the situation will only be what it is now, won't it, Harpur? We don't really risk anything.'

Yes, he *would* have asked, 'What if we don't convince him?' He'd wondered if she realized what an absolute, unpardonable tumble into evil and decay grassing rated as with lads like Melvane, especially when his son had been its victim. If someone did a murmur to the police, that was it – the murmur. For Melvane, the thinking behind it didn't rate. Nobody could explain away the murmur. In Walt's mind, good grassing did not exist, tactical grassing did not exist. Grassing existed and should *not* exist. The punishment of grasses aimed to abolish it for ever by scaring others into silence. And too often it worked.

Harpur had shelved his questions. He couldn't knock down her argument – her 'so-what' argument, which said that, if they did go at once to Melvane and he rejected what they put to him, the position would be the same as if they hadn't tried it. So, all sane reasoning demanded, Try it. And, if she tried it, Harpur knew he should be with her, possibly to make her tale more credible, and possibly to ensure she came away unhurt. He had tried to keep anxieties about Hazel and Iles out of his head when settling this, and more or less succeeded. He would not be armed. How could he draw a weapon for such an outrageous, prohibited journey? But he would be present, and some sort of protection. Some sort would have to do.

Now, present and unarmed in Melvane's fine sitting room, nicely furnished with what Harpur judged to be genuine Regency pieces, he listened to Vera: 'Usually, when we have an officer or officers here, it's all questions, threats and mouth abuse. But that's the Met. They learn savagery and contempt in a police college up Hendon way,' she remarked. 'We call it The Framing Academy.'

Harpur thought the furniture might actually have been properly bought from good antique shops, not thieved. People of Walt's standing sometimes had a sensitivity about keeping robbery loot in their own domestic quarters. Harpur saw some hope in this. Despite everything, they craved innocence. They knew about respectability. For most of their activities they despised and skirted respectability, but they did know about it, and occasionally even gave it an obedient nod.

Melvane lived on a private, gated enclave estate in Dulwich, near a famous school, and not far from where the Thatchers once had a similar kind of property. Prices began at £2 million. 'P.G. Wodehouse and Raymond Chandler went to Dulwich College,' Jane had said as they drove here.

'That right?'

'Authors.'

She had rung ahead to ask if Melvane would see her – a non-traceable call, of course – and mentioned she would bring some law, but in observer role only. Harpur had hoped for a refusal. But Melvane agreed. Why not? The wife might lead to Ballion – a careless, give-away word or two, a trackable vehicle.

In the car, Harpur had said: 'I get a good glow from that.'

'What?'

'People like Melvane – they want to be in a sound, uncrooked setting. The school, the Thatchers, the authors. A suburban paradise. Villains see the sweetness of an OK life. They aim to get there via crime. Some never do, never emerge from their evil. Some make it, though, and then go more or less straight. Think of the House of Lords. The ambition is important, a comfort, in any case. It's the opposite of what Andy Rockmain talks about – that nostalgia for dirt.'

But it was not the kind of comfort Jane Templedon wanted today from Melvane. 'So, have we said enough?' she asked him and Vera. 'You see it now – see it as it was and is?'

'Well, how do we answer something like that, Eleanor?' Melvane said.

'What do you mean?'

'You bring an officer,' Melvane replied. 'All right, he don't seem like them Met louts, all heaviness and classic shoes, but he's still an officer, yes? I'm not going to say in front of him, am I, "Well, thank you, Eleanor, we listened to all of it but don't accept a fucking word and next time I see Ian I'll kill him because a grass is a grass"?'

Jane said: 'No, but –'

146

'And then when something happens to Ian, never mind who done it, who you think they look for? Who you think? Yours fucking truly, that's who,' Melvane replied. 'And in court the officer says, "I heard the accused, Walter George Melvane, threaten the life of Ian Maitland Ballion" or whatever his name is now.'

'I want you to promise nothing *will* happen to Ian because you realize now he is a fine and wholesome friend – to you and Vera and Lester and all the others,' Jane said.

It was the second time Harpur had heard this. In their blockhouse pre-trip conference at the foreshore, Jane told Harpur she would speak to Melvane in exactly these plain, madly hopeful, madly childlike words. He had felt appalled then, he felt appalled now. He had asked himself then and asked himself now how could someone married for years to Ballion imagine this kind of gushing, quaint plea would work with an emperor villain like Walt Melvane? Bizarre, unsettling – the whole blockhouse session went that way. Normally, Harpur met his own supremely talented and supremely well-defended grass, Jack Lamb, there. The difference was, Harpur knew Jack right through, had learned over years to trust what he brought and his interpretation of it. Jack informed only when he considered some impending crime especially vile and vicious, and his tips helped Harpur to rational, strong decisions.

That evening, though, as Jane described her intended journey, Harpur stood there baffled. He lacked any real familiarity with her. What he had amounted chiefly to crude, dossier stuff – university degree, gun club meeting with Ballion as he was, motherdom. Harpur could not trust in her instincts, as he did in Jack's after years of experience together.

She had seemed determined to stay very separate. Even in the cramped, dark space between concrete walls, she maintained a distance and called him Harpur. And there was another difference from Jack. Whereas he had always been brilliant at looking after his safety and personal interests, and *would* always be brilliant at it, Jane Templedon struck Harpur as terrifyingly vulnerable and somehow ignorant of the sort of world she might step into – either ignorant or wilfully blind to it. Yes, Harpur could see she, too, brought a kind of intelligence and strength to problems, but her thinking was desperate, backs-to-the-wall, forced.

Just the same, he found no route around it. She did at least show one resemblance to Jack Lamb. When Harpur met him at the blockhouse, Jack usually gazed out as she had done for a while through one of the gun ports. With Jack, though, it was as if he still expected to see the amphibious, German invading forces, around September 1940, and still expected to throw them back, solo if necessary. Jack loved wearing military kit and would often come to a rendezvous with Harpur in army surplus gear – any nation's army. Jane Templedon did not dress up for the meeting. She had on dark trousers and a denim jacket. When she bent forward to a loophole and gazed towards the horizon, it seemed as if she wanted a vision of the future, not of history, a vision that showed her children, Robert and herself passably secure. She seemed to think this would only happen if she acted.

'All right, we'll go,' Harpur had said. 'Nobody else to know, especially not Robert, especially not Mr Iles.'

'I don't talk to Iles. Not in private. And it would enrage Ian –'

'Robert.'

'It would enrage him if he thought I could read his intentions. And if he knew I'd interceded for him, gone on to his ground, as he'd regard it – sort of mothered him – "Oh, please, Walt, be kindly to my darling boy." He'd believe I had no right to endanger the children by giving Melvane a possible lead – even though he meant to do that himself. He'd think *he* could handle it.'

'You don't think he could?'

'Do you?' she replied.

148

Her doubts were understandable. If Robert Templedon made the Dulwich journey it could only mean his brain had part closed down. No one fully sane would put himself in such peril. And anybody confronting Walt Melvane needed his mind at prime pitch.

Today, in his villa, Melvane said: 'I'm just looking at the situation as a situation.'

'What's that mean?' Jane replied.

'If I said I bought your whole story, instant, straight off, you would go away and your officer would go away, thinking I only said that so easy because the officer was present and I had to do the natural – that being, take care of myself,' Melvane said.

Jane Templedon's face lightened: 'Oh, I see, you mean you *do* accept it, but –'

'This is the thing about Walter,' Vera said. 'Angles. He always spots many angles. Also referred to as "implications".'

Melvane said: 'Put it this way, me and Vera's definitely going to think about it. We're impressed. I can speak for her, I know it. We think you done something brave and thoughtful when you came here. That's the both of you. We're going to dwell on your message, and we thank you for it.'

'Oh, so totally true,' Vera said.

'And I – we – are grateful to you for listening,' Jane said, her voice bright, nearly triumphant.

When they were driving back, Harpur said: 'Jane, get out at the next corner. I'll go around the block and come back for you. Memorize the first half-dozen cars after us now. At least half a dozen. Then, when I've done the circuit, I won't pick you up first time, but I want you to see if one of those six cars has also come around the block and is still behind me. If it is, notice everything you can about it, particularly occupants, of course, plus colour, reg, anything. I'll repeat the drill but second time you come aboard.'

They did it. 'No, nothing,' she said. 'No car stuck with you. Would they know that trick, though?'

'It *might* be in the villains' manual.'

'Is it in the police manual, or is that the same?'

'Or they might have fixed a tracing bug on us,' Harpur replied. He drove, doing a lot of mirror, but could spot nothing that looked like a tail. 'What did you make of Walt?' he asked.

'I thought he couldn't show immediately that he believed us, accepted what we said about Ian – Robert.'

'But?'

'He'll have to consult, won't he – Delicate Royston's lot, Foden's? If it gets around that we've been here and made him change his attitude, he'll look weak, even treacherous. He's been doing all that hate against Robert, hasn't he, ever since the arrests? Pride would stop him from forgetting it at once – from saying he was wrong.'

'But?'

'But, yes, I thought he believed us. And Vera did. It's as if she parrots him, but she's an influence. And you, Harpur, what did you think of them?'

'I can understand why you'd want to see it like that.'

'But?' Yes, but. He dropped her at the railway station, where he had picked her up in the morning. She was supposed to have been visiting relatives. She would take a taxi back to Cormorant Avenue now.

Andrew Rockmain's final session with the children took place next day in the hotel suite. He called the overall process 'benign identity management', though not to the children themselves, of course. This would be the first time Iles and Harpur attended a session. They went with Jane and Robert Templedon. Rockmain considered virtually all the main work had been done and satisfactorily done. He told Iles and Harpur that this would be 'simply a very low-key summation'. Harpur could not be sure how much Rockmain actually believed in his own optimism. Obviously, he would have to hide any doubts, especially from

150

the children themselves. They must be sent towards a beckoning world, alight with confidence, content in their recycled selves. Rockmain had apparently succeeded in transforming other families, so perhaps the endless chirpy blah was justified. On the way to the hotel Iles said: 'Do you know, Col, cunt as he is, Rockmain might have something.'

'What?'

'He definitely might,' Iles replied.

'What?'

'Yes, you're right – they're imponderables. But don't you and I live always among imponderables, Col?'

'Our job is to make them ponderable and ponder them.'

'Sometimes, Harpur, I tire of this secretive, devious work. I long to get into uniform and handle an open, obvious duty – take the salute at passing-out parades, act obsequious to the Lord Lieutenant at a tasteful function, helping him clear his throat before a speech.'

'I think plain clothes best for this kind of meeting. Anonymity is important. The children probably find you less Nazi in a suit. And it gives your tailoring and general ensemble a deserved chance.'

'Well, yes,' Iles said.

'There's your tie, for instance.'

'What?'

'That will be a club tie, I should think, sir – the little shields and the mauve stripes. So it shows you're socially acceptable, despite everything – not blackballed. And then the lightweight – a confirmation of basic taste.' The ACC had on a navy two-piece, possibly alpaca, magnificent around the shoulders, trousers, as ever, cut to show the leanness of his legs. He did a lot of rugby refereeing these days and probably still looked OK in shorts and a credit to his whistle.

'Well, yes, it is,' Iles said. 'And yet, you know, Col,

when I dressed today I had no conscious intention to do a clothes brag.'

'With you, sir, these qualities show themselves by nature – nothing so banal as a deliberate, naff ploy.'

'*Sui generis*, you mean?'

'Along those lines.'

Inside the hotel suite, Rockmain cried with what Harpur thought could actually be called glee: 'Here are Sian Rebecca and Harry Charles, excited at the thought of their new school and new friends! Sian Rebecca and Harry Charles are already known to a good number of people – to their parents, of course, to me, to neighbours in Cormorant Avenue and, as I hear, over the back fence. This is all wonderful, wonderful! Now, many more folk will grow familiar with the names Sian Rebecca and Harry Charles. That is, the other children in the new school and the teachers. And all these relatives, friends, acquaintances don't say to themselves, "Since these are undoubtedly their names, I must call Sian Rebecca Sian Rebecca, or Harry Charles Harry Charles." This is not the way with names, is it? No, indeed, because to all these people the Sian Rebeccaness of Sian Rebecca and the Harry Charlesness of Harry Charles is what makes them who they are. These acquaintances would not be able to think of Sian Rebecca *at all* if they didn't think of her as Sian Rebecca. They would not be able to think of Harry Charles *at all* if they didn't think of him as Harry Charles. The name Sian Rebecca *means* – actually *means* this girl.' He put a hand briefly on the child's shoulder.

In Harpur's view, the grip meant nothing predatory – only that Rockmain wanted to emphasize Sian Rebecca's physical structure, and emphasize also the unique suitability of the abstract term 'Sian Rebecca' for this physical structure. 'The name Harry Charles *means* – actually *means* this lad.' He moved his hand to the top of the boy's head. In Harpur's view, the contact meant nothing predatory – only that Rockmain wanted to emphasize Harry Charles's

152

physical structure, and emphasize also the unique suitability of the abstract term 'Harry Charles' for this physical structure. 'Clearly,' Rockmain cried with believable delight, 'it is the only way they exist for all these people who know them – they *are* Sian Rebecca and Harry Charles. No other names could do, because other names would not be the girl, Sian Rebecca, or the boy, Harry Charles.' He paused, effectively, then said: 'Forgive me, I'm going to go learned for a moment. I expect that in their new school Sian Rebecca and Harry Charles will be taught the classics. Well, here is a Latin phrase for them – *sui generis.*'

'Mr Iles is well into that, as a matter of fact,' Harpur said.

'Several know the tag,' Rockmain replied. 'It means "on its own", "one-off".'

'Mr Iles wouldn't argue,' Harpur said.

'The names Sian Rebecca Templedon and Harry Charles Templedon are *sui generis.* If other names were mentioned they would not, could not, refer to Sian Rebecca Templedon or Harry Charles Templedon because Sian Rebecca Templedon and Harry Charles Templedon *are* Sian Rebecca Templedon and Harry Charles Templedon. And, of course, Sian Rebecca and Harry Charles *know* this. Yes, and more than know it. They *feel* it. This goes right through them, the feeling. They *know* and *feel* they could not be anyone else but Sian Rebecca and Harry Charles. This is so, isn't it, Sian Rebecca? Isn't it, Harry Charles?'

'Yes.'

'Yes.'

'There is a kind of swap process, a merging process,' Rockmain said. 'The names "Sian Rebecca" take to themselves the very nature of Sian Rebecca the person, and the nature of Sian Rebecca the person takes to itself the names "Sian Rebecca". The names "Harry Charles" take to themselves the nature of Harry Charles the person, and the nature of Harry Charles the person takes to itself the names "Harry Charles".' Rockmain looked to the other side of the room. 'And now, let's progress.' Some clothes were laid out on a table. He walked over to it and picked up a school blazer, navy trimmed with red, and showing a discreet badge that featured a bird's head, perhaps a heron, in green and grey, woven on to the top pocket. 'Whose is this, I wonder. I *wonder*. But wait. Perhaps there's a name label – so important when someone is off to a new school. Why here it is, in lovely clear capital letters, SIAN REBECCA TEMPLEDON. Come, Sian.' The child crossed the room to him and put the blazer on over her dress. 'Grand,' Rockmain said. 'Doesn't Sian Rebecca look fine, just fine! This is a blazer that perfectly fits Sian Rebecca, as her names exactly fit her, yet not as totally exactly as her names fit her, because her names *are* her, whereas a blazer is only for sometimes. The name Sian Rebecca is always Sian Rebecca, whereas the blazer can be taken off. But still she does strike us all as splendid in this garment. I think maybe a round of applause is in order.' The five adults in the room clapped for a while, led by Rockmain. Then he held up another blazer and read aloud the label: HARRY CHARLES TEMPLEDON. More praise more clapping.

Iles, sitting in an armchair close to Harpur, leaned across and muttered: 'Obviously, I'll kill the cunt, Col, if anything happens to these kids or their parents because he's fucked things up.'

'He might have something.'

'What might he have, Harpur?'

'Whatever you were thinking of when you said it earlier.'

'Well, yes, he might. But we don't know, do we, Col, can't know? He's the magician, the witch, the dwarf guru, and I've handed over my Templedons to him. But perhaps he would say that without him and his jolly processing, the children at least might not *be* Templedons. Yes, he might say that. It's tricky, Col.'

Harpur always found it terrifying to hear Iles speak of his own ignorance, bafflement and worry. The ACC was not made for indecisiveness, not in police things. A flaky Iles could only mean a flaky world, and whenever the ACC talked like this, Harpur suddenly sensed approaching chaos. Normally, if Harpur sensed approaching chaos he consoled himself with the idea that Iles would repel it, or ignore it into extinction, or reconstitute it as boon. Now, though, glimpses of weakness in the ACC actually seemed to *start* the run-down to chaos.

Des Iles possessed no damn right to grow pitiable or tired, no excuse for feeling troubled by 'imponderables'. Iles had to be up there uniformed or mufti'd, for ever supremely strong and unstoppably malevolent in the cause of good as he saw it, which could quite often be almost the same as the real, genuine good. Oh, definitely quite often almost. Iles had looked on life early and decided that, if he could kick as much shit as feasible out of big villainy, he would make some peace, some decency, and even some wholesomeness possible. Had he lost this golden vision? Was his will sick? What had happened to that Latin stuff – the uniqueness, the on-his-ownness? He sounded like virtually anyone now, almost anyone frail and crushed and scared. God, Iles like anyone? *Anyone?*

A similar appalling collapse of Iles into normality had happened once or twice before, with all the gross shakiness this brought to Harpur. Most terribly, it occurred when an undercover officer, Raymond Street, was exposed and murdered inside a crook firm, and Iles assumed all blame for placing him there.* The Assistant Chief had a talent for blame, mostly loading it on others, of course, but also on to himself now and then. He believed he owed an absolute and eternal duty to protect subordinates and those in his charge. Failure was betrayal. Ray Street had been in his charge. Now, he must look after the Ballion/Templedons, and the responsibility battered him as it might have battered anyone, especially when he let his eyes rest for long on Rockmain, this stunted, waffling mind-artist, and con-

* See *Halo Parade.*

sidered his slippery, glib, constructive ways. Tonight, Rockmain wore a green corduroy suit. This would add to Iles's infuriated mistrust.

When all the Templedons had gone, the ACC, Harpur and Rockmain stayed for a while. Iles said with a bewildering absence of hate towards Rockmain: 'I've been thinking about what you said last time. As I see it, if you're correct, Andy, and Robert Templedon in his guilt spasm wants to put things right with Melvane and the other firms, he'll need a peace offering.'

'Possibly,' Rockmain replied. 'Probably, indeed.'

'Someone must be sacrificed,' Iles said.

'You mean the officer he tipped about the raid, who then helps with the trap?'

'DC Piers Callic of the Met,' Iles said.

'Yes. Robert Maurice Templedon might decide he must kill Callic, as a way back to cred,' Rockmain said. 'I'd considered the possibility, of course. We refer to that kind of deal as "a barter death".' Harpur felt, as he often felt in the presence of these two, that despite their different styles of quirk, each could think faster and further than anyone in sight, including him.

'Which we?' Iles replied.

'Which we what?' Rockmain replied.

'Which we refer to "a barter death"?'

'Oh, you know – psychologist colleagues. It's a textbook term.'

'And you and your brain games can't do anything to turn Templedon away from that?' Iles said.

Rockmain was standing and paced a little now, the green suit seeming to make him especially jaunty, like a traffic light at permanent Go. He stopped and half faced Iles: 'I always have trouble knowing where you're coming from, Desmond.'

Iles considered this for a while, then nodded a couple of times in the style of a mild but intrigued aunt and said: 'Coming from? Coming from. I'm not coming from anywhere. Can't you see, I'm sitting here, you jargonized fucking jerk?'

'Whether you in fact *want* Robert Maurice Templedon to return to his old milieu and to all the hazards this would bring him, so that Mrs Jane Iris Templedon is more available for you, or whether –'

'Listen, Rockmain, *I'm* not your suitable case for treatment,' the Assistant Chief said. 'I'm Iles. You're hired for the Templedons.'

Rockmain held up his tiny, very white hands, one on each side of his face – a peace gesture. 'As a matter of fact, I believe you would set the safety of the Templedons – *all* the Templedons – above any desire to get among Mrs Templedon on an ongoing basis, Desmond, however ripe and tumultuous in you that desire might be,' he said. 'Of course, this might be partly because you've already tried something on there and she's fallen about, hysterical and curt at the idea. But above all I see in you – this is if I were doing a formal, laboratory character analysis of your good self – I see in you a noble, intransigent, everlasting, painfully strict idea of responsibility for any persons under your aegis.'

'Right,' Harpur said.

'So apparent,' Rockmain said.

'Mr Iles went to quite a toff school. It expected to produce leaders. There were classes in how to take care of the little people – pardon the phrase.'

'Someone as smart as Robert Templedon – wouldn't he realize that if he did Callic we'd be on to him at once?' Iles replied.

'He *is* smart,' Rockmain said. '*How* smart, though? He didn't realize that any police officer told about a raid would aim to maximize the catch.'

'*She's* probably smarter than her husband,' Iles said.

'Well, certainly too smart to let you close, ever,' Rockmain replied, 'especially with that Adam's apple.' He paced a little more, then halted again: 'Oh, look, Desmond,

I hope my view of your eternally null chances with her doesn't upset Harpur, who's wisely anxious about his daughter and needs you diverted.'

'Cormorant Avenue,' Iles said. 'Cormorant Avenue. You can see why someone like Ian Ballion would be sickened by Cormorant Avenue.'

'He's not Ian Ballion, he's Robert Maurice Templedon,' Rockmain said.

Iles said: 'But it's the Ian Ballionness of him that would –'

Rockmain began to shout. He became suddenly impressive. His voice had depth. 'We don't fucking well cater for the Ian Ballionness of him, Desmond, nor even concede that the Ian Ballionness of him exists or has ever existed. There is about him now an unmistakable and indeed wholly natural Robert Maurice Templedonness, since that's who he is and for ever will be,' Rockmain replied. 'We must believe this, whatever our fears and doubts. Must believe it, *must*, or where are we? Where, oh where?' He almost sang the words, but like a dirge or a slab of sad opera. Harpur found it moving. Rockmain did worry about the Templedons, knew his restructuring of the Ballions was a frightening gamble. He might even fret about the Templedons as much as Iles did. 'And doesn't Melvane live somewhere similar – that nice Dulwich villa in a security enclave? Suburbia tempts with its smooth siren melody, tempts even thugs, and maybe thugs especially. It wooed you, for example, didn't it, Desmond? Aren't you in *la belle* Rougemont Place?'

'Promise me you'll never turn up there in daylight with that fucking suit on,' Iles replied.

Chapter Fourteen

Thank God he'd hung on to the .22 Beretta. Templedon didn't know this city and finding a street-combat pistol dealer might have been tough. Something like that took time and a lot of very chancy asking around. Tesco's no. Harpur and Iles would probably have nark voices out there who might get in touch to say some stranger had been searching for arms, and might describe the stranger and mention the unlocal accent, plus description.

He had thought of losing the .22, as he had lost Foden's Browning, or some other way. Guns were Ballion, not Templedon. He had to accept that. Had to try to accept that. If you went in for a personality makeover you scrapped outgrown toys. Iles had said early on they hoped to fix him up with a job in selling. He decided then he must switch from an automatic to an automatic calculator and looked around for a decent drop of wet to receive the Beretta. In fact, a very suitable wide and murky tidal river ran right through the centre, not Thames scale but enough, and it would have been easy at night to sink a gun secretly from one of two fine stone bridges. He'd strolled across both several times very late carrying the .22 in his pocket, Robert Maurice Templedon, yet had lacked the satisfaction with his new state, and lacked the will, arm power and voice, to slip the gun out and say, 'I commit this and Ian Maitland Ballion with it to the reasonably deep.' His Beretta might seem of slight calibre and not worth keeping, anyway, except that a .22 did Israeli Prime Minister, Yitzhak Rabin, and Robert Kennedy.

Templedon's lack of satisfaction had grown, of course. It grew quite a bit more at the hotel yesterday as he and Jane watched Rockmain in his crazed, devoted way push every last trace of their previous lives out of the children and replace it with what he called in his demented, professional lingo their Sian Rebeccaness and Harry Charlesness. This kind of shit really worked? Everyone said so. Rockmain was supposed to have successfully transformed God knows how many families by his cocky gibberish.

Naturally, at his own, personal sessions with Rockmain, Templedon was asked very chattily about the guns – not just general questions on weaponry, but specifically a 9 mm Browning and an 8-round .22 Beretta automatic. Evidently some bugger at or near the raid had briefed Rockmain. He might be clever, but not clairvoyant. This information could have come from any of three or four people. Templedon had both guns in his hands when baseball cap man gave him an exit after the hit, and when picked up by the big Vauxhall with Callic and the woman driver aboard on big-load Shogun day. Callic had repeated the advice, or order, from baseball cap man about the guns – 'Get rid.'

In his interview with Rockmain, Templedon told him the two pistols lay for ever useless, the Browning underground, the Beretta underwater. He said he hadn't simply dropped the Beretta from a bridge but flung it out to the middle at high tide from a spot on the bank he would never be able to relocate as an aid to police divers, if it came to that.

Rockmain had given him a long, high-rank stare, a stare that asked, 'You messing me about, matey?' No belief touched his features. Rockmain had that kind of face. It might be a trained face, perhaps self-trained. He could summon anything to it, not just doubt or contempt. At times he looked pally, at times grateful for a listener, at times tireless brainbox, at times half-baked, at times simply jokey and cheerful. Maybe it had been when Rockmain heard and so obviously dismissed Templedon's tale about the Beretta that he started to worry over him and his readjustment to what he'd call Templedonness, more than he did over the children's. If Rockmain suspected Templedon had retained one or both of the guns – and, of course, he must suspect it – he would regard this as *symbolic*. Such elegant, verbalizing vision was his trade. And he'd be correct. It *was* symbolic – but practical, too. Often Rockmain turned out correct, although at first sight he seemed so full of farce and froth.

The Beretta would be the way to see off Callic and open up a route back to Walt Melvane's dark, tricky, priceless esteem, and the esteem of the rest of Walt's family and followers such as Solid, Justin Labbert, the Aspens and so on, as well as those Boon-Mace and Foden connections. When the Krays were big in London, candidates for a gang post had to prove themselves by killing someone. It would be a little like that with Walt now, although what Templedon planned was not just a bit of casual, unmotivated slaughter, but very pukka payback for Callic's cop treachery. Templedon had a full magazine plus a box with another eight .22 rounds. He kept the gun and ammunition among tools in the boot of his car, not wanting Jane to know he still had them. She drove the Saab sometimes but wouldn't go into the tool bag.

Most likely, she spotted his disgust with himself over what happened in the raid. For Templedon to stick to the gun might strike her, too, as symbolic. She knew about guns and their significance – could use one at least as well as himself. She'd be appalled if she came across the Beretta and would guess immediately that he still yearned to make it up to Walt somehow – do penance for Lester and the others – and return to the life and corrupt, uncompromising loyalties Walt stood for. She would not be able to guess the actual target for the Beretta, but she'd know it was a Ballion item, not Templedon, not Cormorant Avenue. He must save her from the pain of too much fucking insight.

He went out to the car on the driveway at 18 Cormorant Avenue, recovered the Beretta from his tool bag and put it in his pocket. It was late and nothing moved in the avenue. As a matter of fact, he took a thorough look every night at vehicles parked nearby, either through the front windows of the house, or on a little walk. He feared Walt Melvane might somehow trace them before Templedon had definitely decided on his reconciliation pilgrimage to that serene estate at Dulwich. *Bring me the head of Piers Callic.*

Templedon did his inventory now. Most people used their driveways or garage, but some families couldn't accommodate all the household cars like that and over-spilled to the kerbside. Plus, there might be visitors, or strangers. Templedon had tried to memorize the regulars, but they were not constant. This impossibility of keeping tabs really troubled him.

Tonight there seemed more than the usual number lined up and obscuring one another. Yes, it troubled him. He stayed with the boot lid of the Saab lifted, as if searching for something in there, but gave a good hard gaze both ways along the avenue, moving his eyes systematically from car to car and allowing each a few seconds for itself. When Rockmain preached the delights of their new existence did the bugger know anything about this non-stop jumpiness? Perhaps he did. Possibly it was one reason he worried over Templedon's willingness to stay Templedon.

As he surveyed the avenue, it made him think of the way he often sensed Jane giving *him* a good hard gaze lately, struggling to read his plans. She saw a lot, and perhaps too much. She was in bed now, though, and possibly asleep. For herself, she seemed to have decided the new life would do since . . . since it had to. Women could be like that. Their history told them, 'This is how things are for you, so get on with it.' Sensible? Perhaps.

162

Subordinate? Possibly. If Jane suspected Templedon wanted to sweetheart Walt Melvane and his chums, it might anger and depress her. She would think Templedon put her and the children at a low point in his feelings because, above all, he longed for old-style fraternity with Walt and the rest again, and yearned to repair his fractured status as a proud, sterling villain. Obviously, that meant one who never grassed. Or did not grass except in what he saw as a good and special cause, a cause he could prove – and prove face-to-face with Walt – to be good and special . . . a good and special cause such as neutralizing the maniac, Foden, so as to save the team for a safer job later.

And was Jane's version of things right? *Did* he set Walt's friendship and approval above all other needs? Probably. Another thing about women – they could do intuition.

All the same, he felt good now about bringing the Beretta out of hibernation. It was a very small slice of progress, but a first slice, and a Ballion slice. Yes a symbol. He'd still seen nothing specific to worry him in the avenue. OK, OK, he could relax. But he stood for a moment longer near the Saab, letting his mind ramble.

Most men he knew in top league robbery felt as he did. They robbed for the family, of course, if they had one – robbed to finance housekeeping, holidays in Mexico, Mercs, state-of-the-art electronic home gear, even kids' education. This didn't mean, though, that the family could ever be supreme and robbery just the caterer, like in a job as, say, roofer or clerk. You gave your maximum to a big hit, and the people you did it with gave theirs, so you had a grand, unique bond, at least as strong as any family link. Lives and freedom depended on that bond. These were associates you honestly and fairly shared out big snatched money with. That showed true understanding of one another and, quite often, trust. This bond could even take in someone like Foden, maybe.

Non-robbers didn't understand the rough but polished

craft properly. Naturally. They couldn't know first hand the spirits-lift that came from snaffling what had been so fucking skilfully and laboriously and possessively piled up and rubber-banded by someone else, the greedy, vain prats. No wonder Lester was hurt and puzzled when Hector refused the Shogun raid. After all, Hector *did* understand about the fine soul-stirs of robbery, and yet he put his mother, playing sick, first. Lester could never have sympathized with this kind of insult, obviously. Templedon himself found it cold behaviour from Hector, even though he'd always been known as devoted to his mother.

Templedon closed the car boot and locked up. Jane probably would not understand about robbery and its eternal, sacred buzz. Yes, she lived with Templedon and might have sensed some of the sweet flavour by that closeness, but this was nothing like actually doing it – the terrifying, larky, triumphant joy of taking – of building money without the bore and servileness of work. Oh, naturally, people in the game promised themselves every time that it would be the last. And occasionally it was, for one reason or the other – one reason or the other being jail, a fall into religion, or injury, or age, or nerve gone for good – which might be the same as age or injury. Many returned to work though. It was a thirst, and not just a crude money thirst. 'One last saunter, to finance me at Malibu and put Redvers through Harrow,' they'd say. 'Yes, one last.' And then there'd be another, and most probably others.

Templedon had started back towards the house when he thought a car parked at the far end of the avenue flashed its lights a couple of times. The vehicle stood half hidden by several others and he couldn't decide what make. The signal might not be for him, but he still saw nobody else about. He walked towards the car. As he grew nearer he identified it as a big, dark-coloured Vauxhall. Of course, he wondered at once whether he had seen it before – different street, different city. This time, though, a man, not a woman, sat at the wheel and seemed to be alone. The headlights flashed again. Christ. Piers Callic?

Templedon felt rage and fear. He had been promised this address, 18 Cormorant Avenue, would stay unknown to any police except Iles, Harpur and Rockmain. Nobody from London should have it. Once details leaked outside the tiny, agreed group, the information could go anywhere, everywhere. Word of mouth was a fast-travelling word and there would be no effective frontier between police and the working firms. Whispers went both ways, sometimes for money, sometimes just for fun or evil or both.

Suddenly, then, the Templedon identities and the Templedon property became deeply convenient and prized to him. He had wanted, half-wanted, to shed this identity and slip back to his Ballion mode, with all its wholesome risks, high, villainous dignity, and splendid, well-tried, grab-all traditions. That ambition had been irresistibly powerful at the last Rockmain session with the children, and until a minute ago. Now, though, as the headlights flashed again, he thought only about their safety – their safety as Sian Rebecca Templedon and Harry Charles Templedon, with no past and a sheltered, refurbished future. The protection in Templedonness had become crucial, entirely unmatchable. Rockmain was rare and magnificent, saintly in his way, the crazy little big-talk, spinning jerk.

Could this really be Callic in the Vauxhall? *Callic*? How? Coincidences like that didn't come, for God's sake. Templedon had gone out to the car for his Beretta and simultaneously the boy the Beretta's meant for shows. Mad . . .

But then Templedon gradually discovered how it *could* be Callic and *was*. No coincidence. No target or not yet. 'Get in a minute, Ian,' he said. 'I'll drive somewhere. It's not good to hang about this street. Sorry, avenue.'

'You're not supposed to know this fucking street, avenue.'

'No, I'm not, but how it is.'

'What's that mean?'

'What?' Callic replied.

'How it is.'

'How it is.' Callic took the Vauxhall slowly past number 18 and around into Chessington Avenue. 'I've brought something for you.'

'What? There's nothing you *can* bring. You're not supposed to be here at all,' Templedon replied.

'True. I wouldn't be.'

'What's that mean, *"wouldn't* be"?'

'Wouldn't be,' Callic said. 'At your feet.'

Templedon had the passenger seat. He looked down and saw a Marks and Spencer carrier bag.

'Take it out,' Callic said. He drew up alongside the railings of a bit of public park at the end of Chessington. Templedon lifted the bag and took from it a Heckler and Koch Parabellum automatic and large box of rounds.

'I imagine you chucked away the pistols after our street incident,' Callic said. 'It's an unbreakable habit for people like you, even if the guns weren't fired.'

'What's that mean – "people like you"?'

'You know.'

'No.'

'The cash-in-transit guild,' Callic replied. He had a chubby, almost benign face, but, as Templedon remembered it, the mouth a bit too tight in repose, and his dark eyes nearly always disbelieving. He wore plentiful dark hair long, tailing back and flattened down over his ears. If you saw someone like this sitting alone in a pub you'd think plainclothes taking a look around, or part owner of a private school, probably safe with children but worried about the accounts and achievement charts. He said: 'Look, this is a genuine, utterly off-the-record call. I feel I owe you. Maybe I didn't play fair. *We* didn't play fair.'

'No fucking maybe about it.'

'All right, things got taken out of my hands, but I could

166

still have done things your way. I put you the wrong side of Walt Melvane. I recognize it. Always have. And I sometimes feel bad, sometimes feel an obligation. It happens – police, grass. There's a responsibility between them.'

Templedon did not like this, the ooze of it. Something devious around. 'What happened to it on the day, then?' he said.

'What?'

'The responsibility.'

'Yes, I understand how you see it,' Callic replied. 'So this is me making amends. And did you?'

'What?'

'Lose the pistols.'

'Yes,' Templedon replied. 'Of course. As you said, a routine. With *people like me*. Unbreakable.'

'It's a good drill. I don't pooh-pooh it. These days Forensic can tell the colour of Uncle Seb's crotch hair from a nephew's gun.'

'This life – the new life here – guns don't come into it, you know, Piers.' He loathed using that name, but some smarm seemed due. He could ooze, too. 'A gun would be a betrayal of what they're trying to do with us, *for* us.'

Callic listened respectfully, his eyes fully unconvinced. He said: 'I don't like to hear you talk like that.'

'How?'

'So fucking *worthy*,' Callic replied.

'Just describing how it is.'

Callic bent a bit closer. 'God, you *didn't* lose them,' he replied.

'I told you, I –'

'Kept the Beretta? Kept both?' With the tips of three fingers he touched the gun through Templedon's pocket cloth. 'Yes, the Beretta.'

'I'm going to dump it. Soon.'

Callic said: 'All right, it's night, and you spot mysterious glim signals in the street. I can see you'd feel the need of a piece. You were getting it from the car boot, were you?

167

You'd located the strange vehicle in your sedate avenue – thought that perhaps you knew it from a former episode, a memorable episode. Yes, it was a police car, so some might have felt safe with it. But you feel it shouldn't be there, anyway, and you're defensive. Good alertness, Ian. What I'd expect. And Foden's Browning? You've got that somewhere, too?' He giggled. 'Anyway, three guns are better than none. I shouldn't call you Ian, should I? Robert Maurice. Do you say Maurice straight or Maur . . . eece, French style?'

'Who's talked?' Templedon replied.

'Nobody. That's what I mean when I say I wouldn't be here except for . . . Oh, luck, really, Ian.'

'Who's fucking talked, Callic?'

'The Heckler's a better stopper than either of those other two.' He glanced around. 'You didn't report this car in the avenue, did you, as per your probable instructions from local officers? I expect they've given you an alarm procedure. Of course. Every resettlement case gets the same programme for alerts, and the same SOS fittings. They've worked it all out – so many supergrass disposals to learn from.'

'What's it about, Callic? I've got to get back. Are you working with the police here?' Things had begun to crumble.

'I felt I owed you. As I said.' His face turned solemn. He had on a dark tweed jacket, dark trousers, black shirt, blue tie. This meeting had not just ooze but kosher gravity.

'Oh, you did what your job said you had to,' Templedon replied, '– maximize the collar. I don't know now how I ever expected otherwise.'

'That's right. But I still felt I owed you,' Callic said. 'There can be debts, one-to-one debts, regardless of the job. Or perhaps *because* of the job – that grass–detective link.'

'The bad stuff's done. Lester's inside. It can't be put right.'

'But perhaps you think it *can* be,' Callic said.

'I don't know how.'

Callic stayed quiet for a short while, maybe running some thoughts around the track. Then he seemed to get an inspiration: 'Did you think of coming up to town and killing me as a nice let's-make-it-up token for Walt? That why you kept the Beretta, even in this gorgeous, tree-girt area? The Browning, too?'

'We have a different existence here,' Templedon replied. 'Killing's no part of it.'

Callic gave a groan at the greasiness, obviously picked up the falsity: 'Hell, you *did* think of doing me! I see the logic.'

'For God's sake, Callic, would I plan something like that after what I've –'

'I'm carrying something myself, you know. I'm entitled in the work I handle. Don't turn hasty because you've got two automatics on you now. I'm good at self-protection. Your new friends wouldn't like it if there was a battle on their ground, in such a charming district. They'd feel negligent.'

'You can take these back with you.' Templedon returned the Heckler and Koch and box of bullets to the carrier bag.

'The gun's unused. Not from the police armoury, although we do like Hecklers. You're safe with it.'

'I'm not safe with anything, am I? Who else knows?'

'What?' Callic replied.

'About the Templedon name. Cormorant Avenue. The whole fucking doomed scheme.'

'Who can know who else knows?'

'But you think someone's coming? Is that what the automatic's for – to look after myself? Your "obligation" to me. You've heard a murmur?'

'No murmurs.'

'Most of these resettlements turn out a hundred per cent efficient,' Templedon replied.

'Mr Rockmain's been talking to you, has he? It's the kind

of thing he'd say. Obviously. Resettlements are his speciality. He has to sell them to the customer.'

'So who's coming to get me, us?' Templedon said.

Callic said: 'This kind of scheme – they can't put a guard on you. Heavies in the avenue, with their earpieces, tireless eyes and thermos flasks – they'd be a give-away. I've done that kind of duty myself back in London. Very, very hard to stay unnoticed.'

'We don't want minders. We're looking for an ordinary existence.' Or perhaps he was looking for a different kind of existence altogether – a back-to-Ballion kind of existence. This was not something to confirm to Callic, though.

'Who's looking for an ordinary existence?' he asked.

'My wife, myself, the children.'

'I've seen your wife lately. This is Jane that was Eleanor, yes?'

'You've been watching the house for a while, have you?'

'Which?' Callic replied.

'Which what?' Templedon said.

'Which house? You said I've been watching the house. Which house do you mean?'

'Cormorant Avenue, of course, for fuck's sake,' Templedon said.

'Well, I did watch that house a bit – as you know. You noticed the Vauxhall, didn't you? But longer term I've been watching another house. And *not* spotted at that one. Or, I don't think so. I'm on foot there, discreet. The point is, watching 18 Cormorant Avenue in the Vauxhall, I *meant* to be noticed, didn't I? Big car like that, foreign to the street, wanted to contact you. Thuswise. Drill was, wait in the street, hoping you'd show. If so, flash the headlights – a greeting. To deliver the Heckler and so on, and to see what your thinking is. Plus to pass on some information. I can't call or phone, can I? Who knows who's watching, listening? As a matter of fact, this is information to do with your

170

wife, Jane-stroke-Eleanor. I've known her by sight, of course, from the time she was just Eleanor and you Ian.'

'Another house? Which other house? What's it to do with Jane?' He was getting a lot of stuff he didn't like from Callic. This sounded like the worst, so far.

'Jane-stroke-Eleanor,' Callic replied. 'I have to say, I'm not sure what it's to do with her. But I thought I should bring the Heckler and Koch, anyway. Because of what I saw. There are eventualities. We've got to consider eventualities in a situation like this. Imponderables.'

'Which other house?'

'And on a street corner. I saw Jane-stroke-Eleanor waiting on a street corner to be picked up,' Callic replied. He hurried his words, as if apologetically. Yes, as if: 'Oh, look, when I say picked up, I don't mean any kind of reflection – picked up in the best sense of that term. Picked up by a police officer, you see, in the course of some sort of operation. An old, doctored Escort, most likely from the pool. This is the Dulwich region. That's the house I've been watching – the *other* house. And then, later, the street corner.'

'Dulwich? You've been watching Walt Melvane's place?'

'Well, wouldn't I?'

'Why would you?'

'Because I want him – have for years,' Callic replied. 'Nice to get Lester, yes. Your tip, a true bonus – to take him like that in the act, and so no need of civvy witnesses to get scared into silence by the family and their enforcer pals. We were *there*, saw it. That's what detection is about these days – not clues and a magnifying glass, but watching it happen. Although Lester's gone, this still leaves Walt, and to a lesser extent – to a much lesser extent – Solid. Walt's the patriarch. Walt's the overlord. He *runs* the whole network and has done for a decade. I wondered whether, under the stress from Lester's arrest, he might do something nice and defiant and stupid, to show the firm's still functioning – possibly with Solid tagging along, and

171

I could nail him, them, general wipe out. Completion. I hate jobs only half finished. So, I watch his house off and on. This is just me. Obviously, I've got other work to do. I'm there when I can be. There are gates to the estate but I can see the house and note entrances and exits. Interestingly, your wife was both.'

'I don't understand it.' Did he? Well, yes. Or probably. 'Is this an obsession with you?'

'What?' Callic said.

'Walt.'

'It's policing. We like to catch villains. We exist to catch villains. It's in the job description, you know. *I* like to catch villains. *I* exist to catch villains. Walt is a villain. Walt is a star villain. You're a villain, but *our* villain, *my* villain.'

'Fuck off, Callic, I –'

'And while I'm watching the Dulwich house, along come Jane-stroke-Eleanor and pretty boy on a call,' Callic replied. 'They go inside. They stay an hour, plus. We were talking of heavies. This officer with Jane-stroke-Eleanor is the heaviest of heavies. He's part of the resettlement gang here, isn't he? I've been able to put a name to him. Harpur. Detective Chief Super Colin Harpur, head of CID in these parts. Built like the rubbish wagon his suit came out of. Amateur haircut. Looks like a boxer. Marciano, the heavyweight world champion once? Seen old newsreels of him? But Harpur's fair-haired. On their way home from Walt's, still in south London, he puts her down, then drives around the block a couple of times so she can note any tail. Standard police ploy. If you're familiar with it – and I'm familiar with it – yes, if you're familiar with it you can counter by a little wise driving. Otherwise, a useful trick. They didn't spot me. You're all right there. Your wife won't know anyone saw her visit Walt – not anyone but Harpur and Walt and his nearest, that is. And anyone Harpur tells, naturally.'

Templedon felt wrong-footed and pathetically weak. God, while he made his fantasy trips to Walt and devised his make-believe cringe speeches, Jane did the actual. It would be like her. She'd never thought much of fantasy. She got on with what needed to be got on with.

Callic said: 'I've progressed a few inquiries here – well, naturally – and hear that Harpur's a sidekick to an ACC Iles. We have to ask, did Iles send her and him? And if we ask that, we then have to ask, Why would he do it? I gather Iles likes to project himself – lovely suits honouring slim, muscular legs . . . crimson scarf in winter worn loose-ended . . . lots of profile poses. Married with a child, but he gets about among women. There's an ethnic tart in the Valencia Esplanade district. Honorée. Possible weakness for one of Harpur's daughters, Hazel? Does Iles now also fancy Jane who was Eleanor? Forgive me, Ian. We have to ask. Beautiful woman. I imagine Jane-stroke-Eleanor wants to see Walt and plead with him to do no vengeance search for you. Or possibly she's afraid you yearn to put things OK with Walt about the raid, or as OK as they can be put, and will visit him yourself. Mind you, she wouldn't guess you'd plan to kill me as a sweetener, would she? That *is* the intention, is it? Or was.'

'Don't be so fucking stupid. How could –'

'She'd simply want to get in first to see Walt and try to soften him, give him the whole original script as created by Ian Maitland Ballion for the Shogun scenes. Perhaps she thought Walt might be easier on a woman, especially a woman with Harpur in tow. It's wifely. Touching. The gossip when you were Ballion said she could shoot. Would she have taken a gun?'

'Don't be insane.'

'All right. Now, Iles is the creator of your new milieu and likes to think of himself as Dr Frankenstein, I hear. Would he want all that jeopardized? Perhaps? Did he encourage Jane-stroke-Eleanor to go, calculating that Walt would probably have her followed back, so that he or some of his people can wipe you out and leave Jane who was Eleanor more available? Harpur might like that scenario, mightn't he? Iles gets turned away from Harpur's daughter. This is why I brought you the pistol, Ian, imagining in my innocence that you might be terribly exposed and gunless. And, of course, before I glimpsed the kill-Callic-as-a sop-to-Walt strategy.'

'It's bollocks.'

'Anyway, even now I think you should keep the H. and K. Even now I feel I owe. Perhaps I'm wrong about your plans for me. I'll gamble.'

Callic pointed towards the carrier bag, indicating Templedon should pick it up. Templedon left it there. 'Yes, total bollocks,' he said. 'Iles would never –'

'Who really knows Iles? Everyone I talk to – when I mention him they say something like, "Oh, God, Iles. He could do anything. Anything plus. And has."'

'He probably isn't aware what –'

'I'm dutiful, Robert Maurice Templedon,' Callic said. 'I have a debt to Ian Maitland Ballion which cannot be forgotten or ignored. This is me trying to pay it – the insights, the pistol, the hanging about in your street at night, the tricky local research. Don't undervalue. Look, let me tell you the sequence – the Dulwich sequence and after. Can I? It goes like this. I see the two call on Walt and then follow them here, despite the street corner trick. I'm trained in tailing and was always OK at it. But no, I don't follow them *both* here. I follow Jane-stroke-Eleanor only here because Harpur drives her back to the station and she takes a taxi. From this I deduce she didn't tell you where she'd really been and who with. Remember her coming home by taxi a few days ago?'

'Taxi? Jane?' Well, there had been an alleged visit to her mother recently, apparently by train. A cab brought her to Cormorant Avenue. 'Don't recall anything like that.'

'I expect you do,' Callic said.

Templedon thought, wings of hair over the ears like Callic's would require much strong brushing to train it into flatness. Callic had patience. Police with patience would always be a pain. They believed time favoured them, as their due, whereas lads like Lester were *given* time, such as fourteen years. People sporting hair like that, so lovingly and poncingly persuaded back, would be a treat to shoot. But Callic probably diagnosed right and this as a location for it must be bad. Besides, Callic might really have a gun himself, and know how to get at it fast. Besides again, you didn't kill someone who'd motored so far to bring you an automatic for whatever motive, and also bring glimpses of your wife on a secret jaunt. This man had soul, possibly. He might be more than just hair slabs above the ears. He might even be more than Mr Treachery.

'Not a simple matter following them – motorway, city roads at both ends, the lot,' Callic said. 'Our manuals insist you need four cars to do a proper tail over any distance if no tracer bug aboard the quarry. Probably right generally. But I managed it. I had a few fair bits of luck. And, as far as I could make out, nobody from Walt's place also followed, though they may have their own tricks. That's the thing. Why I say stay alert, Robert Maurice Templedon. Or perhaps Jane-stroke-Eleanor did persuade Walt you deserved no brutality. Or perhaps they didn't need to tail because Harpur, gladly emissarying for Desmond Iles, let Walt have the address.'

Callic dawdled through these theories. Some came close. He looked formidable in that dark outfit. Templedon couldn't see Callic's shoes properly under the dashboard, but he felt they would be excellent, showing taste. Detectives went in for fine, very dear shoes. It must be to prove they'd absolutely left behind training depot boots and could move with grace in the social scene.

Callic said: 'Then, I do some asking around. People can identify Harpur from my description and I hear about Iles. It took a while because I had to nip back to London and my job – my proper job – now and then. None of the Cormorant neighbours seemed to know the name of these new folk with the Saab and Clio in number 18, but I could see that a house and garden in this avenue, Chessington, backed on to yours so I called there and asked a very nice little girl who answered the door whether she could help me find a family called Amesbury, and were they by any chance in the property over the rear fence from theirs. And the girl said, "No, they're new and they're called Templedon. I know the girl there called Sian Rebecca aged ten, but almost eleven. She came to my party, as a matter of fact, although young. And her mother collected her and was called Mrs Templedon. Sian Rebecca told us her name quite, quite often." Well, Ian, Sian Rebecca's age seemed about as it should be, if I remember your dossier right. She was Rose Diana then.'

'You must be a fucking detective.'

'I didn't really need to discover much more. I knew where you lived and under what name. But I wanted a triple check. It's habit. First names for the rest of you, obviously more difficult. You wouldn't be in the published electoral register yet, but I thought details for the next list might have been forwarded ready by your resettlement managers. They know they have to be quick and thorough with the admin – get the re-created you and yours fully established fast on paper. In this sort of thing, paper's almost more important than flesh and blood. They'd put in the forms on your behalf. It's part of the drill. So, I went to the city hall and said I was looking for a family called Templedon in the Dally Grange district and could they help? We went over the forthcoming register together and there you were, Robert Maurice, Jane Iris, 18 Cormorant. I still haven't got your lad's first names, though – below voting age. But never mind. He's not vital. Except to you, of course. Look after them all, Robert.' He drove Templedon back to the end of Cormorant. Callic leaned across, lifted the carrier and held it out to Templedon. He took it and left the car.

'I couldn't get a phone number for you in all my research,' Callic called softly from the window.

'No, I don't suppose so,' Templedon replied. He walked to the house, opened his car boot and put both pistols and the box of Heckler and Koch bullets in the tool bag with the box of Beretta rounds. Did it amount to a betrayal – betrayal of Jane and the children, of Iles, Harpur, Rockmain? But retaining the Beretta had been that kind of betrayal already if it was one. Adding another gun and more bullets didn't really alter the basics, did it?

He felt himself turning into a world expert on shades of betrayal, starting, clearly, with the Shogun raid. Did some betrayals excuse themselves – or almost? Callic's? Templedon locked up and had a glance both ways along the avenue. Callic and the Vauxhall did not reappear. He must believe he had done all the repayment required by honour – not cop honour, which didn't exist, but Callic honour which might. Might. Oh, very might. Something sly going on there? Why would he leave an extra, excellent gun like the H. and K. if he thought it might be used on himself? Of course, he hadn't known it was extra, believing Templedon had acted to Ballion pattern and junked the Browning and Beretta. He'd discovered his error, though, or part error. Yet he still left the H. and K.

Templedon let himself into the house and sat down for a few minutes with a drink. Of course, most of what Callic said alarmed him. The fact that Callic was in their street and knew their names alarmed him. Yet Templedon also felt some pleasure. It excited him that Jane had carried out her trip on his account. He knew it *was* on his account. She wanted him safe. She wanted the family safe, yes, but mainly she thought of him. The stuff about Iles – possibly true, possibly bullshit, but it did not matter either way. She went to Walt because she could not *not* go. A beautiful compulsion. It was her love for him. God, he prized this, lived by it, whichever identity he might be under. She'd wanted to plead with Walt for him, perhaps thinking as Callic said that a woman's voice might do better with Melvane. The lie she'd told about visiting her mother didn't matter, either. He could see why she would do it. She might fear he'd get enraged with her for meeting Walt. And, all right, yes, she could have imperilled things here, risked a trace back. But he valued her impulsiveness. It was so much Jane. It hadn't all been impetuous, careless urge, though. She took the thug-cop along, someone to guard her and to carry out the no-tail palaver. You wouldn't expect this to beat Callic. He was also a cop and had the same bunch of tricks. Yet, Harpur's ruse might have defeated Walt, or Solid, or other tails from Walt's team.

Templedon thought of one of Lester's words, 'enterprise'. This had been a true enterprise by Jane, an enterprise from her heart. He would not speak of it, not unless she told him. And he didn't want to frighten her by saying how he knew. Callic's arrival meant the Cormorant Avenue cover had gone, at least a fraction. Perhaps because Callic's mission against Walt was a solo one, an obsessive one, the detective would keep confidential what he'd discovered from his lurks at Dulwich. Templedon had to hope so, but knew he should not rely on it. Career-mad people like Callic often hid some of what they knew, even from colleagues. Or especially from colleagues. After all, colleagues were the competition, and keeping stuff from them could be tactical. Templedon went upstairs to bed.

Jane was still awake. 'A night hike?' she said.

'Just to the end of the street – avenue.' He climbed in with her and Jane turned to him eagerly, as if she had been waiting and wondering. Did he smell metallic? 'Yes, charting the neighbourhood.'

'Should you – late, alone?'

'We're new people. The Ballions had danger. But we have prospects.'

She considered this. 'Yes, right. I do begin to feel more or less secure for the first time,' she said. 'Settled. Able to think about other things again.'

'Which?'

'Oh, you know.'

'I'm glad you can think of other things,' he said.

'Yes, I can feel you're glad. And you?'

'What?'

'Do you believe you're more or less secure now? I want that for you, love. Oh, God, I want that for you.'

He saw she was justifying the Dulwich trip to herself. 'I know you want it.'

'So?'

'What?' he said.

'Do you believe you're more or less secure now?'

'We'll be fine,' he said.

'You. I think about *you*. I'd love to see you . . . at ease, all right with yourself. There's no reason for you not to be, none. Nobody can regard you as a rat. You tried to think for all of them, Lester included.'

He would have liked to ask, 'Did you tell Walt that, and did he buy it?' But impossible. 'I'll be fine,' he said.

'You hold off from me,' she said.

He moved closer.

'Your mind,' she said. 'I don't reach you.'

'I couldn't hold off from you, even if I wanted to.'

'That really so, Ian?'

'Robert,' he replied.

'Fuck Robert.'

'Yes, please.'

'That really so?'

'You know, Jane Iris, or Jit, I don't believe I'd ever fucked a girl called Jane Iris before,' he replied.

'Before what?'

'Before you became Jane Iris all those months ago.'

'Oh, many's the man called Robert Maurice I'd been fucked by, as far as I can recall. Specialized in it.'

'Did some of them pronounce it the French way?'

'What?'

'Maur . . . eece.'

'Would you like that?' she said.

179

'I *do* like that.'

'No, not that. I meant being called Maur . . . eece.'

'I think I'll stick with Robert Maurice as Maurice. I'm getting used to my Robert Mauriceness. Just plain, like that. I'd have to go back to Rockmain for guidance on Robert Maur . . . eeceness.'

Joke. They'd always been pretty good with poor jokes, in bed or out. Perhaps poor, cumbersome jokes now meant he and Jane were getting what she called 'settled' in their Cormorant Avenue selves. They could see it all as a far-fetched, idiotic game, though one they had to play, just the same – a very comfortable game, at least until Callic turned up tonight, but Jane didn't know about him and wouldn't if Templedon could prevent it. Although they'd accept resettlement, they'd do it with a giggle. Rockmain set this kind of tone. Half the time he sounded mental, half the time brilliant and very solemn.

During a session with Templedon he had referred to a line from some poet about 'wolves of memory'. Rockmain said his function was to hunt down and slaughter these wolves in Templedon, Jane, the children, or they would pack-run and fang-destroy the present and fine future. This Templedon had thought far out, tripey and full of sense.

'I'm happy now and I'll sleep,' Jane said.

'Post-fuck exhaustion.'

'Don't kid yourself.'

He slept, also. When he came to at about 7 a.m., Templedon immediately thought back to that smug mood of acceptance, jokiness, playfulness, relaxation in the night, wanting to reassemble it as a fixture. But the mood seemed unreachable now. This amazed him. What killed it? Daylight? Callic? Absence of alcohol? Aftermath of sex? Loyalties? Those old London loyalties?

Yes, loyalties, of course those old London loyalties. Did they add up to some of Rockmain's wolves of memory? Possibly. They tooth-tore away all the joshing and dopey trivia. As Templedon grew properly awake, he realized he now had a great location for the killing of Callic. So often the place for these things was crucial. Dear Piers spent periods alone and unlogged near Walt Melvane's Dulwich home, he said. It might have been difficult to stalk him without this pinpointing. Detectives moved around unpredictably according to their cases. Templedon had no home address for him, and he probably would not be in the telephone directory. But his obsession took him back when possible to spy on Walt. To do him here, more or less on Walt's doorstep, would be unmistakably a wholesome and clear tribute to Walt and, yes, Lester. Callic had kindly provided a map reference.

No timetable for this. OK. Templedon could wait unobserved until he showed. Get him before he'd looked about. Templedon wondered which gun. The Heckler and Koch would probably give bigger, more decisive wounds than the Beretta. But Templedon again tried to sort out why Callic had left it, if he thought Templedon might come after him. Templedon saw one, obvious possible answer. The H. and K. didn't work right. Callic was the sort who might supply a weapon knowing it fucking useless, and hope Templedon would try it on . . . try on him what Templedon did mean to try on him in Dulwich. Callic could reciproblast then in what he'd claim was self-defence. Callic had spotted the intent in Templedon, hadn't he, and would ignore the denials? He would always fear reprisals from him for the Shogun raid double-cross, and this might be his way of dealing with that worry. All the talk about obligations and sublime, unwavering cop–grass closeness had been that – talk, only talk. Callic liked traps, didn't he? Ask Lester.

Yet there had been moments yesterday when Templedon felt some gratitude to Callic for coming here with the tale about Jane, and with the gun and, apparently, the honest wish to compensate for two-timing. Templedon had not thought the situation through to the end then. He'd slept

181

on it, hadn't he, and now considered Callic's deception far beyond apology. Ask Lester. And he guessed Callic knew it was far beyond apology and recognized Templedon would get on his track. *Must* get on his track. Callic probably suspected Templedon had kept at least one gun, despite all those references to the cash-in-transit man's routine disposal of weapons. To neutralize the Beretta and/or Browning danger, he brings a H. and K., adjusted into failure. It would provide a harmless reason for Callic to shoot him, as though legitimately protecting himself.

If Templedon did Callic in Dulwich, Walt would be really tickled, surely. Templedon could explain to him and Vera afterwards that the officer had them under personal, long-term watch, aiming at a solo catch to send Walt away for as long as Lester and definitively wipe out the firm. They were certain to see taking Callic's head off so locally as a magnificent intervention by Templedon – almost a kind of room service, and the termination of a dirty, heartless, Callic campaign. The fact that he died while actually on the peep job would bring extra credit, definitely. And it gave an elegance to things if Callic was actually removed by a gun he personally supplied. That idea really warmed Templedon, brought a sweet sense of completeness. It created the right circle of retribution for what this sod did with the Shogun tip.

First thing, though, must be to test the H. and K. somewhere remote. If it failed, Templedon would know he'd read Callic right – and also know Callic expected him near Walt's place. But that was OK. Templedon would have the Beretta, of course, not the useless H. and K., so he could still manage some surprise. If the gun did survive a trial, Templedon might be left with the question of why Callic brought it. A kind of mad gallantry? A challenge? A suicide urge from regret at what he did with Ian Ballion's information? Did it matter?

No question about one thing, though – following this little Dulwich enterprise against Callic, Templedon could be welcomed back as Ian Ballion into the Melvane realm of solidarity, trust and gain. True, regret in Walt's family for Lester would continue, naturally, but without any poisonous blame against Templedon. What had to be considered was that the absence of Lester for so long might soon produce a monarchy problem in Walt's organization. Walt approached retirement and most in the know said Solid probably lacked the skills to succeed him. Now, Templedon wondered if he, Ian Ballion, might slip into the frame for that position once the grassing taint had totally gone. Taking out Callic would demonstrate gun skills as well as terrific planning flair and decisiveness, plus a smart eye for a chance. Leadership.

Chapter Fifteen

'Dad, she doesn't understand about police things.'

'Who?'

'Coral Ann.'

Harpur was driving Jill back from another afternoon at the house in Chessington Avenue – not a party this time, just a get-together and a pious, lead-pellet magpie hunt. 'Which police things?' he replied. Now and then his daughter would have something very useful to say but didn't always seem willing to say it straight. Harpur believed in a decent spell of patience with her.

'She doesn't think about security. That sort of thing,' Jill said.

'What kind of security?'

'Coral Ann should not of given their name.'

'Should not *have given* their name. Whose name?'

'Well, I don't suppose she *would* understand police things, because her father is not a police officer, is he, like you?'

'Whose name, Jill?'

'She shouldn't of. Have.'

'Which police things?'

'Well, for instance, Mrs Templedon,' Jill replied. 'And Sian Rebecca. And all that family, I expect.'

'Coral Ann gave their name to someone?'

'They're a police thing, aren't they?' Jill replied. 'Mrs Templedon came to our house, didn't she?'

'All sorts come to the house, Jill.'

'Yes, but you said she was work. If it's work it's a police thing, isn't it? That's your work. Was she really work, or did you only say so because of Denise and how she gets so jealous of other women?'

'Work,' Harpur said.

'When Denise is angry like that, does she what's known as "withhold her body"? I read about that in a magazine. Some women withhold their bodies when they get ratty over something, and it's best not to upset them – if the man *wants* their body, obviously.'

'Mrs Templedon was definitely work.'

'So, a police thing, like I said. *As* I said.'

'In a way, yes,' Harpur replied.

'Which way?'

'Some aspects of her life – yes, there's a police side to them.'

'Coral Ann could not know it.'

'No, obviously not,' Harpur said.

'Is it secret? But even if she did know it, she would not understand about police things – security and so on. That's what I meant, isn't it, dad?'

'What?'

'She wouldn't know she should be careful.'

'In what way?'

'Saying things,' Jill replied. 'Saying things to someone she did not know at all.'

'Which things?'

'Their name.'

'Whose?' Harpur asked. 'The Templedons'?'

'Yes.'

'What is it about their name?' Harpur said. 'You mean Coral Ann told someone their name? But that's fine, isn't it? Templedon *is* their name. No secret.'

'Dad, there's something funny about that name. I said before – the way Sian Rebecca goes on.'

'Goes on how?'

'Saying she's Sian Rebecca Templedon.' Jill did an imitation of the yapping, precise voice.

'Well, she *is* Sian Rebecca Templedon.'

'Why does she have to keep telling everyone?' Jill said. 'I don't go around saying, "I'm Jill Megan Harpur." I would tell people once, if they asked me. I wouldn't go on and on, like afraid nobody will believe her, or like she's scared she will forget it, forget her own name.'

'As if, not "like". She's younger than you.'

'When I was ten, nearly eleven, did I keep telling people I was Jill Megan Harpur?'

'She might be different.'

'How? Do you mean different from her name?'

'No. Different from you. How could she be different from her name?'

'She was out in the garden.'

'Who?'

'Sian Rebecca Templedon and her brother. Really showing off.'

'Today?'

'We saw from the tree house.'

'You were bopping birds again?'

'Only magpies. They're really cruel and savage, you know, dad. Eating other birds' babies. Sometimes you'll see a bit of a baby dangling from a magpie's mouth. Awful.'

'It's Nature. This is why we have a police force.'

'Yes? Because of Nature? There are police forces because of Nature?'

'To stop people getting savage with one another. Thieving. Killing.'

'Is Nature bad then?'

'Can be, if we let it.'

'So, are thieving and killing parts of Nature?' Jill said.

'If you're a magpie.'

'We're not, are we? What about us? Are they Nature for us?'

'What?'

'Thieving and killing.'

'Some believe so.'

'Who? Only the police?'

'All sorts,' Harpur replied. 'Mr Iles says there's a book about it by a really great thinker called Hobbes right back in history. He preached there had to be laws and people to put the laws in effect so as to stop people trying to take from other people. They had the same troubles then, you see, worrying about how to control things.'

'Which things?'

'Things that might seem quite natural if there was no law, such as the strongest getting away with everything just because they were strong. That's called "jungle law", which means no law at all, only the most powerful doing whatever they like. So we need the other kind of law – real law, police and courts. What the law does is make sure what one person might think is natural doesn't upset the lives of others – or end the lives of others.'

'Does Des Iles read a lot of books?'

'He reads blurbs on the dust covers.'

'Are we like police?'

'Who?'

'Coral Ann and me, with the catapults.'

'Coral Ann and *I*.'

'We're trying to hit their rotten nature out of magpies, aren't we,' Jill replied

'They can't be changed. *We* can be. We have civilization.'

'Are the police civilization, then?' Jill said. 'That's not what some of the kids in school call them.'

'We defend order.'

'Des Iles is interested in order? Des Iles?'

'Of course. Almost always.'

Jill thought about this for a time. It seemed to defeat her. She dropped Iles. 'Sian Rebecca and her brother have got new blazers for their school. The two of them walked

around the garden like a fashion show – like we're supposed to clap or fall out of the tree house we're so excited.'
    'Did you?'
    'Coral wanted to give her a pellet in the throat.'
    'Sweet.'
    'I stopped her.'
    'Good,' Harpur said.
    'Was I like the law? Was it Nature to want to give her
one in the throat because she was so horrible, but
I wouldn't let her?'
    They were stuck in traffic. Harpur would have preferred
to get home quicker, and end this discussion. Yet he felt
that among all the vagueness and drifting Jill might have
something he ought to hear. In her clumping, roundabout,
busy way Jill often did reach topics he should notice. He
tried to guide her back to what she'd been talking about
earlier. 'Perhaps it makes Sian Rebecca happier and more
sure of herself in this new area if she keeps repeating her
name,' Harpur said. Rockmain coached them that way.
Harpur's duty was to back him.
    'A name's just something stuck on like a label, isn't it,
dad? Sian Rebecca's name isn't *her*, is it? It's just her name.
What's that in the play – a rose by any other name smells
just as sweet? You would think Sian Rebecca got to keep
telling people her name so she will, like, *become* her name.'
    '*Has* to keep, not "got to", and no need for "like".'
    'Yes, so she will *become* her name.'
    'I don't know what that means,' Harpur said.
    'Our English teacher told us about an old cartoon in a
magazine where two men are looking at pigs in a sty
enjoying theirselves in the muck, so one man says to the
other: "Rightly are they called pigs."'
    'I don't think the English teacher said "theirselves".
*Them*selves. What's this to do with Sian Rebecca?'
    'Well, the man who speaks is stupid, isn't he, dad? They
are not called pigs because they like muck. They like muck
because they are pigs.'

188

'Still don't get it.'

'Give up, dad. A girl is not made by her name, is she, nor a pig?'

'But names are important.'

'Just so we can tell the difference between things,' Jill replied. The traffic began to move. 'She starts teasing them, instead.'

'Who?'

'Coral Ann.'

'In the tree house?'

'Because I wouldn't let her put a pellet into Sian Rebecca. Coral Ann yelled at them: "I don't think you're really called Templedon at all."'

God. 'Oh, why did she say that?' Harpur tried to keep his voice casual.

'Coral Ann said: "I think you're really called Amesbury. I think you fled with all the crown jewels or gold bars and you changed your name so you won't get caught."'

'Amesbury?' Harpur said. 'What's that about?'

'This is what I mean.'

'What?'

'About Coral Ann not understanding police things.'

'Which police things?'

'Amesbury. It's really stupid.'

'What about Amesbury?'

'Somebody came to Coral's house and asked her if the people over the fence were called Amesbury. She thinks it's a funny name – some crazy joke.'

'And Coral Ann told this caller the name wasn't Amesbury but Templedon?' Harpur said.

'That's what I mean.'

'What?'

'About not understanding police things. If somebody comes to the door and says, "Are they called Amesbury?" you just say, "No," you don't tell them what the name is. When they ask, "Are they called Amesbury?" it could be just a way of asking what their real name is. Or maybe not

189

real, but the name they're *using*. And me – if it was me, I wouldn't say, "Templedon." Of course, that could be because I thought it must be a police thing, knowing about Mrs Templedon at our house, and not for romance reasons, although she's beautiful and smart. Or it could be because I thought there was something funny about the name Templedon seeing the way Sian Rebecca kept on and on saying it. But maybe Coral Ann thought there was something funny about the name, too – that's the Templedon name. We talked about it. This could be why she started the teasing when I say not to shoot her in the throat. The crown jewels and gold bars and Amesbury – all that.'

Harpur pulled in at their resident's spot outside 126 Arthur Street but he didn't leave the car at once. 'So, who called at Coral Ann's house?'

'A man.'

'Not anyone she knew?'

'I don't think so.'

Hell. It looked as if one of the Mclvane crew *had* followed Harpur and Jane Templedon from Dulwich after all and was now completing his research before . . . before what? The round-and-round-the-block ploy to spot a tail had not worked. Perhaps it was naive to think it would. This visitor tracks Jane Templedon home in her taxi but needs a name for her. Neighbours in Cormorant Avenue might not know it yet. He tries the house over the fence and this works, because Coral Ann doesn't understand security, not even at thirteen years of age, because her father isn't a cop. But why would he need the name, the new name, if only here for a hit? He knew the Cormorant Avenue house. That's where the target or targets could be found. This should be enough, shouldn't it? 'What did Coral Ann say about him?' he said.

'Nothing much. Why? Is this an important police thing? I just asked her why she said Amesbury, and she said this man came to their house and said Amesbury, but she told him Templedon.'

'How old was he?' Harpur said. Walter Melvane himself? Solid? They certainly wouldn't need to know the changed name. They would recognize Templedon, once Ballion. As Jill had said, a name was only a label. Might the caller have been someone hired, and needing to report back with full details when he did the job?

'She didn't say his age,' Jill replied.

'Do you think she *would* mention it if he was old? For instance, sixties,' Harpur said.

'Well, perhaps. Shall I ring her up and ask?'

'I might like her to look at some pictures,' Harpur replied.

'It *is* important, is it?' She sounded almost scared by his reaction. 'These would be what is known as file pictures, would they? Do you think you know who he is – someone old? A villain? It's got to be a villain, or you wouldn't be so interested. Someone truly major, dad? Why does he want the Templedons?'

'Just some pictures for Coral Ann to go through.' Harpur thought of Iles and his cherished, prized creation, those Templedons. The ACC would be appallingly hurt, appallingly enraged, if he learned all cover was lost because Harpur not only allowed Jane Templedon to visit Walt Melvane, but went with her. This must look to the Assistant Chief like the most crazed risk, and like the grossest vandalism of a superb project into which he had put all his unique, thoughtful, godlike essence. He would want to lash out. Lashing out was one of his main talents.

Jill said: 'So then, of course, Sian Rebecca goes *really* ape – you can imagine.'

'Dated.'

'What?'

'The slang – "goes ape".'

'Goes whatever then. She starts shouting at us in the tree house. "My name is not Amesbury. My name is Sian Rebecca Templedon." And then more. "This is my brother Harry Charles Templedon." She says her father is called

Robert Maurice Templedon. Many called him Robert, but she called him dad. Her mother was called Jane Iris Templedon. Many called her Jane, but she called her mum. Sometimes her dad called her Jit, because of her initials. This was a nickname. Well, yeah, we would of guessed that, I expect. Templedon was their real, real name, not Amesbury.'

The words tumbled from Jill. But then she paused and when she started up again it was more carefully, slowly. 'Something I don't understand at all came next, dad. Sian Rebecca seemed to get even worse, like mad or a fit? She said: "And my name's not Ballion. I am not Rose Diana Ballion. I am Sian Rebecca Templedon. Always Templedon." It's funny, because she talked about the name Rose before. And then her brother started, and he's saying the same at us. He's saying he's not Larry Raymond Ballion but Harry Charles Templedon.

'And Coral Ann said, "What's Ballion? I never said Ballion. I don't even know how to spell it." And it was true, Coral Ann never said Ballion. All she said was Amesbury. She hadn't ever heard of Ballion. Nor me. Have you heard that name, Ballion, dad? But Sian Rebecca is screaming, "No, I said *not*, *not*, *not* Ballion, didn't I? Not Ballion with two l's. Templedon." She's nearly in tears by now. I mean, dad, just now she was walking around so proud in the blazer and smiling like the Queen and now she's nearly crying and screaming in such a temper. She said, "If you don't believe my name is Sian Rebecca Templedon ask Mr Rockmain. He knows everything about it."

'And Coral Ann said, "About what?" "Mr Rockmain knows everything," Sian Rebecca said. And Coral Ann said, who was Mr Rockmain and was he the one who turned up here at the front door asking? But then Mrs Templedon came out into the garden. She must of heard all the yelling. And Coral Ann said: "Hello, Mrs Templedon. Don't Sian Rebecca and Harry Charles look smart in their new garments?" I mean, dad, "garments"! Coral Ann can be a right smoothie, and we were hiding the catapults behind our backs because even magpies are environmental. Well, Nature, isn't it?'

'*Have* heard, not "of". And what did Mrs Templedon say?'

'Dad, are you like . . . interested in Mrs Templedon?' She held up a hand, apologizing: 'No, no, I know, not "like". Are you interested in Mrs Templedon?'

'In a work sense, as I mentioned,' Harpur replied.

'Sometimes men prefer the more mature woman. She might be your type. I read in a mag about people that can't help getting drawn to each other even when not so very young. She got a lot of life in her although a mother. Denise is clever and great, but she can't be mature yet. She's only a student.'

'Mrs Templedon is new to the area, as you know, and when she had certain problems she needed someone to consult.'

'But the "certain problems" being to do with police things?'

'Yes, involving some police matters.'

'Most people don't have problems about police things just because they are new to an area, do they, dad?'

'We have to be ready to give help. That's what the police are for,' Harpur replied.

'As well as stopping Nature? The man who called at Coral Ann's house asking about them – he's from Mrs Templedon's life before she arrived in this area, is he, dad?'

'I don't know who he is.' A Melvane? A hired heavy? A Boon-Mace? A Foden? Names from the flip-chart – Silvester Aspen, Walt's brother-in-law, Justin Labbert, an associate?

'Mrs Templedon looked so sad when she came into the garden. Sian Rebecca said: "I kept telling them I'm Sian Rebecca Templedon, mum." And her mother said: "Of course, dear, of course." *Really* sad. Coral Ann said this seemed a family that didn't know who they were. I don't understand why she said this. Do *you* understand it, dad? Is someone hunting them?' What he understood was that, because of Coral Ann's ragging, Sian Rebecca and Harry Charles cracked. Memory had rushed them like a wolf pack and the kids did what they could to resist.

Harpur let Jill out of the car at their house. She, Hazel and the boyfriends were due on a good works mission helping redecorate old age pensioners' houses. Harpur went over at once to Cormorant Avenue. Twice he drove past number 18 and saw no signs of calamity. He drove along Chessington Avenue twice, also. A couple of teenage boys did skateboard leaps from road to pavement and vice versa over the kerbstone. No other activity. He stopped his car alongside the railings of a small park and sat there for a good while, watching. His visit could be nothing more than this – simply a loiter and slow cruise through both avenues a couple of times to satisfy himself there were no lurkers, and that number 18 continued to look intact, without signs of break-in or carnage.

Of course, he knew this to be utterly dozy and slack. Anything might have happened inside the house and a casual dawdle and ride-around would never discover it. The ritual could be only that, a ritual, a tic – Harpur trying to console himself for having brought new dangers to Templedon and destroyed Iles's caring cover scheme. He felt a compulsion to do *something*, however token. A check-up on wheels. Yes, vastly, entirely token and useless. Jill rang him on his cell phone from her paint duties to say she had just mobiled Coral Ann also, to check the age of their visitor: thirties not sixties.

Even if the Templedons' cover no longer existed, Harpur could not knock their front door to assure himself they remained all right. Under Iles's anonymity scheme, no such direct contact should take place. If it did, Iles would hear. Robert Templedon might report the breach, seeing it as a danger to his family. And once Iles heard, he would begin his own angry inquiries into why Harpur had carelessly put at hazard the ACC's cherished Templedon project, defying all security rules. He could be given no answer for this, except the even more damaging explanation that Harpur had already carelessly put at hazard the ACC's cherished Templedon project by not just conniving at Jane's journey to meet Walter Melvane, but tagging along, and then failing to lose their tail.

A middle-aged woman came out of a Chessington Avenue villa and approached him. She held a yellow 'Neighbourhood Watch' card to the passenger window. Harpur lowered it. She said: 'Excuse me. We grow anxious about unknown vehicles parked in the avenue, particularly at this spot.'

'Ah.'

'Obviously, I am not a police officer, simply a householder. But we have to be vigilant, you know. Many burglaries. Also sexual liaisons preparatory to misuse of the park. The railings have unfortunate gaps. And, so, what seemed a pleasant amenity when we bought the house has become a nuisance. Only recently, two males in a car here, you see. A large Vauxhall. Not local reg. Perhaps perfectly innocent, as *you* may be, but we wish the avenue and the whole Dally Grange area to be safe and unsleazy.'

'Which two men?'

'Oh, yes, one very conscious of his hair. We all know the type. This is why I mention the park. Dark hair carefully swept back so lovingly over the ears. It's often a sign.'

'Of?'

'Prettifying. Tendencies. I don't object to a man careful about his appearance but –'

'Did you take the number?' Harpur tried to remember whether any of his dossier pictures showed someone with dark hair swept back so strikingly over the ears.

She looked puzzled at the brusqueness of his question and then smiled. 'Oh, are you the police? Are you here

195

because of the nuisance from people and vehicles of that type? Possibly some kind of equipment with them in a carrier bag. *So* unpleasant.'

'Did you take the number?'

'I'm so glad the problem is recognized officially.'

'The police have a duty to see that what some people regard as natural is not allowed to upset others. Do you read Thomas Hobbes at all? He's sharp on unsightly sex in public parks, particularly parks abutting villa avenues. You took the number?'

'Certainly. Neighbourhood Watch would be in vain if all we did was watch, wouldn't it?' She produced a notebook from her handbag, copied a registration number on to a spare page and tore it out for Harpur.

'I'm going to wait here for a time, so no need to be concerned about me any longer,' he said. 'Perhaps I'll have a walk around.' He pointed. 'Don't you find these skateboarders as much a pest as sex rovers? And noisier.'

'But skateboarding is wholesome, bodybuilding. These are my sons, as a matter of fact.'

'That's all right then.' When she had gone, he phoned in to the computer and asked for a registration trace. The reply declared the number valid but ownership details were blocked. That usually meant a vehicle used by the police or intelligence services. As far as Harpur could recall, no headquarters vehicle had this number. He felt confused. Of course, Neighbourhood Watch might be right and the two in the car had nothing to do with the Templedons, just a love couple either winding up to or down from the park – probably up to, given the still suave state of hair wings over the ears.

Harpur left his car and walked around the corner into Cormorant Avenue. It was dusk. Could he make himself difficult to see? At number 18 he kept going but managed a good glance through the downstairs front room window. The curtains were back and lights on. A big television set flashed. To one side of it and watching the screen stood

Harry Charles in his blazer. Things must be normal. Harpur went to the end of the avenue, then crossed over and walked back on the other side. He returned to his car. Two other vehicles were parked near it now, a Ford Focus ahead, a Volkswagen estate behind. Neighbourhood Watch stood bent over near the passenger window of the Focus talking to its occupants, a man and woman. A couple of men sat in the front seats of the VW. It looked as if the Focus pair had refused to open the passenger window, forcing her to shout. She was not bad at that. She felt entitled. She owned property. Harpur picked up phrases he heard earlier: 'simply a householder', 'perhaps perfectly innocent', 'Dally Grange area to be safe and unsleazy'. Harpur would have liked to make every area safe and unsleazy. That's what police were for. Ask Iles. Ask Thomas Hobbes. Harpur didn't see, though, that couples lining themselves up for sex in the park made this area unsafe or sleazy, and Iles probably wouldn't either. Hobbes? Certain aspects of Nature could do without too much curtailing. There were people who liked the open air and why not. Neighbourhood Watch had spoken of gaps in the railings – perhaps uprights forced apart by the romantic and desperate. Some people had nowhere *but* the open air. Being 'simply a householder' often turned out not simple at all, because householders grew harsh and narrow when they thought the value of their avenue castle might shrink. Neighbourhood Investment Watch.

He started his car. As he did, the passenger door was pulled open and Jane Templedon took the seat alongside him, quickly folding her long body down. 'I saw you go past the house and followed. I guessed that's what you wanted. Yes?'

'Just a stroll.'

'Look.' She had a small parcel with her wrapped in what might be the plastic dust cover for a computer screen. She opened this up. Harpur saw a .22 Beretta and a 9 mm Heckler and Koch Parabellum automatic. ' I thought it was

197

money,' she said. 'Wrong. I went looking for cash and found these.'

He switched off. 'Which cash?'

'It could have been a packet of money in the boot of the car. Hidden among tools.'

'Would you mind covering the guns again now?' Harpur replied. 'This lady might come and talk to us. If she sees those she'll wonder. She believes I'm the police.'

'Well, you *are* the police.'

'But she'll assume she's got it wrong if she sees guns. Might imagine we're here to do a hold-up. Bonnie and Clyde. She's all tense. Do you recognize her? Could she recognize you?'

'No.'

'You might bump into her one day when you're with Robert.'

'So?' she said.

'You're sitting in a car at night with a man who's not your husband.'

'So? You don't look that kind of man.'

'Oh?'

'Sorry.'

'Does Iles?'

She folded the plastic back over the pistols. 'I didn't want that kind of money, you see, and Robert would know this. So I thought he'd hide it – take it, hide it, spend it in unnoticeable dribs and drabs.'

'Which kind of money?'

'If we're Templedons we're Templedons. Entire.' She groaned, but softly and briefly and gave a slight, shamed grin. 'Do I sound like bloody Rockmain? He's right, though. He looks and sounds half soaked, but he's spot on. We have to enter into the change properly. That sort of money could be no part of our new lives.'

'Which sort?'

'Normally I would never go ferreting in Robert's car boot. You understand this? I'm not some snoop. But such money – it would be like a return, like a relapse. Intolerable. I had to see. If I found a fat amount I'd have known what it was.'

'What? How did you know the package was there, anyway – whatever it contained?'

'I thought Robert's cut from the raid,' she said.

'From the Shogun raid?'

'How much cash in the Shogun? Two million plus? And two million plus that its owner can't wrangle about, because he made it in a dodgy way, perhaps imported it in a dodgy way. The raid police – they were bound to corner a ration for themselves, weren't they? Perks. That's traditional. As a cop, you'll know the routine.'

'Which?'

'Detectives' percentage of tricky loot.'

At once Harpur said: 'No, the police are not like that. Our function is to bring order where, without us, only strength and natural selfishness would prevail.'

'Oh, God, someone's been reading Hobbes and feeding you chunks. Rockmain, the idiot-genius intellectual? Iles, the dandy lech philosopher? I thought Robert would probably be due a pay-off for what he did. Of course. Grasses collect, don't they? It's a long time after but that often happens, doesn't it?'

'What?'

'The delay. They postpone the share-out for months in case people start spending like fools, and everyone can guess where it comes from. So, I wondered if now was the moment for Robert's reward.'

'You know the swag game, then, do you?'

'Bound to. And there's a scene in one of those US gang movies where a hood buys a flash new car right after a job and Robert de Niro as boss gets furious. *Goodfellas*?'

'But they wouldn't have any idea where you live.'

'He'd tell them, wouldn't he? We're talking money, for God's sake. A lot of zeros. He's not going to stay hidden away, is he? "Kindly deliver my slice here."' She attempted a clipped, male voice. She wore her fair hair very short, and Harpur considered that a good idea, not for all women but for women as pleasant-looking as Jane Templedon. The hair framed her face without obscuring any part of it. In her case, this worked nicely because obscuring any part of it would be stupid. When she thought she'd made a hefty point to Harpur she turned full on to him, her eyes light blue, sharp and impatient, occasionally gleaming with insolence. Iles would adore this. He could get excellent empathy with people he thought despised him, especially women. He wanted their insights on himself. What the insights showed did not count much, as long as they were about *him*, and thoroughly about him. Iles knew he was worthwhile. They didn't need to agree, just to give him exclusivity.

Once, he had spoken to Harpur about what he said the Church called 'the principle of plenitude' in the world. This stipulated that, for the creation to be perfect, it had to contain something of everything – and so, apparently unattractive items like blowflies and dandruff. Similarly, Iles said, there was a due place for folk who despised him, and Iles more than accepted this, he regarded it as crucial and a revelation. Their hatred made him complete.

The insolence in Jane Templedon's eyes came when she spoke about the 'traditional' cornering of unaccountable loot in a raid by the police, and when she ridiculed Harpur's plummy, self-righteous answer. She had a straight, fine nose. Her skin was pale and unlined, her mouth mobile, quick and firm on to the words she wanted, and able to give some of them power to sting and tear.

Harpur tried to read in Jane's features the clash that ought to exist between her education and the crooked life Ian Ballion had brought her. It struck him as not suitable somehow that a woman familiar with the works of Thomas Hobbes should be digging illegal automatics out of a car boot tool bag thinking them moolah. But Harpur knew he occasionally set too great a value on an education, not having bothered with much of a one himself. He couldn't really spot any hint of turmoil in Jane's face. He had searched for it on the Dulwich journey and in the Templedon meetings and at the blockhouse, but never found anything. She was a woman who opted for a specific way of things and took to it totally. Months ago she'd been all-out Ballion, now all-out Templedon.

'How did he get it?' Harpur said.

'What?'

'The package.'

'That's why you were up at the house, walking the avenue both ways in a fluster, isn't it – regardless of security instructions?' she replied. 'You knew we'd had a visitor.'

'I became a bit uneasy about you all. I'm like that. No special reason. In fact, no reason – just a restlessness. I thought that in the dark I could chance it, just to quieten my mind.' It seemed unnecessary to mention the inquiring caller at Coral Ann's place.

'I don't know how you knew, but you did.'

'Which visitor?'

'Not to number 18 itself, but in the avenue.'

'Who?'

'Not clear. Robert went out to him and they drove some-where. One of the big Vauxhalls? That's important. *A big Vauxhall.* In the raid, when Robert did his run, he found a big Vauxhall waiting for him at the end of the street. It wouldn't be in the court transcripts, of course. But he told me.'

'An unmarked police car?' Might the stranger in the avenues be a cop, then, not a pathfinder from one of the firms, after all? But a London cop? Why?

'A Vauxhall chauffeured him away from the ambush. A lifeline for their informant. Yes, I say informant. Robert wouldn't like this. But it's how the Met think of him. How you think of him? Why not? After all, you're giving us the retired supergrass treatment, aren't you?'

'We say Covert Human Intelligence Source.'

'But *I* don't have to regard him like that. He doesn't regard himself like that.'

If Harpur could find anything at all but fight and disdain in her face it was devotion to Templedon. That appeared often. Iles would regret it, resent it. 'You watched when Robert went to the car? From a window? Did you get its number?' Harpur said.

'I keep an eye. How I saw you. Listen, Harpur, I don't spy on Robert and I don't grass on him. But I was scared – scared at first it was to do with his plan for a say-sorry trip to Melvane. I wondered if that's where the two of them would go. This was before I'd identified the Vauxhall. When they drove away I could see it properly. Robert came back pretty soon, though, with something for his car boot.' She took a piece of paper from the pocket of her jeans. 'Here's the reg,' she said.

He glanced a it: 'Yes.'

'What do you mean, "Yes"?'

'I've seen it.'

'How? Are you out in front?'

'Tell me about the man in the Vauxhall,' Harpur replied.

'It was night and he didn't leave the car. Hard to see much of his face. But I remember a lot of dark hair.'

'Swept back behind the ears?' Harpur said.

'Yes, you *do* know all this. It *is* why you ignored security, isn't it?'

'Mr Iles will understand about that.'

'Will he get told?'

'Mr Iles *would* understand,' Harpur replied. Oh, yeah?

Neighbourhood Watch left the Focus and walked down towards them. She paused and this time Jane lowered the window. 'Ah, you've acquired a female colleague for your work here,' the patrol said to Harpur. 'Good. In fact, brilliant. The nuisance is both hetero and homo. A woman's presence will be useful.' She nodded down at the plastic cover on Jane's lap. 'Is this a recorder, to get their damn dirty cries of fulfilment and ecstasy as evidence?'

'Pocket flame-thrower,' Jane replied. 'You've heard of a scorched earth policy? This is scorched arse.' She closed the window. Neighbourhood Watch went on to the VW.

Harpur said: 'They could be a partnership, Vauxhall Man and Robert. Vauxhall Man might think he owes Robert something. Not money. Not necessarily. I don't believe any was skimmed. But, a gun for Robert to look after himself and the family? The bond between detective and grass can be powerful, genuine, enduring. Vauxhall Man possibly felt guilty about what he did with Robert's information. Maybe he's into recompense.'

'Why?'

'Why what?'

'Why don't you believe any was skimmed?'

'I don't.'

'Faith in the Force?'

'It's not my Force,' Harpur replied.

'Faith in the Service?'

'Some of that, yes. And I'd have heard if money went adrift.'

'How? Nobody could know except the people in the Shogun and the raid police themselves.'

'God, you stick at things, don't you?' Harpur replied.

'Do you know that line from Conrad about the mind and instincts of a burglar resembling the mind and instincts of a police officer?'

'Conrad who?'

'You *do* know it, do you?'

'It's one of those comforts crooks give themselves. They like to believe taint is general.'

'Conrad wasn't a crook,' she said.

'It's one of those comforts crooks give themselves.'

'Vauxhall Man brought guns, not *a* gun,' she said.

'One of them might have been there already. I expect Ian – Robert – had a pistol at the raid, though he didn't fire, of

203

course. That might mean he felt all right holding on to it. No matchable, evidential bullets around. Vauxhall Man might not realize Ian – Robert – kept this original weapon. Normally, it's a basic drill for cash-in-transit people to separate themselves at once from a raid gun. Vauxhall Man would think Robert was wide open, unarmed. It's a nice gesture. Good grey-area policing.'

'Vauxhall Man seems very big-hearted, for a cop.'

'That's what I mean – the bond. It's authentic. Golden. But there could be another side. Vauxhall Man might be hunting Melvane himself – Plenipotentiary of Onset, a mighty, long-life crime syndicate up there. So, your visitor calculates that if he arms Robert there's a chance Melvane or Solid or both will get blasted suppose they come hunting. A villain dynasty totally eliminated – Lester in jail for ever, Walt and Solid dead or disabled. That would be the hope. I gather the Met have been stalking Walt for ten years plus. His last conviction 1992, though he's still directing Onset non-stop and a real tease. Major scale. What else has he got for career? Of course, it might be Robert who gets gunned instead. That possibility already exists, though. Your visitor brings him no extra risk.'

She lost her jauntiness. 'But Melvane and his wife seemed to listen and accept what I – what *we* – told them,' she said. She spoke plaintively, obviously craving his agreement.

He couldn't give it. 'They listened. Of course they listened. In case you said something that helped find Robert.'

'I didn't. So how can Melvane come looking?' she said. 'He doesn't know where we are, and Robert wouldn't tell him, even if he told the police up there who could bring his money share.'

'Vauxhall Man knows where you are. We were followed. Sorry. This is a clever lad. Suppose he leaks your address to Melvane – to make sure he gets here and meets a barrage from Robert.'

'Vauxhall Man is a detective, yes?'

'That's what you're telling me – in the exit car for Robert at the robbery.'

'How come a detective's at Melvane's place in Dulwich then, and able to follow us? Do you mean he's a bought creature – secretly on Melvane's staff?'

'No. I think he wants to collar Melvane. He has him under surveillance. Different kind of Neighbourhood Watch. He sees us arrive and tails us back, despite my textbook tricks.'

She turned away from him, as though exhausted by the chatter. 'God, Harpur, I feel like such an amateur.'

'*He's* not.'

'Neither are you.' She glanced down at her lap. 'Look, I was going to hand over the guns. I don't want them, or the money, if it's ever offered.'

'Yes, you should hand them over.'

'There was ammunition as well.'

'I expect so.'

She put her hand hard on the package, as though ready for a battle. 'No. Now I don't think I *will* surrender them.'

'Does it feel like a betrayal of him?'

'It feels moronic.'

Harpur said: 'If you surrender them, I can make it easy for you with him – point out that you have no choice. But if you return them to the Saab I can do him for illegal possession, you a possible accessory.'

'He has to be able to look after himself, look after us.'

'That's a Ballion thought, not Templedon. *We* have responsibility for looking after you now. Mr Iles made you. Mr Iles will preserve you.'

Some of her aggression came back. 'All right, I did say we have to take on the Templedon role fully, no back-sliding. But we could get just as shot as Templedons, if Walt and Solid turn up. When a bullet's got your name on, it will kill whether the name's Ballion or Templedon.

You *can't* look after us, can you? Put guards on the house and everyone will guess this must be an ex-grass and family.'

'Does it matter, if the cover's gone?' Harpur said.

'*Would* you put guards on? Would Iles let you? He believes he made us. Yes, he thinks his work must stand alone, independent, whole, or what sort of sickly achievement is it?'

'This is a a tricky one.'

'I'll put the guns back in the Saab boot,' she said. 'For now, anyway. He might turn rough if they're missing. He'd guess I'd taken them.' Her voice went brassy for a moment: 'You wouldn't really get him, us, for illegal possession, would you? You're bigger than that, aren't you? Aren't you?'

'What's he like with a handgun?'

'We're both all right. We met in the university shooting club. He dropped out.'

'Of the gun club?'

'Of university. He thought he could see quicker ways to making a career, and no loan burden.'

Harpur said: 'I ask about his marksman skills because Mr Iles wouldn't want innocent bystanders hit or someone's old red setter if it comes to a shoot-out with Walt Melvane and/or Solid. Iles abominates fracas. Mention his name in a pub or do-it-yourself store and people will reply, "Oh, isn't he the one who abominates fracas?" Order is his big and enduring mission. He dotes on peace in the streets – *and* avenues – as well as devising new families.'

She left his car with the pistols and Harpur went home. The house was empty. A note from Denise on the kitchen table said she had gone in her Fiat to pick up Hazel, Jill and their boyfriends from the weekly good works session. The church organized this. Harpur did not greatly mind good works but fretted about his daughters' connection with a church, any church. He'd had enough of that himself when a child. Enforced religion darkened so many days for him then. All that stuff about shedding of blood and death as the wages of sin.

He mixed a gin and cider in a half-pint glass and pretended to argue with himself over whether he should tell Iles the Templedon cover was probably finished. Harpur knew he had a duty to tell him, but also knew he could never risk it. Iles would ask the questions and ultimately out it must come that someone had followed Jane Templedon and Harpur back from a weak-minded, give-away visit to Walter Melvane's. Ultimately had always been a time-spot Harpur tried to avoid, especially with the Assistant Chief. Although Iles almost certainly liked more people than he loathed, he did loathe quite a few. He would loathe Harpur to a possibly dangerous point, if he discovered about the trip to Dulwich, the caller at Coral Ann's house, and the seeming link between Robert Templedon and Vauxhall Man – presumably the door knocker at Coral Ann's. But by now, of course, Harpur realized that this invader of the avenues – thirties rather than sixties – was not Walt Melvane or similar, but probably a detective from the Met.

Iles's aversions could fluctuate. Harpur knew the ACC already detested him periodically, because of that episode a while back with Sarah Iles, his wife. Only periodically, though, and this was vital. Iles would be comradely now and then, and not just as a possible way of getting to Hazel. More or less the same thing went for Iles's attitude to Francis Garland, a chief inspector, who'd also had some pleasant evenings and so on with Sarah, though not at the same time as Harpur, obviously. Yet Iles admired Garland as an officer and trusted him with big cases. Most judges and lawyers Iles did abominate continuously, of course, and people in the Home Office, especially the head of it, and anyone who menaced, hurt or killed one of the ACC's subordinates. Harpur did not want to join those who qualified for Iles's constant enmity and felt he would

207

if the Assistant Chief learned of that Dulwich journey and its results.

This evening, Harpur had been home from the avenues for only about ten minutes when Iles himself turned up. Harpur knew he should have expected it. The ACC was aware of the help-a-pensioner scheme, and would often call on Hazel's nights with the paintbrush because it excited him to sweat level to see her in dungarees and with smudges on fabric and her skin – and possibly in her hair if she forgot a bobble hat. Iles did not seem to need any special colour or colours of paint for these deep tremors. It was the artisan appearance that got him going. If her hand or lower arm were streaked he would feel entitled to rub at the paint with his fingers in an almost wholly benign cleansing frenzy, while tut-tutting sympathetically about the friction. Jill used to get in a bigger mess, but Iles never showed interest. Hazel took it all without too much embarrassment. Harpur had never seen the ACC touch any part of her legs or upper body. Hazel's boyfriend, Scott, loathed Iles.

Tonight, the ACC had on a royal blue, open-necked shirt, unquestionably custom-made, tapered grey flannels, and black Galileo slip-ons, say £350 a pair. 'You'll be amused at news I bring, Col,' he said. 'I know you can be surprisingly ironic for someone of your meat and potatoes background.'

'I get it from one of my aunties.'

'I'm amused myself.'

'You, too, can be surprisingly ironic, sir. Many say this. In the canteen or lounge bar I'll often hear someone muse interestedly, "Mr Iles? Mr Iles? Ah, yes – isn't he the one who can be surprisingly ironic?" Others suggest "He could be surprisingly ironic" should be on your gravestone.'

'A move afoot to make me other than *Mr* Iles, Col.'

'Beatification?'

Harpur mixed a drink for him. Iles liked what he called 'the old tart's refresher', port and lemon, and Harpur always made sure he had stocks of both on Hazel's decorating days. In any case, Jill regularly checked there were bottles of each. Hazel would never have asked or revealed concern. Jill said Hazel was in what one of the magazines called 'denial'. Jill had flair as a hostess and never complained about the lack of attention to the paint on her. She took this as what happened, or didn't happen, to younger sisters. Jill seemed to believe her day as someone interestingly smudged might come.

'At the rumour level only, for now. But let's say, beefy rumour, shall we?' Iles said.

'These are the best.'

'I thought to myself, I must run this past Col.'

'Thank you, sir. What?'

'Oh, yes. I gather there have been soundings.'

'That so, sir?'

'Soundings are what they take for this sort of thing,' Iles replied.

'Which sort, sir? Who take?'

'Oh, yes.' Iles did some profile. He was about to lift the glass to his mouth but seemed to realize suddenly that this would clutter the line of him and lowered his hand. 'I hear a knighthood, Col.'

'Wonderful!' Harpur replied. And why *not* a knighthood for Iles?

'When I say "soundings" – they ask folk as to the suitability of possible recipients. That's their job, the awards people. They ask around.'

'You might scrape through, even so.'

'Obviously, they wouldn't ask someone like you, Harpur.'

'Because I know too much?'

'They want advice from figures of quite notable standing.'

'Right.' Just the same, Harpur saw that if things went desperately wrong on the Templedon situation because of him it would probably fuck things up for Iles. 'Rumour level only', no matter how beefy, meant the offer stayed very conditional and could be rescinded. 'Grand, sir. *So* deserved.' Harpur meant it. Of course he meant it. Somehow the perfection and saintliness of the Assistant Chief's work with the Templedons must be kept intact, at least until the knighthood rumour turned concrete. '*Sir* Desmond,' Harpur said. 'It sounds robust. And the new Chief's already a knight, so there'll be no envy bile from above.'

'You see how it happened, do you, Col?'

'On account of your –'

'They hate me, of course.'

'Who, sir?'

'*Who*? But you know, don't you, Harpur? The mighty, the tainted, the wankers up there.' He waved a hand loosely. It took in God, the Trinity, the Cabinet, with special reference to the Home Secretary, and then offered general reference to all politicians, every Police Authority.

'They hate you but they're set to give you a knighthood?' Harpur said. 'How's that, then, sir?'

'I never hold it against you that you fail to see subtleties, Harpur. In a way, it's endearing. It shows you can't be accused of over-sophistication.'

'This is a relief, sir.'

'They hate me for the almost magical success of the Templedon project. Jealousy. By the freighter load. That's their most obvious grievance.'

'Awful.' Yes, awful if the project fell deeply sick and died.

'But much, much more important, Col, they hate me for my drugs policy.'

'Hate you for it. But they're coming round to it.'

'Naturally they are. Why they hate me. I was there years before them. Jealousy, sheepishness, shame, Col, by the pantechnicon load. Describe my drugs policy, Harpur.'

'You mean blind-eyeing the trade in exchange for peace on the streets? Your live-and-let-live pacts with barons like

Panicking Ralph Ember and Manse Shale? The Non-Fracas Treaty?'*

'I preached that drugs were here to stay, so accept this and make sure the business works inside a due, controlled framework.'

'Hobbes, isn't it, sir? Didn't he sound off in his time about, first, acknowledging, then, effectively regulating H. and E. and ganja?'

'They declared my thinking abominable, immoral, illegal, degenerate and impractical. But, now, you see, a revelation comes to them in Westminster and Whitehall. What do you think it is, Col?'

'That Tom Hobbes is the boy?'

'It is –' He went into sing-song tone to repeat his own words. 'It is, *drugs are here to stay, so accept this and make sure the business works inside a due, controlled framework.* That's to be national policy from now on. They won't put it quite as forthrightly as that, of course – not their style, the fucking weasels – but it's so. They've learned. They've collapsed. They've embraced what was obvious to me so long ago.'

'You must be well used to running ahead of the field. I should think at Staff College they called you –'

'Consequently, some shit-faced, conniving adviser around the corridors-of-power-and-cover-my-arse in Westminster says: "We'd better give that fucking Iles a fucking gong. This way, we can make out he undertook a kind of pilot policy on drugs for the rest of the country at our request. It worked, so now we can have some relaxation of the law on substance trading. And we pat our well-beloved Ilesy on his subservient back for running the experiment, which the electorate will be led to believe we, of course, ordered, and give him a nice title to retire on. That should stop the fucker crowing over us in the public prints and saying we dithered and dodged and attacked his policies non-stop before caving in to them." I see myself as rather like Charles VI of France, you know, Col.'

* See *Easy Streets.*

'Ah! I wondered who it was you reminded me of, sir. But yes, yes! As well as Dr Frankenstein, of course.'

'They called him Charles the Mad, but also Charles the Well-Beloved. These sods regarded me as Desmond the Mad. Now they want to switch and see me as Desmond the Well-Beloved.'

'*Sir* Desmond.' So, yes, yes, it would be even more impossible to tell the ACC that his Ballion-Templedon triumph had changed to a potential catastrophe, and because of Harpur. Iles was a great policeman and sparklingly devious workmate. His lovely pleasure at the idea of collecting an earned honour from those terrified not to give it to him must be preserved if preservable. To shatter this sweet scenario would amount to foul cruelty and Harpur could not contemplate hurting him again, following that chapter with Sarah – and regardless of his creepiness with Hazel. Of course, it might be impossible to keep the facts of the fuck-up from him for ever. But the ACC's momentary delight must at present have respectful, intensive care. His beautiful clothes and shoes made him appear more vulnerable. He ponced about brilliantly in this pricey gear, yet a word wrong could put him on his arse, the magnificent soles of those Galileos up for inspection, the Sirdom a goner.

'They abominate my triumphs, Col. As you say, I'm always in advance of them. It infuriates. Their hate is natural – part of that "principle of plenitude" I think we spoke of. It is necessary to the total scheme. It is integral. I do understand the agony they get from realizing they are fourth class minds.'

'Who exactly?'

'And there's something reciprocal from me, obviously. *I* hate *them*. You'd expect that, wouldn't you? But also obviously I'll take what the clowns have been compelled to give. Churlishness can have no part of Desmond Iles.'

'Which clowns exactly?' Yes, who had proposed Iles should be silenced and soothed by accolade? The new

Chief, Sir Matthew? Did Iles hate him so soon? Iles definitely did not small-mindedly, poisonously, hate all Chiefs simply because they *were* Chiefs and above him. For instance, Iles in his way had seemed fond of the previous Chief, Mark Lane. Always in that reign, the ACC strove to save Lane from complete mental collapse, while pushing him near enough to it for Iles to pinch many powers beyond his rank and get his own policies going. Toleration of drugs dealing in exchange for no turf wars had been one of these, the main one.

In fact, though, Iles failed to keep Lane from disintegration, and he did suffer a full breakdown for months. The ACC was probably a cause of that, though perhaps not *all* the cause, only the major cause. Iles had been authentically sad about Lane's state, once the Chief collapsed. 'This is a good man who should have chosen another kind of work, Col, such as cushion stuffer or aircraft design,' Iles had told Harpur. Lane was eventually promoted to the Inspectorate of Constabulary, and with a knighthood. Iles had been genuinely pleased to see him given a nice fade-out billet. Iles did try to hate selectively, not from mere mania or boredom. Harpur wanted to dodge selection.

'Perhaps a knighthood will come to *you*, eventually, Col.'

'Thank you, sir.'

'All kinds get them now.'

'This is heartening.'

'If they approached me with soundings about you, Harpur, I'd almost certainly try to be humane.'

'Thank you, sir.'

'Because they're going to offer it to me, don't think clothes or looks or hair styling are factors and would exclude yourself.'

'Do they know about you banging Honorée in a police vehicle on waste ground off Valencia Esplanade?'

Iles seemed mellow and confident, happy with his port and lemon. Harpur longed for him to stay like this. The knighthood prospect must go through, must not get

213

mashed by a Templedon fiasco. The title might change Iles, make him believe he could move up into full Chiefdom himself, and beyond. Several Chiefs had knighthoods. But it would be very unusual for an ACC. This would really pump up his morale. Although Iles detested the rank of Assistant, with all its demeaning overtones-undertones, and all its bum-sucking 's' sounds, Harpur believed that until now the ACC knew this was as far as he would go, and – the strange, vital point – felt it to be as far as he *should* go. Despite his constant arrogance and pirouetting, Iles had seemed to accept that he could not manage high-level command. He'd often worked against Lane, and yet he needed Lane. Iles's destiny was Assistant – or Assssissssstant, as he would hiss the indignity of it some-times. He appeared sure he had been born to second stringdom. To date, he lacked the confidence of a top dog. Iles had quoted with passion and lavish self-pity that verse from Psalm 13, 'How long shall mine enemy be exalted over me?' The question seemed to suggest there might be a change. The fact was, though, Iles had always needed somebody exalted above him – maybe not an enemy, just *somebody.* Lane. And then the new Chief.

But perhaps now, as *Sir* Des, he might emerge, full of contempt for what the awarders awarded, but also splen-did and splendidly boosted and able to run a system for himself. This would be a true advance. Iles had always needed that boss presence above him, because a capable boss would run a decent, enduring organization. Inside such an organization and not quite at its top, Iles operated more or less as he liked if he could get away with it, and only sometimes with rectitude. But Harpur had always sensed an abiding dread in him that his own ungovernable behaviour might establish a standard, suggest a norm. He was Iles and unique, and uniquely fallible, and uniquely aware of his faults. He wanted someone over him per-manently and officially to represent the system – so that Iles could abuse it, but abuse it only so far and in the cause

214

of what he, Iles, and sometimes only he, Iles, saw as good policing.

Of course, the ACC would rate as egomaniac yet his frantic obsession with himself had always included the ability to spot how far his ego could safely carry him. Harpur's school – like what Iles had referred to as the university of life – had not done much poetry, but he recalled a line, 'the proper study of Mankind is Man'. Iles believed that as a piece of Mankind *his* proper study was Iles – proper, loving and very tough on Des Iles. On *Sir* Des Iles he might get less tough. Harpur thought he would make a great, uncorruptible, uncatastrophic, unhinged Chief, preferably somewhere else, and a long way from Hazel. Harpur knew he must not jinx such a belated, possible progress from ACC to Chief by too much niggling truth at this stage.

Denise arrived with the girls and Scott and Darren, Jill's boyfriend. 'I do believe you're getting to be an expert artisan, Hazel,' Iles muttered in disappointment. 'Hardly a new paint trace anywhere.'

'She's been trying hard, so as not to get pawed by hangers-about,' Hazel's boyfriend, Scott, said.

'Cut it,' Hazel said.

'We've been discussing hate, as a matter of fact,' Iles said.

'Dad's no good at that,' Jill replied. 'Never has been.'

'Hate as a positive, constructive thing,' Iles said, 'like honesty or the ability to ride a bike.'

'Hate? My mother hates all police,' Scott said. 'I think that's stupid. Out of proportion.'

'We'll still turn up if she calls us when set on by brigands,' Iles said.

'I tell her there are bound to be one or two reasonable officers,' Scott replied.

'Well, yes, I've heard people praise Harpur,' Iles said. 'And it's not mere pity.'

'Mr Harpur *is* one, yes,' Scott said.

'But you'd have to say that because of Hazel, wouldn't you, Scott?' Iles replied.

'And you'd have to say it because of Hazel, wouldn't you, Mr Iles?' Scott said.

'Who's the other?' Iles asked.

'The other what?' Scott said.

'You said there must be one or *two* reasonable officers. Who's the other?' Iles asked.

'I can't just answer something like that straight off, can I?' Scott replied. 'I'd need to do research.'

'We talked about hate as a motivating force,' Iles replied.

'Yes,' Scott said.

'What?' Jill asked.

'What what?' Iles replied.

'That word – what-do-you-call-it, "motivating". What has hate been motivating lately?'

'Something rather good,' Iles said. 'There are people who hate me, you know.'

'Get away,' Scott said and whistled.

'And, because they hate me, they're going to offer something they think will make me easier to manage, less difficult and dangerous,' Iles said.

'They'll electronic tag you at last?' Scott asked.

'To achieve something good out of something bad, such as hatred, is quite a religious idea,' Denise said.

'Many do see me in that kind of light, I've been told,' Iles replied.

'Hate is unchristian,' Jill said.

'Don't let's bring all that into it,' Harpur said. 'Anyway, the Bible tells us to hate evil.'

'That's our role,' Iles said, 'to hate, combat and remove it, even if Scott's mother hates *us* for doing so.'

'I think Jill's right,' Denise said later to Harpur in bed. 'You're not capable of hate.' Despite the chill from Scott, Iles had offered to drive both boys home when Harpur had done some big yawns and the conversation thinned.

216

'But I'm capable of love,' he replied.

'Oh, of course. Mostly.'

'You're only here mostly.'

'Well, yes, there's a reason.'

'It can't be much good.'

'This is going to sound vain, Colin.'

'You don't usually mind that.'

'The difficulty is, I'm a young girl with what I've been told by my college tutors is true potential.'

'Did one of them, male, want to discuss your true potential in some cosy little room over a drink with the door locked?' Harpur replied.

'I shouldn't absolutely tie myself to anyone at present.'

'That I do hate,' Harpur replied.

'What?'

'When you say such things.'

'I don't often.'

'It seems often,' Harpur said. 'At which stage might you be able to tie yourself absolutely?'

'Sometimes I feel it would be so grand.'

'It would be,' Harpur said.

'And so I'm going to think about it plenty.'

'I suppose I'll settle for that. *We'll* settle for that.'

'Who?'

'The girls and I, of course.'

'I know I'd be well loved here.'

'Well, there you are then.'

'And yet I've got these damn beckoning horizons,' she said.

'The tutor keeps telling you about them, too, does he? If you look closely at one of these beckoning horizons you'll see something stiff and sticking up, like a ship's mast over the skyline. It belongs to the tutor and, yes, it's beckoning. Am I on one of them?'

'What?'

'These horizons.'

'Oh, much, much closer than that.'

'I don't mean now this moment.'

'Let's think about the nowness of now, all right, Colin?' she said. 'Closeness. Yes, such closeness.'

'Do you think it's a fault?'

'What?'

'Not hating much. Iles believes hate is a crucial component – giving or taking. Do I lack a dimension?'

'I think your dimensions are adequate.'

'Why should I go about hating?'

'Just concentrate on the loving then for the moment,' she replied.

'The moment?'

'You know what I mean.'

'No,' he said.

'More than the moment.'

'Much more?'

'If possible.'

Next day, Iles drove, with Rockmain as front passenger and Harpur in the back. They followed the Templedons' car at a wise distance, as agreed with them. School run for Sian Rebecca and Harry Charles. Their parents were taking them to register and settle in at Matthew Arnold Interdenominational, a fifty mile each way trip. Iles had decided the Templedons must not make it alone. After what Jane told Harpur about cover collapse, he agreed. He would have understood Iles's feelings, even without that. This family – it *belonged* to Iles. He built it. He had to keep it complete in his sight and protection for as long as could be managed. And, as Assistant Chief, he could manage something for as long as this – an escort to the Matthew Arnold school gates. No further. These Templedon children in their uniforms must join the school simply as Templedon children. The Matthew Arnold knew of no police connection, and shouldn't. Secrecy procedures had to be carried on, although Harpur realized they might be absurd now – carried on for the ACC's sake as much as anyone's. Let him glory in his possible step. But he could not go banging about in the school, flashing his prodigious care and corny grandeur, checking security and dishing out emergency call numbers to the staff, as he'd certainly like to. Ordinariness for Sian Rebecca and Harry Charles was vital.

'Christ, Col, imagine if they saw Rockmain,' Iles had said just before he joined them in the ACC's Rover. 'Those lips. I don't expect you've ever heard of the Matthew Arnold who gives this school his name – absolutely no reflection on you. But he did a lot of considerable stuff in Victorian days and believed in sweetness and light. His chief theme, Col. Can anyone beat it? Sweetness and light.' Iles stretched out the words giving them their full chime and insanity. 'The school bearing his name will be keen to enshrine those qualities. Do you see what I mean about the grossness of taking someone with looks like Rockmain's into such a venue?'

'Yes, I *have* heard of Matthew Arnold. Someone read one of his poems at my wife's funeral – "Strew on her roses, roses."'

'Arnold excelled on the posthumous. Another of his themes. Think of *Sohrab* and *Balder Dead*. And *Thyrsis*, naturally.'

'Always,' Harpur replied. Rockmain had wanted to come because, like Iles, he believed the Templedons arrived in the world through him, and considered he should be present at their first expedition to the wider life. Iles probably objected, and vastly resented his claim to responsibility for the Templedons. But surprisingly often the ACC gave way to a sense of what was due, and even displayed kindness. Iles would recognize that Rockmain put the work in and deserved to witness its results, if only from a distance. Iles worried continuously about the self-esteem of others, including a twat's like Rockmain.

'I hear hints of a laurel, Desmond,' Rockmain said as they stuck with the Saab.

'*So* brilliantly deserved, Andy. And nobody can say you angled for it by dressing tastefully,' Iles replied.

'Not me.'

'Not you? *Me*? Good God! What about this then, Col?'

'It takes some believing sir,' Harpur replied. Iles obviously wanted it treated as news. 'And yet, that might seem grudging of me. After all, they gave Mick Jagger a knighthood, didn't they? And think of the people who get peerages.'

The Templedons entered the school grounds and Iles, Rockmain and Harpur waited according to plan in a layby. Harpur saw Iles was devastated by the disappearance of the children. He obviously feared for them. *His* fear scared Harpur.

Rockmain said: 'They decided you deserved an honour for recognizing before themselves that the drugs fight was lost. You'd be sharp at spotting opportunities in defeat. Capitulation has a valid place in leadership, and you headed the sad retreat with galloping distinction, Desmond. I don't think there's any question of your associates in the trafficking game, Panicking Ralph Ember and Mansel Shale, qualifying for a title, though – or, at least, not immediately. I understand the old Chief, Lane, backed your candidature from his new power point.'

'A sweet, conscientious, addled man,' Iles said. 'He opposed me at the time. Now, out of fair's-fair, he wants to say sorry.'

'You shouldn't blame yourself entirely for the pulverizing of his mind, sir,' Harpur replied. 'It was only your nature, nothing plotted.'

'Thanks, Col.'

'Whereas I hear Lane's wife did everything she could to fuck up your elevation,' Rockmain said.

'Poor infirm thing,' Iles replied.

'She talks to people about you – influential people – your cuckoldom, complemented by careless promiscuity. You don't emerge with distinction – a weak and rather dismal figure, Des. Didn't you have crabs for a while? A great deal of scuttlebutt comes my way.'

'I expect she does talk,' Iles replied. 'A lovely woman but not in the sexual sense. Oh, perhaps that's unkind and too sweeping. Not in the sexual sense as far as I'm concerned. Arse like a washboard. I don't know about Harpur, though. He's fairly avid and will take anything available. Mrs Lane could not forgive my rebuff, I'm afraid. She's entitled to bitterness at her age.'

The ACC had decided that, because they were far from their own ground, it would be no security breach if the five of them stopped for a pub lunch on the way back. He could be ardent and docile passing Jane Templedon the cruet. During the meal he seemed to recover from loss of the children. Somehow he must have convinced himself they were safe. Harpur could not see how he'd managed that – though, of course, Iles knew less than Harpur did. Or Harpur *hoped* Iles knew less than he did.

The ACC would pick up the bill. He might reclaim from the Templedon budget or do it simply as Iles. He could often be lordly and dismissive about expenses. Rockmain, eating spaghetti tuna, said: 'It has to be admitted that some kind of schizophrenic stress – using that term very loosely, very – such stress can affect people who undertake the programme you – Jane, Robert – and the children have experienced recently, and especially the children. I can't be more specific than "some kind". As a letter in the *Guardian* pointed out recently –'

'You read not just the *Guardian* itself but *letters* to the *Guardian*?' Iles cried.

'Pointed out recently,' Rockmain said, 'there is no known, exact physiological basis for schizophrenia.'

'God, schizophrenic stress in the kids?' Templedon said.

'I think it's what we expected, surely, Rob,' Jane said. She touched his wrist. Iles saw it and his face fell into agony for seconds.

Rockmain said: 'I mention this not to depress or frighten

you but to urge that, should such symptoms occur – possibly notified by the school nurse, for instance – should such symptoms occur, either in the children or in yourselves, you must inform me at once via Mr Iles or Mr Harpur, either of whom can be designated my go-between.'

'Thank you, Andy,' Iles said.

'It is as much my bag to deal with post-change trauma as it is to effect the changes in the first place,' Rockmain said. 'I will return immediately in those circumstances, if I deem it necessary.'

'You do have an on-tap look to you, Andy,' Iles replied.

'But how naive it would be to suppose that once the set processes of resettlement have been completed the whole transformation is therefore tidy and secure. Back-up, back-up, back-up. If I could be said to have a mantra, Back-up is it.'

'This is fine of you, but typical,' Iles said. 'Mantras suit you.'

'Schizo,' Robert said. 'Sick-in-the-head children. Oh, hell.'

'We can contain such episodes,' Rockmain said. 'Episodes is all they are. Unfortunate, fleeting, controllable throwbacks. The death agony gurgle of those wolves of memory.'

'Larkin?' Iles said.

'Schizophrenia, schizoid,' Rockmain replied, while dealing damn well in his small-mouthed way with the meal. Harpur considered it showed real word-forming ability to get hefty terms like that out around such food, regardless of Iles's disgust at Rockmain's lips. 'I'd like to say something retrospectively about these terms. Fear not, I'm not going to turn pedantic on you –'

'Splendid,' Iles said.

'– not going to turn pedantic on you and preach that, in fact, schizophrenia, schizoid are specific mental conditions having not much to do with what in ordinary talk folk refer to as "split personality",' Rockmain said. 'But I do have to recognize that this is how these precise medical labels are used currently – schizophrenic meaning in such uninformed, everyday talk someone who seems to have two sides to their personality, and possibly two *warring* sides. So, in order to get ease of comprehension, I've taken for now the common interpretations of the terms.'

'Thank you, Andy,' Iles said.

Schizo? Didn't that term – used in what Rockmain called its common interpretation – supremely suit Iles? At coffee, Harpur opted out and said he must check the car. Rockmain's briefcase containing all Templedon documentation lay in the boot of the ACC's Rover, because they would drop Rockmain off at the station for his London train. Harpur told them he worried about it. Iles gave him the keys. In fact, though, Harpur went to the Templedon Saab and used his own break-in bunch. He always carried this. Perhaps Jane and Conrad were right about the common kinks of police and burglars. Harpur had a good eye for keys, located one straight off to fit the Saab boot, and opened it without jogging the alarm. He found both pistols and the ammunition. He left the ammunition. It would be difficult to conceal a box of bullets. Even with only the guns in his pockets he might look bulged. There were advantages in Harpur's kind of reach-me-down suits, which Iles wept and guffawed over. They rarely had a consistent, discoverable line, and a bit of extra misshapenness might not be noticed, even by Iles.

To insist the other day with Jane Templedon on confiscating these weapons would have been crudely heavy. Nevertheless, pistols should have nothing to do with the new Templedon identity. They were part of a former, discarded self. Schizo. Harpur could not be party to a gun fight in the street, and one in which Robert Templedon, outnumbered, might get slaughtered. A street battle centring on an ex-supergrass for whom Iles had responsibility would slaughter Iles's knighthood chances, too, particularly if Robert lost it. Someone had to look after Iles

– someone who recognized that although the ACC's offensiveness and vanity were wholly authentic and worked at, they did not occupy him totally. Room also existed in him for speckles of self-doubt, nerviness, crippling hesitance.

Harpur relocked the boot, then immediately opened it again and put the guns back. He found he had suffered the same kind of second thoughts as Jane's. How could he leave Templedon unable to guard himself when it was Harpur's fault the new dangers existed at all? He had not really attempted to stop Jane going to Dulwich and in fact compounded the breach of secrecy by accompanying her. And, God, that inept attempt to get rid of any tail! He recalled telling himself a moment ago that he must not permit Templedon the means for a street fight, and shuddered now at the shitty primness of it. At least an armed Templedon would have a chance if it did come to a street fight.

All right, such gun play could destroy Iles's hopes of a knighthood. Harpur did want the ACC to land it, and not only because he might then look for a Chiefdom and get promoted away from Hazel. Iles had earned recognition. Priorities, though. These required safety, or as near as could be got to it, for the Templedons. As to Iles and the award, Well-Beloved Desmond should use his well-belovedness on those with power to help secure his fine prospects.

Chapter Sixteen

That big-word lunchtime lecture by Rockmain in the pub – it convinced Robert Maurice Templedon even more he must get back to what he was, Ian Maitland Ballion. End this Templedon game. Rockmain made the change-over sound as if it could trigger a mind disease which, so the bugger said, didn't really add up to one. Like, 'Let's call it schizophrenia, but that's not what it really is, only similar.' Well, too fucking similar. Templedon wanted a return route for him and for Jane and the children to where they came from. And he'd make that route by the method he'd already fixed. Hunt and kill Callic, who brought this shambles on them, then explain it all to Walt Melvane, with Callic's death the chief piece of evidence for what he wanted to prove. Perhaps Jane had already tried to prove it to Walt and got nowhere. But this new visit would be a clincher.

Templedon had watched in misery as the kids walked off to their classrooms at the Matthew Arnold. Their eyes seemed weary. Their mouths were clamped. Did they feel scared to open them, in case too much came out? That bloody uniform – so slick and cliquey. Anyone who sent children away to school must feel a remoteness from them. Maybe the parents who did it regularly grew hardened. Maybe some of them liked the remoteness because they could run their lives as they wanted in term-time. Perhaps he'd been a little remote from the children himself as Ballion. But now he found he resented the distance and felt the distance seemed greater because *his* children were bound to sink deeper into the Templedon myth, while he stayed incurably nostalgic for the old, dangerous, London simplicities. And if the kids did *not* sink further into being Templedons, they might suffer those foul head flips described by Rockmain – talked down by Rockmain, but horrible to hear about, even in his slippery, clouded words.

Of course, Templedon did not know when Callic might be in position for his freelance surveillance stints near Melvane's place. They were irregular. Drive to London and hang about Dulwich – this was the plan. Templedon could not stay permanently. Jane would want an explanation otherwise, and his absence from home might also be noticed by the police. He realized that Jane might have sensed he wanted to make the trip to Melvane. Perhaps she went first hoping to make his visit unnecessary. Harpur went with her. She probably told him what she suspected. That would mean Harpur must be alert now to any unexplained absence of Templedon. He had to make the journeys when he could, stay for as long as he judged all right, and count on finally coinciding with Callic. And coincide with him when Callic's concentration was on Walt Melvane, not on his own safety. Templedon hoped for that. Of course, Callic might be expecting him. Had he brought the pistol to tempt Templedon up there?

Templedon decided he would try the Heckler and Koch Parabellum now. If it turned out faulty he'd know as a certainty what Callic planned. The chance remained that this handy gift was a ploy. Templedon went over again what might be Callic's thinking. He probably suspected from the day of the raid that Templedon must come after him for the betrayal. And so his scheme – locate Templedon, get to him and, in the cause of apparent apology and cop–grass loyalty, confer a middle-hefty handgun for self-defence, but a gun sure to fuck up when Templedon tried to use it. There would be excellent legal cause for Callic to defend himself and open fire on Templedon, though. Any court was sure to accept that Callic might fear the H. and K. could suddenly start functioning properly immediately after a failure.

If the 9 mm *did* turn out faulty in trials, substitute the Beretta. And if the H. and K proved all right, he would take it with him to London. Although the .22 Beretta could certainly kill when fired from a good hand, the Parabellum's bigger calibre rounds would be more likely to do the full damage – particularly if Templedon could get off two or three shots. And if he couldn't, it became even more important the one bullet maximized. Thanks, Callic. This killing had something precious to prove. It should show Walt that Templedon never really went over and longed to be back as Ballion with him.

Templedon took the Saab out into the countryside. Although the geography was unfamiliar, he toured about until he found a good stretch of woodland with a drivable track leading to its edge. Here he parked. He planned to walk further in among the trees with the gun and try some secret targeting. He opened the boot and pulled the tool bag open, then stood back amazed. Neither gun was there, nor any of the ammunition. He felt dazed and sick, almost blacked out. He scrabbled about a bit in the boot but realized he would not find them. He knew at once what had happened. Thank God for the trees. He needed one of them to lean against. Jane, only Jane, could have taken the pistols. She sometimes drove the Saab and had a key. And had she searched the boot? Why? Did she see him place the weapon there? Did she also see him meet Callic in the Vauxhall? It would all be visible from a front upstairs window. Spectating? And spectating before she made love so eagerly with him that night? Jesus, what kind of deceit was that?

His shock became rage. In her businesslike style, she had swallowed the Templedon changes, and this was her way of ensuring he did too. Deliberately, furtively, what she had done was disarm him. She evidently thought that from now on she would take over management and control of the Templedon identity. She'd become little Rockmain's sidekick. Or that sod Iles's. He wanted her. This had been obvious from the beginning and even more obvious at the pub lunch. Something under way there? Did she scoop the guns to please him? Did Iles actually *want* Templedon unprotected, despite all that rubbish about the family as his precious creation? This old recurrent question. He did not actually throw up, and his sudden frailty and confusion disappeared. Only the vast anger with Jane remained. He drove fast back to 18 Cormorant Avenue and let himself into the house, not sure what he would say, but something final. She'd been in the sitting room when he went out and he pushed that door open, ready for a real face-to-face.

'Come in, Ian, dear,' Walter Melvane said.

'Yes, come on in, make yourself at home, like,' Solid said. 'Grand place, but you deserve it from the law, don't you?'

They were sitting with Jane between them on the smart, black leather chesterfield. The three looked packed together, almost comic. Only almost. Walt and Solid held what could be Smith and Wesson automatics, shielded from the windows by their bodies, although very available. Absurd, but Templedon realized he felt a special insult because these bits of high-placed low life should invade the neat respectability of their sitting room, their fine *Templedon* sitting room, their 'grand place'. They brought with them the smell of that hard and dirty life he had been thirsting for until only minutes ago. Now, represented here by them, it seemed an affront. What was that Rockmain had said about schizophrenia? For the Melvanes to be crowding Jane on the chesterfield looked not just comic but a crude mockery of the happy furniture scheme. Templedon did what he was told and went into the room. He stayed standing.

Walter said: 'Solid's going to frisk you, Ian. You're a bit of a bad beast, aren't you? A peril.'

'How did you get here?' Templedon said. Solid stood, holding the Smith and Wesson down by his trouser leg and crossed the room to search him. 'Callic gave you the address?' Templedon asked. 'Some understanding between you?'

'I don't know if you heard this, Ian, but your missus came to visit us, with an officer. Big, lout-looking lad. Perhaps we tailed them back. Solid's good at gumshoeing by car. Oh, Callic got the address, too, have he?'

'You fucking know he has,' Templedon said.

'How would he come by it then?' Walt replied.

'He's not carrying nothing,' Solid said, finishing the search. He did not look solid. He was slight, round-faced, his dark hair parted centrally, and with a slab of it curling down each temple. He had on a navy or black fleece zipped to the neck. He could have been called Sensitive. Or Runt.

Templedon's anger had become pointless, but, oh, God he could have done with the guns. 'Jane, you went to see the Melvanes?' Play dumb even now, though he was not sure why.

She said: 'I had to. It was —'

'"Jane" you call her?' Walter replied. 'Although we're here and know she's Eleanor. They've really done a job with you. Anyway, I got to say, she definitely tried to talk your case, Ian. It was kind of . . . well, noble. Yes, I repeat, noble. Like a wife *ought* to be. You're lucky there and it's a pity you won't be able to enjoy . . . But it couldn't work, could it – what she said? It did sound good but . . . but Lester's locked up. You done it. You got to be dealt with for that. Custom and practice, Ian.'

'Like holy,' Solid said.

'It goes beyond husband and wife, don't it, Ian?' Walter said. 'It's the procedure. This is what got to happen to grasses. There can't be no varying or where's the structure of things, where's system? It would be chaos.'

Solid said: 'Dad always worries his nut about structure and system and the start of chaos. It's leadership. I'm learning all that stuff now Lester's in the . . . Oh, yes. I wouldn't be surprised you might of been thinking about the leadership yourself, Ian. Not on. Not fucking on. Family. Well, obviously not on now.'

'We're going for a spin in your car, Ian,' Walt said. 'The four of us. Luckily, we got another vehicle waiting near where you, Eleanor, Solid and me are going. But you won't be joining us in that vehicle.'

'And yours might get burned out,' Solid said. This bit of it seemed to excite him and he smiled, a strong heir-apparent sort of smile.

Chapter Seventeen

In one or two ways Iles was like the old Chief, Mark Lane, though Harpur did not mention this to him often. Lane had always liked to visit the site of any crime he regarded as more than just itself. By this he meant that it seemed to typify – this was the key term, 'typify' – it seemed to typify some kind of drift into general hellishness. He saw such crimes, in fact, as terrible symbols. Lane feared non-stop that a kind of national, or world-wide falling apart might somehow begin here in his domain and destroy all good structure and system. And not *just* world-wide. Maybe cosmic. When the old Chief insisted on these visits it was because he wished to look personally for signs that a seemingly one-off, simple offence might actually be what he called 'the start of general chaos'. Iles used to help such notions along in him, of course, and delightedly encouraged all his dreads and depressions.

Now, though, just as Lane might have done, Iles came out with Harpur to look at these two bodies and the torched vehicle. Car burns occurred frequently here, so it had not caused much interest when a blaze started on the hillside last night. What else was the countryside for, except to offer take-and-drive-away pyre sites? Harpur knew the place pretty well – the remains of a Second World War anti-aircraft battery emplacement. It was another spot where he sometimes met his own supreme grass, Jack Lamb. The concrete road laid sixty-plus years ago for army lorries remained usable.

Iles said: 'You think two cars here originally, Col?'

'That's how it seems to Francis Garland, sir – from the tyre marks. Francis handled the preliminary stuff as duty officer.'

Iles considered this. He said: 'Do you suppose, Col, that anywhere else in Britain or, indeed, the Commonwealth, there is another Assistant Chief Constable who has to depend for information on a major case from two shaggers around who took turns with his wife?' Iles's voice climbed towards one of his screams. He and Harpur stood near conifers and the sound seemed to soar a respectable distance up the trunks and then become lost in thick, high, dulling foliage. 'Was it for that kind of treatment that I joined the Force and –'

'The tyre observations have to be part guess, sir,' Harpur replied. 'Plenty of people drive here – ramblers, lovers, bird watchers.'

'You say these two and whoever killed them arrived together in one of the cars?'

'Again we' re guessing. There's a great mix of footprints. We think they left the car and were shot more or less where they lie. Then we assume this car was set alight. That's how Francis sees it, and I agree.'

'When my wife talks about him or you now, Harpur, I can promise you, absolutely promise you – it is without the least –'

'The Met people are on their way,' Harpur replied.

'Cockahoop, I suppose.' Iles went forward and peered down at the bodies.

'They do like it, yes, sir.'

'And both these lads holding unfired S. and W.s? Do I identify the weapons right?' Iles asked.

'We wondered if it was to be an execution party that became somehow turned against the executioners.'

'We know the executed. Who switched to executioners? Who turned the script around, then?' Iles asked.

Harpur still felt it had been rethink-right to leave the

guns for Templedon in the Saab. He'd presumably be dead now, otherwise. 'That's the question, sir, isn't it?' he answered. 'This is going to be a tough one. Perhaps impossible.'

'Yes, I wouldn't be surprised. Impossible,' Iles said. 'Best like that? Small calibre wounds? Beretta .22?'

'The likelihood. To be confirmed. Immaculate shooting. Head in each case. At least two bullets each.'

'Yes, I can see. Do we know anyone with a Beretta?'

'Not common at all.' Harpur wondered why Templedon had risked using the smaller gun. Perhaps it was the first he could grab. But grab it how? Had Templedon taken the guns from the boot to have them ready in case a vengeance party came? Resourceful lad. Now and then the law couldn't cope on its own. Occasionally, a natural survival impulse from someone not part of official counter-crime forces might be needed. It would be *very* natural, wouldn't it, to eliminate a pair who had arrived to eliminate *him*? Yes, Nature wasn't all bad, regardless of what philosopher Hobbes said. Hadn't her loving, interventionist nature – Nature – driven Jane Templedon to make that trip to London and plead for Robert? Maybe the results had seemed bad, for a while. But now? Walt and Solid might not be here, conveniently dead, if she and Harpur hadn't given them, or given someone, a lead to Cormorant Avenue. It was not in Jane's character, her nature, passively to let things happen. As Jill said, Jane had a lot of life. These two didn't because *she* did, and made the Dulwich voyage. Incidentally, Jane knew about the guns in the boot, didn't she? Harpur wondered why he'd thought only of Robert as executioner.

Iles stood gazing down at the corpses for a while longer, entirely free from smirk. He rarely crowed at deaths, regardless of whose. The ACC knew about decorum and often let it infringe on him a little.

Harpur said: 'The knighthood, sir. I've been wondering whether Mrs Lane can make something bad and damaging

233

of this as regards your reputation. Possibly you should think of some counter measure. If she digs around – and that's how she is, isn't it, she does dig around? Suppose she digs around and discovers these two are related to Lester Melvane and that there may in consequence be a link to your supergrass family. Rockmain has heard she's intent on hindering your elevation for old time's sake – and this would seem very likely so, wouldn't it? She's not a gent, like Mark Lane. These deaths – well, through them she might be able to make it look as though your Templedon operation had dark, very faulty, smelly elements, and is not as first thought trouble-free and pure. Not an unmixed, knighthood-worthy triumph, as it appeared until this. She would whisper such matters to her husband. She's good at whispering to him, isn't she, and he was always good at tuning in? She'll besmirch you and he might backtrack on his recommendation. I'm surprised she hasn't been able to smash his support for you already, aren't you?'

Iles bent for a closer look at Solid. 'I grieve to have these on our ground, Col. And yet it's splendid, too, isn't it?' He straightened. 'Oh, thank you for that analysis of my situation.' He began to howl up towards the topmost tree greenery again. 'Look, Harpur, I believe – yes, I do believe such comments well intentioned, despite your skittish pollution of my wife. Nowadays, whenever Sarah and I discuss you, and this happens occasionally, she will –'

'Mr Lane is a fine man of integrity, but he must have felt torn about endorsing you. Although, from a sense of justice, he would want now to recognize your wisdom on drugs so early, he will also recall how you consistently and joyfully treated him like a cunt, sir. His attitude to you could be touch-and-go. Some hostility from Mrs Lane – some *additional* hostility – might make him reconsider. In the normal way, sir, such malice would be immaterial, since it is the kind of thing expected from Mrs Lane, and because you, in what Rockmain would probably call your

234

"youness", can withstand such attacks. But landing a knighthood is a delicate matter, even though all sorts of oddballs do get there.'

'Which sort would you say I am, Col?'

'What?'

'Oddball.'

'Oh, honest, definitely not Sectionable yet for mental trouble, very tastefully garbed, Adam's appled, wholly devoted to your work and those you lead, prick-driven to an embarrassing degree.'

'Yes.' Iles gathered some leaves and spread them carefully over Walter Melvane's and Solid's faces, as if he could not bear to look any longer on their uncheery eyes. He said: 'Did this itemized account of me as me just come to you spontaneously like that, Col, or was it prepared?'

'They'd have these traits in their database when considering the knighthood, sir. They probably don't like giving one to somebody out-and-out mad, but I think you'll be OK.'

'The law says they have to disclose what they hold in a database, doesn't it, Harpur?'

'Certainly. But there'd be no point in insisting on an inspection, would there, because you already know your qualities as listed.'

'Parts I did recognize.'

'Which, sir? The Adam's apple? "Tastefully garbed" or "prick-driven"?'

'Certainly Mrs Lane is a lady who knows how to whisper,' Iles replied. 'Certainly she has unmatched besmirching flair, whether or not the object of this besmirching – one's self – has anything to be reasonably besmirched for. What does that imperious cow care? Destruction is her aim and the spread of woe. She could star in the Book of Revelation. But the impacts of these deaths – Walter Melvane, Solid – could go either way, surely. All right, yes, they might be said to have connections with the Templedon assignment – unclear connections, but connections.

Possibly Mrs Lane will try to introduce a note of her own typical disharmony, the sad blot. Think of things another way, though, Col. Here, nicely mortuarized, we have one of the most inveterate, controlling London villains, plus his probable successor. They have been obliterated on our territory in totally mysterious conditions and thus a continuing, vile insult to the State has been nicely put a very definite end to. What the Metropolitan, in all their fucking, big-mouth grandeur, could not manage has been done for them here. I feel I – we – should pick up some reflected glory for that, don't you? My claim to a title might in fact have been furthered. Can you see that, Harpur? They'll say, "Ah, yes, Desy Iles, wasn't he the one who arranged the marvellous erasure of Onset?" Good God, you might be in for something yourself since you've certainly been in attendance and relevant.'

'Thank you, sir.'

'Possibly a commendation scroll in gothic script or inscribed tankard.'

Chapter Eighteen

Although Robert Templedon still felt mostly proud of Jane's Dulwich jaunt to see Melvane, he did query its wisdom with her once, a long while after. 'Damn dangerous, Jane.'

She came back at him hard: 'It worked, didn't it?'

'Worked?'

'They wouldn't have found us.'

'No, they wouldn't. The risk was –'

'They're dead. They'd be alive and still a threat, otherwise. We won.'

'I suppose so,' he said. He couldn't really argue.

'We won, no matter how it happened. It could be through the one you call Callic, or through tailing by Walt or Walt's lot. God, what a procession if they followed us themselves! First, Harpur and I, then Callic, then the Melvane car.'

Today, no procession at all. Jane and Robert drove alone in the Saab to the Matthew Arnold for their first weekend visit to the children, an escort unnecessary now. They had decided to take Sian and Harry out to the pub where Rockmain did his schizophrenia-no-no-no-or-only-a-bit spiel. Although, yes, there had been that flicker of debate with Jane weeks ago, Templedon now felt pretty good. It was a true and lasting comfort to have a wife who could not only steal your own automatics but use one of them so beautifully, before resuming ordinary Cormorant Avenue and Matthew Arnold life. When he asked what she did with the pistols her only answer was, 'They're gone. For good. For good in both senses. Our gun club days are finished, aren't they, Robert?'

Oh, hell, but it had been a bad time walking from the Saab that late afternoon with Walt and Solid up at the old army emplacement. Luckily, though, those two gave nearly all their vigilance to him, 'the bad beast', not to Jane. Error. Error. They'd seemed a bit scared of him. Templedon could believe this. Well, obviously, he used to be a big-timer, didn't he? Lester would have mentioned to them what he could do.

Back home after the brilliant, quick end of Walt and Solid, Jane had told Robert they never even searched her while the three waited in the sitting room for him. She described Walt's behaviour then as 'sort of . . . yes, sort of gentlemanly'.

'Oh, sure.'

'He came over as apologetic about giving me a tough time,' Jane replied. 'An almost-chevalier. Some of these major people in the firms are like that, off and on, aren't they? It seemed ungrateful to put bullets into him so soon afterwards, but what else?'

'He'd understand.'

'Poor Vera,' she had said. 'Alone tonight.'

'That's the game.'

'She and Walt sympathized with what I said on the London trip with Harpur. Walt told me that.'

'But the rules,' Templedon replied. 'It would be the rules, wouldn't it? Always the fucking rules.'

'Yes, the rules. He explained they could not allow special terms for any grass, or utter break-up would result. One small failure might start universal rot. Of course, he had to say it all again when you arrived home – he felt so regretful, ashamed. That's Walter, not Solid. Solid was . . . just solid. As if no choice existed. The "procedure". Walt jibbed at what they had to do – but they'd have done it. Their response was laid down by eternal villain etiquette, lapses banned. God, though, such a pair of oafs to let me walk behind them, even for a couple of seconds, when we left the Saab.'

And the Beretta, fairly easy to hide in the pocket of her chinos, despite its long nose. Where had she kept the guns after taking them from the Saab? He did ask, but was given no answer. She probably picked the smaller calibre weapon to prove the refinement of her shooting. She could be like that. Tidiness would appeal – a couple of small holes apiece very close together in the skull. Or possibly she knew so much about small arms she could instantly see the H. and K. had been doctored somehow and wouldn't do the job.

As they neared the Matthew Arnold now, Jane said: 'You know, I'm still glad we didn't cremate them in their Jag.'

'Lugging the bodies and piling them in – yes, crude. Plus blood and bone bits over us. Dicey.'

'Disrespectful to Walt.'

'That wouldn't have bothered me. He'd had plenty of respect in life.'

'Not so much a kindly funeral pile as waste disposal,' she said. 'You know, his false teeth came half out on impact – either the shots or hitting the ground. I pushed them back in. This was a leadership figure. All right, he let himself get killed through sloppiness, but Walt still deserved some dignity.'

'Yes, I saw you with the teeth. Definitely, he had his own kind of greatness.'

'Just the same, a good idea to torch the car as car. They intended to set ours alight to complete their . . . their statement, I suppose it should be called. Revenge statement. So, we achieved a neatness with *our* statement. The bodies would be the main part of that, obviously, but the fire a footnote.'

'Neatness does come into things, doesn't it?' Robert said. 'Satisfying. Strange, really. Balance – the way I'd thought of shooting Callic with a gun he personally brought me.'

239

'Sometimes things seem to move in their own circular fashion. A bit eerie.'

'This would have been the Heckler and Koch, if it worked. That Parabellum might have been a real, heartfelt, let-bygones-be-bygones gift, or might have been a set-me-up trick. Did you look at it, try it?'

'And burning their car was bound to bring someone out to look, in the long run,' Jane replied. 'I wouldn't like to think of the corpses lying there undiscovered. Not Walt's. Rats. Foxes. Weather. Again, a matter of dignity.'

At the pub lunch, Sian Rebecca said: 'Oh, many, many new friends.'

'Wonderful,' Templedon said.

'Yes,' Harry Charles said. 'A lot.'

'What do they think of your names?' Templedon asked.

'What? What do you mean, dad?' Sian Rebecca said.

'Sian Rebecca Templedon. Harry Charles Templedon,' Robert replied.

'Well, they don't think anything about them,' Sian Rebecca said. 'That's just who I am, isn't it? This table doesn't think about being a table – because that's what it is, a table.'

'Do they teach you stuff like that in the Matthew Arnold?' Templedon said.

'And "Sian Rebecca" is the same,' Sian Rebecca said. 'It's just who I am.'

'Or "Harry Charles",' Harry Charles said.

'That's a fact,' Jane said.